Crossing Hell's Bridge.
Reaching U.S. Heaven.

ISBN-13: 978-1482649741
ISBN-10: 1482649748

Visit Dr. Luke A.M. Brown & Mrs. Berthalicia Fonseca-Brown at www.TheNon-SilenceoftheLAMB.com.

Crossing Hell's Bridge. Reaching U.S. Heaven.

Berthalicia Fonseca

DEDICATION

Our late mother:
Mrs. Estelle Streete Brown

For the record, we owe our success to
Moreen Williams, Dolcie Garwood,
Gretchen Reid, Dr. Michael Simonds,
Dr. Pamela Garjian, and Dr. Miguel Buxeda.

Our editor, William Greenleaf

THANK YOU

Also dedicated to our late sisters:
Beverly Allen
Myrette Williams

And to our late nephew:
Caple Allan-Browdie

Prologue

Cascade was a rustic, picturesque town, steeped in beauty and located in the parish of Hanover at the northwestern end of Jamaica, West Indies. It was a small, tranquil village full of trees, colorful bamboo, and a large variety of vegetation. Set in a green valley encircled by uncontaminated virgin mountains, the quiet town was defined by the village square, which lay on the outskirts.

As the gateway of the village, the square had a narrow, T-shaped intersection and was the only means of entering the town. All public and private transportation passed through this square on the way to other larger cities or towns.

At that time the main public transportation in Cascade consisted of old, overloaded country buses that were stuffed with goods and large baskets of freshly harvested farm produce. These ugly buses would approach the town square from the west in the mornings and return from the east in the evenings, briefly stopping to drop off or pick up passengers at the town square. The passengers walked to and from these public transports via the third leg of the T-shaped road, which pointed southward.

Travelers leaving the village would have their luggage stacked up in messy piles on the roadside waiting for the bus to arrive. There were a few small and medium-sized local shops located at the town square. This was where most of these travelers would stop to shop while they waited for their transportation to arrive.

As the battered buses approached, they blew their horns in warning. People could hear them from miles away, and everyone would gather their luggage and stand at attention, all eyes steadfastly focused in the direction from which they expected the eye-catching vehicle. As the dilapidated, antediluvian vehicle appeared in sight, the people could see piles of loads already on top of it. At times, it would be so overstocked that it would lean to one side as if it were about to turn over.

Strangely, those exiting the bus had just about the same amount of luggage as those boarding the bus. During the loading and unloading, it was sometimes difficult to tell who was coming and who was leaving. After the dust had settled, the bus would drive off and disappear with the previous crowd, leaving the crowd of new arrivals standing in the village square. They would fetch their loads and place them on their backs, shoulders, or heads, then stroll away inland into the Cascade hills, valleys, and mountains via the third leg of the T-shaped crossroads.

The sunbaked road leading into Cascade was paved, but filled with potholes. Taking the road meant a heart-stirring adventure with breathtaking scenery on either side. Farther inland, the road became more mountainous, with scenic hillside landscapes and awe-inspiring views of the sea.

Despite Cascade's natural beauty and pure fresh air, in Essie's opinion it was not a place to live. Besides wanting to escape her abusive family, Essie believed Cascade was much too small. She dreamed of a place and a time where she could stretch her wings and fly away to be a part of a bigger and better world. Essie dreamed of living in a big city.

Chapter 1

Essie and her whole family were more than ecstatic when Gena came to Jamaica to take Myrtle with her to the United States. They all knew that would be the only way Myrtle would survive her risky lifestyle. Moreover, they knew that she would get the best health care and medications for her heart.

Myrtle was happy too. She had hoped that Dr. NcNelly, the man who had funded the Glenworth house, would take her and the rest of the family to the United States, but that hadn't happened. That was part of her broken dreams. Eventually, she had totally given up on going to the US to live a better life.

However, Gena had never given up on Myrtle's dream. That was the main driving force in the first place that motivated Gena to be a pioneer and make a way for her family to live in the United States.

Gena, being the oldest child, knew everything about her family's highs and lows. She knew that her little sister was heartbroken and disappointed with life. Myrtle often mentioned that she felt as if her life was merely one big mistake. Gena knew that Myrtle felt like ending her life because nothing mattered anymore.

Gena herself was also hurting inside, just like Myrtle, so she told herself that she owed it to Myrtle to make the dream happen the first chance she got. That was when she got the bold idea to get a visa for the Bahamas and then leave from there on a cruise ship to the United States. Once she got to the United States, she would get herself together and then come back for Myrtle.

It worked out almost as planned. When Gena felt like she was about to be crippled with fear, as she attempted to stow away on the cruise ship from the Bahamas to the United States, she thought about her little sister and how Myrtle needed her. She knew she had to be strong for her. When Gena was being abused, teased, and threatened on the ship, she found her strength by thinking about how Myrtle needed her. That was all that mattered to her then. Gena made it successfully through a lot of struggles because she thought of saving Myrtle and delivering her to the US in a sound state of mind before it was too late. This thought was always foremost in Gena's thoughts.

But Myrtle wasn't the first family member Gena brought to the US. An opportunity came up for her to file for her little brother Leonard, who desperately wanted to be a doctor and who was a much easier candidate to work with at that particular time.

It was not Gena's plan to get Leonard as the first emigrant in her family to the United States. Neither was Denise supposed to be the second emigrant. But when the opportunities presented themselves, Gena astutely and brilliantly capitalized on them. Gena's only intention initially was to make it to the United States at any cost and get her sister Myrtle, whom she knew was suffering, there, too.

Therefore, when Gena went to Jamaica to get Myrtle, she was focused and fearless like a soldier on a special rescue mission. She was determined to rescue her little sister from emotional captivity. Gena had looked forward to this mission for years. She had spent many sleepless nights thinking about how she would deliver her sister from her despair in Jamaica.

By the time Gena got to Jamaica, she was as prepared as a lawyer going to court to defend an innocent man who was wrongly accused, or a special squad poised to embark upon a mission to rescue an innocent captive.

She gave Myrtle a passport book and told her that she wouldn't have to worry about anything. All she had to do was listen to Gena keenly and do exactly what she said she should do. If she did that, then their mission to the United States through immigration at the airport would be successful. Gena also gave her a piece of paper with some vital facts that she would need to know within one week. These were facts about Myrtle's new name and identity.

During the week that Gena was in Jamaica, she and Myrtle rehearsed their strategy repeatedly. Gena called Myrtle by her new name to see if she would respond promptly to it. Early on the morning of their flight, Gena took Myrtle to the dentist. He extracted one of Myrtle's teeth with very little Novocain, and within a few hours, one side of Myrtle's face was swollen.

She was in excruciating pain. Unfortunately, this was part of the plan, necessary to make their mission successful. Myrtle's deep Jamaican accent could be a real liability, especially considering that she would be playing the role of a native-born American in front of the US immigration officer.

7

Once they got onto the plane, Myrtle's face was so swollen, she was virtually unidentifiable. When they got to immigration, the well-mannered young white officer was very compassionate because he could almost feel the pain that Myrtle was going through. Therefore, he hurried to process their documents. Never in his wildest dreams could he have imagined that anyone would have gone to such great lengths in order to make it to the land of freedom and equal opportunity. But if he had realized the truth, he would at least have felt that Myrtle deserved a chance of freedom for wanting it so badly. He certainly would not have wanted to be a hindrance in such a driven person's pathway.

They made it out of the airport. Myrtle was delivered by Gena to US soil, where the streets were paved with gold. Myrtle was very happy, but more than that, Gena was finally free, free to live her life because she knew she had successfully done what Dr. McNelly had failed to do.

Chapter 2

DECADES EARLIER...

After a five-hour bus ride through the hills and mountains, fourteen-year-old Essie arrived in Montego Bay, the second largest city on the island of Jamaica. The megalopolis was the most popular tourist vacation area on the island, a place full of neon lights and glorious white-sand beaches.

Essie felt that all her life she had been a misplaced piece of a jigsaw puzzle, until now. This was the right place for her, the place where she belonged. It was a mind-bending, uncanny feeling because, in the midst of a confusing, industriously busy city, with nowhere to go, Essie felt content and right at home.

Essie had worked it all out in her head. She would make her way to a busy shopping center and find a kind-looking lady, one who seemed to need a helping hand, maybe with many kids. She would ask her for a job. Essie was willing to work for food and shelter. She would do anything, whatever it took to survive. After all, that was what she had been doing all her life anyway. She'd been living with her resentful adoptive family in Cascade, receiving food and shelter in exchange for hard—very hard—labor. Essie realized that her overworked, abusive environment back home was a blessing in disguise; it had prepared her for anything that the big city might pitch at her. Nothing could be worse than what she had left behind.

Essie walked for some time, searching until she found the perfect place. She boldly walked up to a middle-aged lady and made her best plea. "Good evening, miss. My name is Essie from the town of Cascade. I'm here looking for a job. Could you help me? I can do your housekeeping. You don't even have to pay me, because I'm willing to work for food and shelter."

"Lard pickni," the lady said, "move from in front ta me and go home to yuh parents. What a nice-looking child like you doing pon the street? Mi nuh want no liability pon mi self ya mi child. No sirree, I don't have no time for foolishness."

Essie quickly realized that, although people might be decently dressed and look pleasant enough, they were busy, selfish, and self-centered. Some of them wouldn't even stop to listen to her. Either they were overly concerned for her, or they treated her with scorn, as if she were a con artist or about to rob them of their purses. They seemed to be afraid of her, something she had not expected.

Although Essie knew the big-city lifestyle was in her genes, she slowly but surely lost confidence in her big plan. Every time another person shunned her, she felt her belief in those big dreams shrink a little. It wasn't long before she realized that she really hadn't worked everything out properly; indeed, she had no backup plan but to head home. But at six in the evening, it was far too late. The last bus back to Cascade had left at four, almost two hours earlier.

Essie's excitement rapidly turned into panic, and fear raced through her empty stomach. The reality of the situation hit her hard, and she was bitterly disappointed.

What should she do now? Where would she sleep tonight? She could not hide her fear; it showed in her face.

From the corner of her eyes, Essie noticed a grubby, dirty old man watching her from across the street. She walked faster, but the crazy-looking man started following her. He crossed the road to her side and increased his speed. Essie immediately crossed to the other side, but he did the same, rapidly closing the distance between them. She started running as fast as she could.

She held out her hand and stopped the first car coming her way. She told the driver, a big, fat black man, she had nowhere to stay and frantically begged him to help her get away from her pursuer.

Initially the driver's rough, hairy face wore a mean look, but when he saw Essie's old brown suitcase and the panic in her eyes, he smiled. "Okay, babes, jump right in. I'll take care of you."

Essie wasn't too sure what he meant, but she had no choice. She tried telling herself that he could be the Good Samaritan she'd prayed for. She hopped into the back of the vehicle, relieved; she was going to make it after all. She introduced herself to the driver. "My name is Essie. I'm from Cascade in Hanover. What is your name, sir?"

"Big John," he muttered.

Big John didn't seem to be in any mood for deep conversation, so Essie kept quiet, observing the passing scenery and strange, busy people. Emotionally exhausted, she leaned her head back and promptly fell asleep in the car.

11

The evil man drove to a quiet, desolate area, where he stopped and went to the back of the car. He intended to take full advantage of Essie's vulnerability. By this time, his vile thoughts were unstoppable. He knew what he was about to do was wrong, but it didn't matter now. His revolting life was on the wrong road anyway.

He'd spent many years in prison for virtually the same crime. He had very bad memories of his time behind bars, and he didn't wish to go back there, but he had no control over his repugnant carnal desires. He had wanted to do good this time, but he couldn't control himself. The opportunity had presented itself to him like a cake on his birthday.

He knew for sure that he was going to burn in hell for his evil deeds. But most of all, he knew that he could not stop now.

Chapter 3

After Essie's life-threatening encounter with Big John and her rude awakening to life in the big city, her ambitious plan came through after all.

She found a job working for a kind, charming woman in her late thirties named Sandra Ferguson. A registered nurse, the woman was married to a dentist, Dr. Roan Ferguson. He was much older, perhaps forty-five, and was tall, dark, handsome, and cordial. The pair, who had three children, worked at the large hospital where Essie had been admitted after being attacked. They lived nearby in a highly desirable, upscale neighborhood and enjoyed an enviable upper-middle-class lifestyle in a well-appointed two-story home.

They were a good, loving family.

The children's names were Lee, Jonathan, and Mary. Lee was a well-behaved boy about five years old. Jonathan was older, around seven, and also mannerly and well behaved. Mary, the oldest child, was a shy girl of nine.

The Fergusons had had no luck with babysitters, but when they heard Essie's story in the hospital, they decided to give her a chance. Moreover, that was their way of helping her while giving back to society.

They made Essie feel welcome in their home. They gave her a room located on the first floor and explained the rules of the house and what they expected of her. They even promised to pay her a small weekly salary.

"Essie, can you cook?" Nurse Ferguson asked.

"Yes, Nurse," Essie said. "I was the main cook in my family, responsible for meal preparation each night."

Essie once again reflected on her overworked lifestyle in Cascade, seeing it as more of a preparation for her future than as a punishment. She was happy to let the Fergusons know how well she cooked. Cooking was a delight for her, and she didn't really consider it work. It was always the fun part of her day.

"Okay then, Essie, along with taking care of the kids, we'll expect you to cook for us sometimes when I'm not home in time. Can you manage that?"

"Sure, Nurse. No problem."

Essie thanked God for giving her this job working for such a wonderful family. She did wonder, though, why she had had to undergo such a horrific experience first with that terrible man. She thought about the barrier she'd overcome in order to get to this job. She felt as if the Fergusons' home was the Promised Land, but the devil had the keys to the gate.

Why couldn't I have met this family at the shopping center on my first day here? Essie wondered. *Was it too much to ask for a better life? Is that an example of the cost I'll pay each time good things happen to me? Would it have been better for me to have stayed in Cascade? Did I do the right thing to search for a good life at whatever cost?*

Essie made up her mind then and there. She

would not give up hope because of the high, unfair price she had paid for finding the good that lurked behind the next door in her life. She promised to find strength from her past experiences in order to fight the unforeseeable future. She believed she deserved a good life, and she wouldn't settle for anything less than the best she could have. She would continue to reach high and work hard toward that end.

Essie loved every minute of her life in Montego Bay. As each day passed, she learned more about the big city. Although she was a city girl at heart, she loved nature, and Montego Bay had lots of it to replenish her soul. After all, she was on an island where the change in seasons was marked only by newly flowering plants, blossoming trees, and the proud peacocks strutting around freely.

She liked to visit Rocklands Bird Sanctuary, a bird lover's paradise. It was nestled in the hills of Anchovy, just outside of Montego Bay, within the borders of the parish of Saint James. She was dazzled by the Jamaican national hummingbird, with its stunning emerald-green chest and ruby-red beak. She gazed at the one perched on her finger and listened to the soothing hum of the other birds all around her. She could easily stay here for hours, but instead, she chose to continue her stroll off the beaten path of Saint James.

On another nature stroll, Essie observed the beautiful Montego Bay gardens, complete with turquoise water ponds and spectacular cascading waterfalls. She pitched small gravel stones into a pond with broad green leaves floating around its edges. She watched as each stone plunged into the pond and the water rippled outward. She smiled at the beauty of nature and frowned at the little crooked sign posted at the top of a two-by-two stick, about two and a half feet tall, planted into the ground. It read, *Please do not throw anything into the pond, and do not feed the ducks.*

The tropical garden overflowed with crotons, bamboos, ferns, cocoa plants, indigo, and the forget-me-not wild maca plant.

Essie was now deep in the forest of Montego Bay, with its scenic backdrop of rocks and woodland. She observed the unspoiled nature of God as she traveled along the undeveloped dirt road. She listened to the waterfalls and the gurgle of nearby creeks, and to the water trickling down the bushy hillside and over shady branches. She made her way through the old riverbed and tropical foliage enveloped by towering green trees.

Although she loved every minute of Montego Bay, she sometimes got homesick as she thought of her nature getaway in the countryside of Cascade. She remembered those occasions when she would journey deep into the countryside through shadowed corridors and beneath tall, swaying trees. Hidden in the woodlands was the great Rocky Point River that plunged down a narrow gorge, with its blue-green waters splashing along the smooth black-and-gray rocks of the irrigating riverbanks. Being in the forest never failed to give Essie a serene feeling of oneness with nature.

Living in Montego Bay, Essie never took anything for granted. She went to the beautiful white-sand beaches every Sunday she could while the Fergusons were at church.

She also liked to take leisurely walks along the city streets. Montego Bay was divided into three distinct parts: the city with its crowded streets, the Hip Strip, and the outlying hotels and villas on the beaches and hillsides.

While strolling through the busy tourist paradise known as the Hip Strip, one of the first things that caught her attention was the iconic aquatic playground of Jimmy Buffett's Margaritaville, where tourists and locals alike rode down an enormous water slide and participated enthusiastically in other extreme water sports.

Essie observed a bunch of people dancing to the loud reggae sounds of Bob Marley and stopped to read a sign that said, *Come to Margaritaville where there is a thin line between Saturday and Sunday morning.* She smiled because she understood that it was true. Sunbathers partied during the weekdays and partied twice as much on weekends. On the weekends, they partied all night, up to the breaking of dawn.

Essie continued along the one-and-a-half-mile stretch of vintage hotels, some remodeled to look modern, as she observed the island lovers sunbathing and partying along the narrow road.

Essie often volunteered to do the grocery shopping for the family and any other errands that needed to be done. She did this so that she could learn more about the fascinating city of Montego Bay, second only in size to Kingston.

On her walks, she observed the crowded, colorful, and lively setting of the central-city streets—an indication of how vital, noisy, and lively this Jamaica city was. Although Montego Bay was famous for its beaches, beach bars, gourmet restaurants, and nightlife, it also had its industrious side. Cars packed the streets, trying to get through.

Essie observed the authentic city charm and adored it in all its glory. It was exhilarating to see exquisite Jamaican/Spanish architecture in the central parade. She enjoyed Sam Sharpe Square, a friendly cobblestoned hub of activity, the meeting place of all the townspeople and taxicabs. It showcased a cage that was formerly a jail for runaway slaves and the ruins of the courthouse, built in 1804 and destroyed by fire a few decades earlier, but now rebuilt to restore its charming beauty.

As she ambled down the busy streets, Essie noticed the architecture on both sides. Interspersed with modern buildings were the previous century's wooden gingerbread houses.

Country folks often flocked to the city to visit the markets, shops, and banks. These were some of the same country folks from Cascade who traveled on old, overcrowded, dilapidated buses. In addition, the busy streets hosted guests from hotels and cruise ships as they made their way to shops and crafts markets. They hosted housewives and office girls, as well as street hagglers.

In the crowded marketplace, country folks sold their natural produce from homemade vending stalls. The venders, who filled an area three or four blocks long, squatted on the ground or on very low stools with their baskets full of produce between their open legs. They beckoned Essie to patronize their small entrepreneurial businesses. The pungent, sometimes rotten, scent of overripe mangoes and bananas hung heavily in the air. The local market was full of customers busy testing and tasting guineps and sweet and sour saps, as well as nesberries, before they bought.

Essie enjoyed the fun of haggling over the price before she bought her yellow yams, cassavas, and sweet potatoes. She enjoyed a good deal at the overcrowded produce marketplace. She enjoyed the tropical island uniqueness in all its glory.

In the big city, trusted friends didn't come easy. However, Essie made a few along the way. One of them was Stedman, a handsome Indian-Jamaican boy, brown skinned and about four years older than Essie. He was a kindhearted person with a great sense of humor. Another was Cherry. Cherry was Essie's age, a typical Jamaican girl, dark skinned and average looking, but a truly supportive and attentive friend.

Essie looked forward to meeting her friends every Sunday. She would make plans with Stedman or Cherry on the previous Sunday for things they would do or places they would go the following Sunday.

They made an effort to visit a different beach each week. Sometimes they would go to the park to watch a soccer game or enjoy whatever entertainment was being held there. Essie developed a love for the beautiful white-sand beaches, as well as the exciting game of soccer. She never understood the rules very well, but she loved all the quick action, and it was obvious whenever someone made a goal. She couldn't explain much more than that, but she enjoyed it very much.

One Sunday, the three arranged to meet at Doctor's Cave Beach. Stedman, the first to arrive, hurried to the water's edge and waded in, frolicking in the gloriously soothing sea. He floated on a large inner tube pulled from an old truck tire, his arms on either side of it and his head bobbing in the center. He stayed fairly close to the shore, the tips of his toes barely touching the sand, and paddled around in circles, swooping down the faces of the little waves.

He was having a great time when he saw Essie arrive. By this time, she had evolved into a beautiful girl, tall and shapely. She had the perfect beach body—the figure of movie star Raquel Welch. She wore a one-piece, tight-fitting black bathing suit, with a white towel draped over her shoulders.

"Hey, big-hip girl. I'm over here." Stedman waved to Essie.

"I saw you, Steddy. I saw you as soon as I came through the gate. I saw your little head in the middle of your big black tube. You look like a black-eyed pea in a large pot." Essie dropped her towel on the sand and ran across the white beach toward him. She stopped abruptly at the water's edge and looked down as if seeing something strange.

"What is it, Essie?"

"Oh, it's a little bitsy sea crab crawling on the sand. It's so cute. I'm going to pick it up."

"Leave the poor crab alone."

"No! I like to catch them and put them in a glass bottle."

"But you don't have a bottle."

"That's true, Steddy. You're right. I should leave it alone."

"Why don't you come into the water? It's so warm and nice."

"No, it's not. It's cold. You're lying, Steddy." Essie tested the water with her foot.

"Essie, I'm not lying. It's warm where I am. Remember, you have to dip your whole body into the water for the first time, and then you'll see that it's really warm."

"You know, a friend of mine used to say, 'Never test the water with both feet.'"

"Or else what?"

"Or else you'll get burned or drown, or whatever. It's just a saying. Don't get technical with me, Steddy."

"Okay, Miss Pretty," Stedman said with a grin, "I'll leave you and your country phrases alone. Very soon you'll be telling me that one hand of a banana is better than two bunches."

"Are you teasing me, Steddy? You know I don't like to be called country. I'm a big-city girl like everybody now." Essie protested against Stedman's unwelcome humor.

"Okay, Miss Big-hips, Big-city Girl."

"Where is Cherry?" Essie asked, finally realizing that Stedman was playing alone in the beautiful

20

sky-blue waters of Doctor's Cave Beach.

"I don't know. She's not here yet."

"I hope she comes. I could kill her if she doesn't show up like last Sunday."

"Talking about the devil, there she comes through the gate," Stedman said as he spotted Cherry in a sexy pink two-piece bathing suit, with a white towel around her waist.

"Oh great, here she comes."

"Yes, Miss Miserable is here."

"No, she's not," Essie said. "Just leave my friend alone."

"Hey, bad-minded people," Cherry called out to her friends as she approached them, "I can hear you. You're talking bad things about me. You all can't stand to see a girl make a grand entrance."

"Oh no, Cherry, not me. Steddy is calling you miserable."

"Stedman? Let him gwane. Let him go on. You don't see he's a big troublemaker, that one? He needs a big lick inna him head." Cherry joined them in the water, and she and Essie mischievously held on to one side of Stedman's floating tube as they tried to hoist him out of it. They spent the rest of their time playing and catching up on the past week's events.

"Cherry, what happened to you last week?" Essie asked.

"Nothing. Just some schoolwork that I needed to catch up on."

"Mo Bay High School is getting tougher these days," Stedman said.

"Yes, sir. I can't wait to finish that school. They give too much extra schoolwork on weekends. They're trying to kill me, marsa."

"I need to go back to school one of these days so I can get some subjects and go on to college," said Essie, confessing her dreams to her friends.

"That's a good idea," Cherry said.

"You know, I went to a cricket match the other day, and it was very good." Stedman tried to steer the conversation in a different direction. He never was much of a school type and had started working in the hotel industry at seventeen.

"Where was the game?" Cherry asked.

"At Jarrett Park."

"Who was playing?" Essie also wanted to know about the game.

"It was a big match, man. It was the West Indies playing Pakistan," Stedman explained. "It was a kind of test match."

"Is it still going on?" Cherry asked.

"No, it was just a three-day match. It's finished now."

"Wow. I wish I'd known about it." Essie's voice was low with regret.

"But Essie, you don't like cricket; you like soccer," Stedman said.

"Essie doesn't know what she likes, Stedman!" Cherry exclaimed.

"Yes, I do. I like cricket a lot, but I love soccer more."

"Okay, next time I'll tell you about it in advance. Oh, and by the way, there's a big soccer match next week at Jarrett Park. We could go there next Sunday."

"Okay, I'm in," said Essie.

"Who's playing?" Cherry asked, wanting to make sure it was worth her time.

"Some team from Kingston's supposed to play Montego Bay Soccer Club."

Cherry smiled. "Oh, that should be good. I'm in, too."

"What time is the match?"

"Starts around four p.m."

"Where do you want to get together?" Cherry asked Stedman.

"How about at the front gate? A good friend will be working there, so we won't have to pay anything to get inside."

They continued to have a wonderful beach day, and as it drew to a close, they turned their thoughts to meeting the following Sunday.

At eighteen, Essie enjoyed her life. For the first time, she felt it was worth living, and she embraced it to its fullest. She felt confident, and it showed. Her one regret was not completing her schooling before she had run away from Cascade. If she'd done so, she could take advantage of the many opportunities the big city offered. She could have continued her studies in Montego Bay and moved on to college to start a professional career.

Her eyes had opened to the ways of the world, and she wanted more, including bigger and better dreams. She was well aware of her beauty, but she knew her looks could only get her so far. On the other hand, if she had a good education, she could definitely secure a bright future for herself. Thus, she started planning to return to school as soon as possible.

As time progressed, Stedman and Essie got closer and closer. One Sunday, while at the beach, they even confronted each other about the direction of their casual relationship. It was at a secluded spot facing the golden sunset, where they lay on the sand laughing and having fun. Eventually, Stedman started telling her how he truly felt and that he'd love for her to be his girlfriend.

Essie had been attracted to him all along, but was afraid to let him know. Hearing him say how much he loved and desired her was like sweet music to her

23

ears. She leaned over and softly kissed his lips. "I was hoping you'd say that."

"Why?"

"Because I already felt a special desire for you." A shy but somewhat seductive smile played on her lips as she glanced at him, then quickly looked away.

"So why didn't you tell me?"

"Well . . ." She started to explain, but then stopped. Her face flushed with embarrassment, and her body became frigidly awkward. She tried to find a position that would ease the tension she felt. She was about to embark on a topic she had never quite touched on before.

"Well what?" Stedman asked eagerly.

"Well, I wasn't sure." She hesitated, then corrected herself. "Honestly, I was afraid that you didn't feel the same about me."

Stedman knew her words were true and came deep from her heart, because her voice had changed. She started panting heavily. She tried hiding it, but her heavy breathing was too obvious to ignore.

"Believe it or not," he said, "I was attracted to you from the first day that I laid eyes on you at Sunset Beach Place, but I didn't have the guts to tell you until now. Essie, I loved you then. I've loved you all along. I love you now, and I'll love you forever."

"Wow!" Essie exclaimed with a confident, flirtatious smile. "Four years is a long time." It sure felt good to be loved. It gave her chills to hear those words from Stedman.

They held each other close and kissed passionately. Stedman rested his hand on Essie's leg and caressed her knee while still deeply engaged in their passionate kisses. Essie had her beach towel wrapped around her waist like a skirt. With one hand, he slowly but skillfully raised the towel to unveil Essie's long, sexy legs. He had dreamed of doing this many times before. Now that he had her in his arms, it felt a million times better. His heart raced with excitement, and his manhood awoke. He wanted Essie's body right then. His body ached to explore her inner soul.

He slowly and ever so softly ran his fingers along the inside of her legs. He could feel Essie's pulse hammering under his fingers. She needed him also. Her body ached with the pain of urgent desire. Essie drew a deep breath, then gave a big sigh as Stedman touched her pulsating body once more. His trembling fingers touched the exquisite softness of her innermost thigh where her shimmering legs met. She sighed deeply and quivered in response to each sensuous touch.

One thing led to another, and they made love on the white sand of Cornwall Beach. It was a perfect finish to a wonderful romantic evening. With a passion of its own, the sea washed over their bodies, matching the intense motion of their rhythm, rising higher and harder until they reached the final moment, spasms rippling through them. The sun disappeared into the sea, leaving pink and gold sunset skies.

They felt each other's love and had no doubt it was real.

Chapter 4

Essie's favorite food was Jamaica's national dish, which was made of ackee combined with pieces of cod. The two were put into a Dutch pot or deep frying pan to be simmered down with various seasonings, including onion, black pepper, tomatoes, and a little hot sauce. Essie loved her ackee and saltfish with a variety of side dishes, but her favorite was plain white rice. To her, it was a tantalizing combination. It was most delightful, and she would give up anything in exchange for her favorite meal.

Therefore, it was a stunning surprise when she turned down the Fergusons' offer to have dinner with them one evening. Essie had diligently prepared the ackee and saltfish and presented the food at the table, but she declined to join the family for their meal.

That was so unusual, it caused Nurse Ferguson to inquire about her health. "Essie, my dear child, are you feeling okay?"

"Yes, Nurse Ferguson."

"You've never turned away your favorite dish before. What's wrong?"

"Nothing. I just don't feel like eating it today."

"What are you going to eat instead?"

"I'll just eat a piece of bread and a pear for now, and maybe later I'll have some plain rice with butter."

"Okay, suit yourself, child. All I know is that something isn't right."

Essie also wondered what was wrong with her. She couldn't imagine turning down her favorite meal, but she had no appetite for ackee. The sight and smell of it nauseated her.

For the next few weeks, Nurse Ferguson noticed that Essie's behavior changed significantly. She slept an awful lot, often forgetting to do chores around the house, and spent excessive time in her bedroom. She even forgot to pick Mary up from school one evening as instructed. This oversight caused a lot of chaos and panic, as Mary was not picked up until two hours later than usual.

Nurse Ferguson got very upset and called Essie aside to tell her that she had to leave. And so Essie was fired from the best job she ever had. Sadness overwhelmed her, followed by confusion and loss. She didn't know what to do, but she admitted they were right. She knew her work performance was no longer acceptable, but she couldn't seem to do much about it. Her body was changing. She'd gained significant weight and tired more and more quickly. She called Cherry to see if she could help her with a place to stay temporarily until she could get another job.

Cherry, who lived with her parents, asked them if her friend could stay a few days at their home. They agreed, saying it was all right as long as it was only for a few days. Essie was grateful and happy to hear the good news. She and Cherry packed her belongings at the Fergusons' and went to Cherry's home. Essie was still confused, unsure of where to go or what to do next.

As Essie was carrying a box into the bedroom at Cherry's home, she fell to the ground.

Cherry saw her fall and started yelling. "Help! Mommy! Daddy! Help! Essie fainted." Cherry feared it was due to exhaustion. Cherry's parents hurried downstairs and saw Essie lying on the floor. They rushed her to the hospital. It was there that the doctors diagnosed her with a miscarriage. She had been three months pregnant.

Maybe Nurse Ferguson knew it all along, Essie thought. *That could be the real reason why she fired me. She didn't want to be bothered with a maternal situation on the job.* Essie hadn't planned for a baby, but to know she'd just lost one made her very sad.

When Stedman heard, he was also sad because he would have loved to have his first child with a pretty girl like Essie. He immediately rushed to the hospital to see her. When he got there, he found her in tears.

"Stedman, I'm sorry I lost your baby."

Stedman comforted her. "Essie, my love, don't cry. I love you, and I want you to come and live with me. We'll have another baby and be a family."

Essie hugged him and cried on his shoulder.

Chapter 5

At fourteen, Essie was a strikingly beautiful young woman. She had a glorious face with a light complexion and exceptional features, yet a humble appearance that allowed her to wear a subtle, pleasant expression wherever she went. A small, straight nose defined her stunning profile. A small but noticeable mole close to the left side of her upper lip complemented her bright hazel eyes—wise eyes that appeared to change color in the tropical sunshine. Her skin was as cool as the fresh country breeze in the early morning.

Essie's glittering black hair extended over her shoulders and flowed down to the center of her back. She was like a little Jamaican terrestrial mermaid on this tropical island. In the small country town of Cascade where she had grown up, it was a rarity to see females with such long, resplendent hair. Most young girls wore their hair in a single ponytail because their hair was significantly challenged both in length and texture.

Very tall, with long, skinny legs, Essie had the body of a sixteen-year-old. She had started developing more rapidly than her peers, and although not yet fully developed, she already boasted a bigger bosom than her friends. Essie realized very early that she stood out in Cascade. There was no other like her. Everywhere she went, people noticed her.

Essie had a shy, childish smile, but when she laughed, she would light up with glee, and her happiness could be seen from a mile away. She laughed hard and loud, holding nothing back. She loved a good joke and would be the only one laughing long after everyone else had stopped.

However, Essie was not talkative. She was a humble, thoughtful, and rather polite child. She made friends easily, although she enjoyed being alone. Sometimes she would sit by the back porch in her huge backyard and stare out over the serene, variegated green mountaintops, deep in thought, lost in her own little world like Alice in Wonderland.

She often wondered about her biological mother. Even a black-and-white photo would be consoling to her, if only there were one around. Essie got her beautiful features from her mother, Doris Lynn, a tall, skinny, light-skinned, gorgeous young lady. A perfect mixture of ethnicities, she exhibited Indian, Chinese, and Jamaican features. This explained Essie's long, straight hair and other unique attributes.

Doris Lynn had just turned eighteen years of age when she became pregnant with Essie. Essie's father was always a mystery. Doris never told anyone how she got pregnant or named her baby's father. When asked about it, she would quickly change the subject. If she was pushed too hard, she would shut down and not speak at all. Sometimes she didn't speak to anyone for weeks. Nevertheless, everyone in her family supported her pregnancy. After all, she was of grown age and didn't need anyone's consent to start her own family.

Her family remained tolerant and patient with

her. They all hoped that after she delivered the baby, she would be less emotional and would open up communication on that oh-so-critical paternal topic.

This made the shocking news from the Lucie General Hospital on the rainy, misty eve of March 26, 1922, all the more difficult to take. Frozen at first when she heard the bad report, Doris's mother stood perfectly still, as if afraid any movement would cause her to shatter. She stayed as still as if she were wrapped tightly in a sheet of wine glasses that were stacked from side by side and from head to toe. Or as if she were confined by wine glasses from the ground up, one on top of the other, which would fall and shatter if she moved as much as an inch. The only part of her that still moved was her heart, and even her heart was totally out of sync, like a grandfather clock left in an empty house, chiming loud and clear, but completely off rhythm.

Doris died while giving birth to Essie on that lonely, miserable night. No one knew all the details of her death or what exactly happened. Heartbroken and distraught, the family mourned and wept the loss of their loved one. For many weeks and months, long after Doris's funeral, they were deeply depressed, left with so many unanswered questions.

Chapter 6

"Essie, wake up. Momma said you need to clean the house today."

"Rachael, what time is it?" Essie mumbled as she vigorously rubbed her sleepy eyes.

"Time fi get up yuh red dundus pickny," Rachael said to her stepsister in a raw Jamaican patois dialect. "Time to get up, you red-speckled colored child." It was 6:00 a.m. on a Sunday when Rachael went to Essie's room because she was having difficulty sleeping.

"Really, Rachael, what time is it? It seems much too early to wake up."

"It is time to get up, you lazy scoundrel," Rachael said with a mean expression on her face.

"What time is it?" Essie asked again. "I'll clean the house. I do it all the time. I just wondered if you know what time it is."

"Lazy pork head," Rachael said rudely. "If you want to know the time, why don't you go find out for yourself?"

Frustrated, groggy, and sleepy, Essie crawled

slowly out of bed and poked her head into the living room, stealing a quick peek at the loudly ticking bright-orange clock on the wall. Her hair stood out from her head in disarray, blocking her view. She wiped a tendril from her face so she could see the time more clearly. Did it say 6:05?

Essie could not believe that Rachael, who should have been sleeping, was up and awake, forcing her to get up to clean the house. Essie rubbed her eyes again in disbelief. It just didn't make any sense. Maybe she wasn't reading the time properly. Yes, it said 6:05.

She took a curious peek through the window to see how it looked outside. She had a clear view, with the aid of the disappearing moonlight, of the old rusty washbasin that was once white in color but now brown and half buried in the ground, like a shallow grave. It was the old familiar landmark of the Streetes' make-believe property boundary on the right side of the house.

It was still dark but with a misty, smoky appearance, a foretaste of the approaching dawn. It was much too early to clean the house, especially on a Sunday morning. Essie knew that she couldn't clean now even if she wanted to honor Rachael's wish. Everyone in the Streete family was still asleep, except Rachael, and cleaning would only serve to rudely awaken them. Then she would really be in trouble.

Essie went back to her room and saw Rachael standing at the door with an empty bucket hanging from her left hand. She wondered what dirty trick she was up to now. "Rachael, it's only a little after six. Why are you up so early? Can't sleep?"

"No, I woke up, so I have to make sure that you are awake also. You've been living on our family for free. Life is too easy for you. If I'm up, then you must also be up. Get used to it, you orphan scoundrel."

"Rachael, why don't you just go back to bed and

try to get some sleep? Count sheep if you have to. When you get up so early, what good does that do you?"

"Makes me feel much better, pig face."

Pig face? Essie thought to herself. *Me? She's talking about herself being fat as a pig. And if our faces were to be compared side by side, whose face would most likely resemble a pig?*

It was only a thought, since she dared not breathe a word of such terrible truth. "Okay, I'm going back to bed, Cinderella," Essie said sarcastically.

"Have a nice wet dream, pig face," Rachael said, barely stepping aside enough to let Essie squeeze through. Rachael then stood at the door with an evil grin on her face, waiting to see Essie's next reaction.

"Oh my God. My bed is soaked. Rachael, what did you do? Did you pour all this water into my bed? You have gone too far now. This is not funny. I'll have to tell Aunt Rose as soon as she wakes up."

"I'll tell Momma that you did it. You got angry with me, and you wet your bed. Prepare for a beating from Dad. As I said, have a nice wet dream." Rachael chuckled as she left for bed.

Essie knew she was right. Aunt Rose would only call Uncle Amos to straighten things out. It would no doubt end with an unfair flogging that she could certainly do without.

Essie turned her mattress onto the other side so that the water could drain and the bed could eventually dry out. She lay on the floor, a deep sadness overtaking her.

***

Another hungry mouth to feed was the last thing anyone in Doris Lynn's family wanted. It is said that one has to be poor to know the luxury of giving. They felt very sorry for their orphan grandchild, but the Lynns had no room or time to raise another child. They already had a large household, and to make matters worse, they were very poor.

Doris's parents, Vera and Danny Lynn, were destitute farmers whose scope of farming was so small, it seemed as if they farmed solely for themselves. The little piece of nutrient-shy land that comprised their backyard barely yielded a harvest adequate to feed the impoverished family of six in their overcrowded household. At the time of Doris's death, Vera and Danny Lynn had four children, not including Doris. They all crammed into a dilapidated two-bedroom country house made of mismatched pieces of wood and rusty sheets of zinc. Propped up on four-by-four stilts, the color-shy, sun-drenched old house crowned the top of the hillside, close to the main road.

The Lynns were not willing or able to take on any more responsibilities. Already in over their heads with financial burdens of their own, they had nothing more to give.

On the other hand, Aunt Rose, Vera's youngest of three sisters, was more than willing and able to help raise Vera's orphan granddaughter. Aunt Rose had been married to Amos Streete, a skillful handyman and carpenter, for ten years. They had two girls: Rachael, seven, and Renee, five. They lived in a modest four-bedroom house that Amos had built ten years earlier. Moreover, they had been trying to conceive another child, but had two failed attempts. So Aunt Rose was more than willing and able to take little baby Essie into their home.

Essie was a pleasant addition to Aunt Rose's family. They were proud of their pretty little newly adopted baby girl, and Rachael and Renee were happy to have a new baby sister. They took turns carefully holding and playing with young Essie. She was like a new pet in their home, as far as Rachael and Renee were concerned. They nicknamed her Pretty. Essie was the perfect addition to their lives.

This blissful union, however, changed as Essie grew older and more beautiful. Like the evil stepsisters in the Cinderella story, Essie's stepsisters became jealous of her, and their jealousy got stronger as time went on. They did everything in their power to stifle Essie's beauty so they could feel better about themselves.

Unfortunately, the whole Streete family was jealous of Essie. They tried to suppress her confidence any way they could.

Essie tried hard to ignore them, but she often broke down and cried. When the family went to town to shop or to have fun, they would leave Essie alone in the house. Sometimes all she could do was cry and hope for better days.

One of the things Essie disliked most was carrying water from the public water pipes. She did it in order to keep the water tanks or reservoirs full at home. It was one of the most demanding tasks she had to do because she had to carry the water in a large bucket on her head back and forth for more than two miles each time.

Essie's older sisters almost never had to do this task. It seemed so unfair. Whenever she would complain about it, Aunt Rose would shout at her and threaten to call Amos.

This caused Essie to tremble and shake with a deep fear. Amos didn't need any good reason to beat her. He'd just grab a belt or a stick and start furiously whipping her as hard as he could.

For these reasons and more, Essie dreamed of a better place. She knew she had to leave. She didn't know where to go or by what means she would get there, but she knew it was just a matter of time. Clearly no longer accepted, she felt the longer she stayed, the more she would strain her welcome.

Chapter 7

Now fully grown, Essie lived with Stedman, her first step toward maturity and independence. Each day, she learned more about herself and how to adequately please her man.

"Hello! I'm home."

"Hey, Steddy! How was work today?" Essie always met Stedman at the door with a warm hug and a long, welcoming kiss. She wore a sexy midriff T-shirt that showed off her flat teenage belly. To complement her barely-there shirt, she sported sexy, tight-fitting, blue-and-white French-cut underwear. She gave Stedman a welcome fit for a king, and he loved every minute of it.

"Work was okay. There's nothing special to talk about. It was just another hard day working for the money."

"Did you get any tips today?"

"Yes, but not much."

"Okay, honey. Just sit in the chair. I'll get your shoes off for you."

"Thank you, Essie, my dear. I thought about you

all day long. I couldn't wait to get home to see you. I missed you so much."

"I have a surprise for you, Steddy." Essie stooped down to untie his shoes.

"I can see my surprise staring right at me."

"No, not that! I have a bigger surprise for you."

"What could be bigger or better than that sexy camel toe that you have barely hiding from me? I've been thinking about you all day at work. Essie, do you know you rock my world?"

"Come with me." Essie rose and put Stedman's shoes away in the corner. She then took his hand and led him to the dining area. "Surprise!"

"Wow! You did all that for me? Essie, you are so romantic. I really love it." Stedman admired the large bouquet of flowers on the dining table and the bottle of wine sitting in the ice bucket. The table was nicely decorated with burning candles and red and white rose petals all around the edge. "But what's the occasion?"

"We're celebrating our love today. That's all."

"So why aren't you dressed up?"

"I'm okay; you're overdressed for the occasion."

"This is an informal dinner celebration? It's a first for me, but I like it."

"This is my style, my way of celebrating our love. Have a seat, and I'll fetch the food from the kitchen. I've already prepared it."

Essie dashed to the kitchen for the food, while Stedman took a seat. She always made him feel like a king, having learned very early that a happy home makes a happy life. She could not control what went on at work, but she could make Stedman's home life a pleasant one.

Essie rushed back to the table with his hot plate of food. "I prepared your favorite—oxtail with rice and peas." The familiar sweet-smelling aroma stimulated his nostrils and his appetite as it filled the air. Stedman was in heaven. He had his favorite meal and his beautiful girlfriend at a special romantic occasion at home. What more could a man ask for in life?

The night only got better. Essie led Stedman to their bedroom after their romantic dinner. The bed was nicely made up and decorated all over with red and white rose petals.

"Here, Steddy, honey. This is your dessert." Essie stepped out of her underwear, climbed onto the bed, knelt down on her knees, and laid her head on the soft surface of the bed.

Stedman was instantly erect. He eagerly dropped his pants to the floor and approached her. His whole body was filled with warm, tingling satisfaction as he plunged his huge manhood deep into Essie's glorious soul.

They were truly in love, and it showed. Essie gave all her love and affection to Stedman, and he gave her no less in return. She felt truly loved and secure with him.

Stedman had a nice, comfortable two-bedroom apartment in the upscale downtown area of Baldwin Heights, and Essie was delighted to share his home and his life. He was a proficient, skillfully trained waiter in a large, popular hotel called Half Moon Resort. His pay wasn't great, but he sometimes made quite a bundle in tips. Therefore, he could easily afford a decent lifestyle for them. This also meant he was willing and able to take care of her and a child or two if they came along.

Indeed, Stedman confessed to Essie that he would love to have two or three kids before he turned twenty-five. His dad had always told him that was the best time to have one's children, and that was the main reason why he started working at seventeen. Starting so young and working so hard ensured that he could comfortably afford a nice home and have decent savings in the bank to start an early family.

He loved kids, and he wished to have some of his own, especially now that he had a beautiful woman in his life. He wasted no time trying to get Essie pregnant again.

Essie got pregnant within nine months of moving in with Stedman, and this time she knew it, having educated herself on all the signs to look for. Essie did everything right to the best of her knowledge. She ate properly and got plenty of bed rest. She even visited her doctor twice to make sure everything was good with the baby. That was more often than the average expectant mother saw a doctor in that era.

It was a terrible surprise, therefore, when she had a miscarriage in her fifth month while taking a bath at home. Essie was shocked and couldn't understand how a stillbirth could happen unprovoked. She thought everything negative a woman could think. She started blaming herself, thinking that she was not made to bear children. She feared it was not God's plan for her. At only nineteen, she knew her age wasn't the problem. There were so many girls who were much younger than her having children with no problem.

Stedman came home from work that day to find her in tears. Heartbroken, she told him the miserable news. By now, Essie knew how badly Stedman wanted her to have his child, and she felt very sorry for him.

Stedman calmed and comforted her, saying he would always be there for her, with or without children. It didn't really matter to him. It was her love that mattered most.

However, a year later when Essie got pregnant for the third time, but was unable to bring her pregnancy to term, Stedman reneged on his promise. He told her that although he loved her dearly, she would have to leave. He had a new girlfriend who was pregnant with his child.

Essie was devastated, but she knew there was no way she could repair their relationship without bearing him children. When he said someone else out there was already pregnant by him, she gave up, although she didn't believe that part of his story. She thought it was a convenient excuse to get her to leave—and soon. In the end, it didn't matter. He wanted her out of his life, and that was a fact. He wanted kids, and she could not bear them. It was as simple as that.

Essie understood Stedman's point of view. Wretched and heartbroken, she wasn't angry with him—not until she discovered that his story was true, indeed. "Steddy, how you could say you love me and yet be out there cheating your ass off?" She was furious.

"I do. Well, I did." Stedman searched for the right answer as he tried to explain himself.

"You're no freakin' good, mon, ya know dat?" Essie shouted. "You're a fraud an' a no-good, low-down liar. I wish ya'd burn in hell."

"Essie, I didn't intend for us to end up this way, but you gave me no choice."

"*What*? I gave you no *choice*?" Essie's eyes blazed red as fire, and her heart pounded with rage.

"You knew kids were important to me, and you deceived me. You knew you couldn't have children, but you didn't tell me anything was wrong with you. Your uterus is, well, *condemned*. There, I said it. It needed to be said. At first I thought it was my fault, but after three times with the same result, I had to see if I had anything to do with you losing my babies. That's why I took Cherry up on her offer. I just wanted to know that I can have healthy kids just like everyone else." Stedman remained calm as he explained his viewpoint to Essie.

"Cherry? Oh my God! No! My friend Cherry! I

cannot believe my ears." Essie was stunned. Cherry and Stedman were having a baby? The anger within her would not be healed in a lifetime. She was beyond angry now. She staggered out the door, ran around to the back of their apartment building, and started to sob.

Essie became depressed knowing her best friend and her lover had betrayed her in such a despicable way. It was the worst feeling in the world. It was bad enough to lose the first love of her life, but she knew she'd get over him. There were many more fish in the sea, and she was a very good catch. However, it was different losing her best friend at the same time and in the way that she had lost her. Who could she go to now? To whom would she turn for help and comfort?

One of the first things Essie had learned was not to trust anyone. Then she had met Cherry, and things had changed. She'd met a real and true friend; at least, that was what she had thought.

Still heartsick and sorely tried, Essie decided that she needed to find a suitable career. She pleaded with Stedman to give her some time to find a job. She remembered a magnificent cake that she'd skillfully baked for a party at Dr. Ferguson's home. How excited everyone was about that cake! Maybe she could work as a chef at a good hotel.

She searched all over Montego Bay for a job in the culinary arena, and eventually, with the help of Stedman's connections, landed her first chef job at Round Hill Hotel. With the money earned during her first pay period, she put money down on a one-bedroom apartment located close by the hotel.

Essie turned her disappointments and hurt emotions into working passion. It was as if she put her pain and sorrow into her position as a chef, and she did very well. Her manager liked her skill and enthusiasm. Essie had always known that she would be a very good chef. She loved to cook, and it showed in her excitement about a good, tasty meal.

If a meal wasn't good, she was the first to let it be known. She just couldn't hold back her personal opinion about the taste of certain foods. She viewed a dish as a symphony. Each part of it needed to come together at the precise time and complement the other parts. Cooking was like a piece of music where each instrument, like each ingredient, added its own beautiful sound. She believed that anyone could prepare an edible meal using good ingredients, yet only a top chef could take the very same ordinary ingredients and produce an unforgettable gourmet meal.

Essie cared about the quality of the outcome and refused to accept ordinary results. She believed in the basics and learning the details because she believed the details resulted in the perfectly cooked roast or pitch-perfect sauces. She put great thought into each plate of food she prepared.

Everyone who knew Essie knew she was obsessed with food. People trusted her because she had a unique and discerning personal taste. When a meal was good, she would openly remark about it, praising the chef or whoever provided it. She became excited at times and would go on about how good a meal tasted. It surprised no one when she turned out to be a popular, noteworthy chef in a large hotel.

Although enthralled by the culinary fine arts, Essie had never gone to school to study cooking. Her ability was a purely natural skill. In addition to her innate culinary instincts, Essie furthered her education about food by teaching herself through various cookbooks from the library. She loved to try a brand new recipe and would spread the book open in the kitchen and start making the new dish, line for line, while she hummed a song or lullaby to herself. She would add a little ingredient into the pot or oven, and then rush back to the book to see what was next. She enjoyed every minute of cooking.

When she was in the kitchen, she was more entertaining than the popular TV chef Emeril Lagasse, but without the "Bam!" and the juggling knives. For Essie, being a chef was more fun than it was work. She was promoted to head chef early on at Round Hill Hotel. Essie had discovered her hidden talent, and she began to let it shine.

She had few regrets about her turbulent breakup with Stedman. As a matter of fact, she was grateful for the day when she was forced to go out and seek a job, because it had helped her find her real God-given talent in life.

Chapter 8

Essie was thrilled about her newfound culinary career, and discovering her natural calling felt like finding gold in a hidden treasure box. Yet every now and then, she had a sad spell. Sometimes she sat in the corner by herself, feeling sad about how life had started so unfairly for her. More than anything else, she had a strong and growing concern about her sterility problem. As a female, she felt cursed by God for not being able to have children. Worse than that, she felt that she would always be shunned by men for being sterile.

It was at this point in her life that Essie developed the bad habit of smoking. It helped her to think more clearly during her sad mood swings, and it just felt right.

One day, while on her daily errands, Essie decided to take a cigarette break, and finding a pleasant spot, sat on the wall and gazed out over the town. Deep in thought and reflecting on how her life was going, she was interrupted by a minister who walked up to her and introduced himself.

"Hello, pretty young lady. My name is Reverend

Paul Murray. What's yours?"

"Essie, sir," she replied cordially, a bewildered look on her face.

"You look a bit sad today."

"I'm okay, sir."

The reverend persisted. "Tell me, my child, what's on your mind?"

Essie took a good look at the well-mannered and rather handsome black middle-aged minister. "Are you the pastor at Holy Cross Church of God in Mount Salem?"

"Yes, my dear child. Have you ever been to my church?"

"Yes, sir. I attended your Easter ceremony last year."

"Really?"

"I went with Nurse Ferguson and her family."

"Great. I'm very happy to hear you attended my church once before, but Miss Essie, it doesn't have to be an Easter celebration for you to attend."

"I know, sir."

"I would like you to pay us a visit next Sunday if you can."

Essie thought for a long while, then responded with a request of her own. "Pastor, I have a question for you."

"What is it, my child?"

"Why am I cursed by God?"

"No! No! Never say that again. That is not true. You are a special child of God. If you were not special, He would not have sent me here to talk with you today."

"Well, if I'm so special, why can't I have children?"

The reverend closed his eyes and turned his face upward in a dramatic way as he whispered a quick prayer to God. "Do you believe in God, my child?"

"Yes, sir," she said without hesitation.

"Well, let's go somewhere and talk about this matter. Where do you live? Is it very close by here?"

"Yes, sir."

The reverend stood up and turned to look around him, wanting to ensure their privacy. It was as if he were about to do or say the unforgivable. "The Lord is telling me right now that I should touch you so you can be healed."

Those words sounded good to Essie's ears, and she nodded several times. "I live not very far from here," she said, relief and joy on her face. "Let me take you home." Essie led the way to her house.

They held hands and prayed briefly. After the short prayer session, Reverend Murray turned to her. "Essie, my child, do you believe in God?"

"Yes, sir."

"Essie, my child, do you believe in miracles?"

"Yes, sir."

"Then my child, take off those worldly condemned clothes you're wearing and let me heal you through the grace of God."

Essie was shocked to hear those words from the good minister, but at this point she had nothing to lose. So she obeyed him and undressed except for her panties and brassiere.

"All of it, my dear child, all of it. Take off all your sinful, forsaken clothes," he said, shouting in a strong, demanding tone.

"Okay, Reverend." Essie reluctantly complied.

"Essie, you are like a pretty, unspoiled flower that was planted by the rough terrain or by the wayside. Do you believe in God?" he asked again.

This time she did not respond.

"Essie, my child, do you believe in miracles?"

This time Essie started to laugh. Ripples of mirth

burst from her throat, a kind of laughter that was unique to Essie: strong, loud, and seemingly endless. "Pastor, get on with your business. Let's just get it over with."

"Well then, kindly turn your back to me and bend over while I get myself ready, my child," he said in a soft and provocative voice. As usual, he altered his tone of voice to match the action he needed.

Essie did what the good minister said without question.

"Oh Lord! Oh Lord! Thank you for choosing me today to do thy work. Praise be to God in the most high. Thank you, Lord. Thank you, Lord. Thank you, Lord."

Chapter 9

A tyrant must put on the appearance of uncommon devotion to religion. Subjects are less apprehensive of illegal treatment from a ruler whom they consider God-fearing and pious. On the other hand, they do less easily move against him, believing that he has the gods on his side.
Aristotle

After Essie's strange and eerie encounter with the Reverend Paul Murray, her faith in God became even more questionable than ever, and she was completely confused. She couldn't understand what had happened to her and concluded it was just another bizarre occurrence in her life.

However, when she missed her menstruation on the following month, Essie started believing again. As corny as it sounded, she believed it was a miracle of God, and this time, she would bring the pregnancy to term. She felt happy again, but hesitated to raise her hopes too high.

Essie wanted to let Reverend Murray know the

good news, but the only way she knew of getting in touch with him was to go to his church. So she decided to attend services on the following Sunday with the hope of speaking to him. She knew she'd have to be discreet. She shivered when she thought about how strange the situation was. She felt like a religious groupie chasing after a high-status celebrity.

She went to church as planned, but the reverend wasn't there. At the end of the service, one of the deacons informed her that Reverend Murray had just emigrated to Canada with his wife and kids. Essie never said why she wanted to speak with him. She just went home with the knowledge that she needed. She realized that Reverend Murray was leaving the island, so just before he left, he had to get his kicks or his game on with some easy, naive chick. He was just like all the other guys who would say or do anything to get under a female's dress.

Essie had her answer, and she realized that she would have to deal with this pregnancy by herself. It was an unsatisfactory situation, to be sure, but she felt quite contented with what she considered to be a trade-off with God. God was giving her a baby, but the baby would not have a father. She accepted her fate in life and would step up to the plate and be both mother and father to her miracle baby.

The only worry Essie had was how to deal with work and her bills in the final stage of her pregnancy. The answer came to her from one of her coworkers at the Round Hill Hotel. His real name was Richard Browdie, but everyone called him Longman. He was very tall and skinny—a handsome, light-skinned, charming chap in his late twenties. Hence the nickname.

Longman found out that Essie was pregnant after speaking to her one day at work. He'd always admired her beauty and her strict work ethic and had wanted to approach her earlier, but was too timid to do so. Therefore, by the time he got himself to speak to her on a personal basis, he was very disappointed to find out that he had made his move just a little too late. Another man had obviously beaten him to the punch, because she was now pregnant.

However, as they continued talking, he realized that the baby's father would not be in Essie's life. This gave him some hope. He knew within himself that he cared enough about Essie to date her even with a child. Although he really wished that the baby was his, he and Essie grew to be friends and lovers over the next four months. By this time, Essie's pregnancy had become obvious and was a grave concern to her manager at work.

One day, Longman went on his lunch break and found Essie in tears. The manager was pressuring her to quit her job due to her pregnancy and slow productivity. Longman encouraged her to go ahead and quit. She could come and live with him in his one-bedroom apartment over on the other side of town. They were already dating anyway, so he thought he might as well take on the full responsibility of being a father to her baby and build a serious relationship with her. He promised to take care of her and that she would not have to worry about anything.

Comforted by Longman's thoughtful words, Essie eventually took his advice and quit her job. She moved in with him when she was in her seventh month of pregnancy.

The one-bedroom apartment was a little tight for her and Longman. Essie worried about how it would work out when the baby came, but she was relieved and happy that at least she and her baby would have a roof over their heads and someone to take care of them.

When the baby was born, Longman was thrilled

and supportive, as he had promised. He was a good father to the baby, although he decided not to let her carry his last name. Instead, he encouraged Essie to name the baby, a pretty little black-skinned girl, after the reverend. The miracle baby became Gena Murray. Essie was the one who decided on Gena, a short form of genie. According to the English dictionary, a genie is a supernatural spirit that often takes human form, serving the person who calls on it. Essie truly believed that God had sent Gena to her, and she was her miracle baby, the answer to her dreams.

Happy with her baby and her relationship with Longman, Essie couldn't have asked for a better outcome. She only had one growing concern with Longman. He was a nice guy and excellent provider, but he had a drinking problem that grew worse with time.

After Essie had lived with him for about eight months, he began to come home on Friday nights—which was his payday—noisy, roaring drunk. Essie paid no attention until one night, he came home very drunk and wanted to make love to her. When she told him she was not in the mood, he demanded that she leave his house immediately and that she take her precious baby with her. He thought Essie preferred the baby over him. After all he had done for her and the baby, the least she could do was attend to his needs.

Essie calmed him down and gave him what he wanted, but from that time onward, she knew in her heart that a stupefied, staggering drunk was no father for her baby girl. This was not the way she wanted to live, nor was it the way she wanted her daughter to grow up.

She began to make plans, and the second time Longman came home woozy, drunken, and rowdy, demanding she do whatever he said or leave his house, she assured him she and the baby would leave soon. She redoubled her efforts to find a job, and by pure chance, met Mr. Allen, a popular barber who had his own business and was doing well for himself.

Chapter 10

Essie sat on a bench in the middle of downtown Montego Bay. She wore a short, multicolored miniskirt and a thin, white, sleeveless cotton blouse. She'd pulled her hair back and combed it into a long ponytail, and her tiny, sexy feet wore a pair of cute white pumps. She crossed her legs tight like a lady in a content mood.

Their eyes met, and they smiled. Mr. Allen walked over to her. "Hello, sexy lady, what's your name?"

"Essie. And yours?"

"I'm John Allen. I own the barbershop just down the street."

"Oh, really? I know where it is. I've passed by there many times."

"Could I offer you some lunch at the hillside plaza? I'd planned to eat a solitary meal, but I'd much prefer the company of a pretty young lady like you. Would you join me?"

"Sure. Why not?"

The lunch date went well, and the after-lunch was even better. They went for a walk by the ocean and eventually picked a private spot to stop and chat. They spent all afternoon getting to know each other, and the evening ended with Essie placing a sensuous kiss on Mr. Allen's lips. They made arrangements to meet for lunch the next day.

After the second lunch, they went straight to Mr. Allen's home. He headed to the kitchen to get Essie a drink, but she was already burning up with sexual heat, so she stripped off her clothes as she entered the door.

Mr. Allen had dreamed of something like this since he first met Essie yesterday. He slowly pressed his lips to hers. She opened her mouth and ran the tip of her tongue, tentative and soft, along his lower lip. He leaned into her, searching with his tongue as she opened her mouth wider. She tasted like sweet bubble gum, and her mouth was soft and yielding, inviting him in. Mr. Allen kissed her long and deep, reveling in the sensation of her tender lips against his. They made wild, sensational love right there on the kitchen floor. Gratified and pleased, they lay together, exhausted.

Not long after Essie met John Allen Sr., she moved from Longman's apartment into his home. John was a noble, sincere, upright family man with two kids of his own. He was fresh out of a divorce and had lost custody of his kids to his ex-wife in a hefty divorce agreement. The settlement was enough for his ex-wife and kids to live a very comfortable life. Therefore, he had no guilt about starting his life over with someone else, even with someone who already had a child who was not his own.

John was a handsome man in his early forties—light-skinned, conscientious, and intelligent. There was one outstanding thing about his appearance: he had beautiful wavy hair. Being a barber and the owner of a busy shop in the heart of Montego Bay, he kept his hair neat and attractive at all times. Any woman would be happy to have him father her children, and Essie was no exception. Within a month of living with John, she became pregnant with her second child. John never questioned the closeness of Essie's pregnancy to her last time with Longman, but she had doubts.

Essie was a fair-minded, forthright person who understood the big advantage that a mother had over the father of a child. Obviously, she was the only one who knew without a doubt that the child was hers. It was one of the sweetest and most wonderful joys of being a biological parent. She thought that if she could give that same certainty to the father of her children, it would no doubt be a great gift.

Essie believed that blind trust, when it came to paternity, was not necessarily love; it could simply be selfish female manipulation of a relationship, or even worse, a means for a female to intentionally hide the true paternity of her child. Therefore, if she truly loved her man, she would request a paternity test for her child. She would do it so the father could enjoy the same happiness and certainty as the mother.

If it were left up to Essie, the law of the land would require all babies to be tested for paternal confirmation immediately after birth. This was why she told John about her concerns.

Mr. Allen insisted that it was his child, but he was willing to compromise with Essie and give the baby two surnames. Therefore, the baby's official name was Junior J. Allen-Browdie to reflect Longman as a possible father.

As Junior grew older, his looks became more pronounced, mirroring John Allen, right down to his beautiful wavy hair. John had been right all along. He never had an ounce of doubt and was confident and happy about his first boy child. He loved him very much, but being the intelligent father that he was, he showed equal love and attention to both children.

About nine months after Junior's birth, Essie conceived another child. She delivered the baby the day after Christmas in 1953. This time it was a girl, a pretty little baby who looked just like Essie. They named her Betty Allen. John felt like he had regained everything that he had lost to his damnable ex-wife. He now had a much prettier, younger, and kinder woman in his life and three beautiful kids. He would take his new family everywhere he went because they were his pride and joy. Essie made John a happy man.

Essie was happy too, until John's terrible ex-wife came back into their lives and began causing trouble in their relationship. Audrey became angry when she noticed how proud John was of his new family. Jealous, she couldn't bear to see him so happy with his new life and independence. Audrey started sending her kids over to John with various different demands. Suddenly, she wanted to force the kids back into his life—not for his affection or benefit or for any good reason, but to cause trouble in his life.

Although John loved all his kids—Essie's first child and the two he had with her, plus his two daughters by Audrey—he would not let his ex-wife's evil plan disrupt his newfound happiness.

When she couldn't disrupt John's life by manipulating the kids, Audrey started verbally attacking Essie, and even threatened to fight her if she saw her on the streets. Essie tried to ignore her, but Audrey kept on bothering her. Eventually, Essie got fed up.

Essie heard rumors through the grapevine that John had an affair with a lady who reportedly visited his barbershop much too often. For obvious reasons, Essie's relationship with John suffered, and Essie decided to accept an offer made to her by a man she met while shopping one day. He was a rich black businessman named Conroy Levy, who lived out of town. He offered to take care of her and her three kids by getting an apartment for her in Montego Bay. That way, when he was in town, he would have a family and a place he could call his second home. Although she knew it would hurt John badly, she took Conroy Levy up on his offer and moved to her own apartment, which he completely subsidized.

This arrangement worked out well for Essie because she felt a little more independent. Moreover, she only saw Conroy Levy once a month when he came into town to do business. When he was in town, Essie would attend to his every need, but particularly, to his sexual desires. She often welcomed him in lingerie. "Hello, sweetheart. How was your drive into town?"

"It was tiresome, my dear. Thank you for asking."

She stood in the doorway wearing a short, black transparent dress which revealed her bright-red panties with layers of frills on the backside.

"You smell great, my love, and you look even better. I love your sexy outfit." He leaned in and kissed Essie on her lips.

"All for you, my sweetheart." Essie kissed him back and jiggled her voluptuous boobs in his face. "Come in. Let me have your shoes. The kids are with a friend of mine, so we're absolutely alone." She turned around and wiggled her body in a sexy way as she led Conroy inside to the bedroom and removed his shoes. "I missed you, sweetheart. I've been preparing for your arrival."

"I see. The room is smartly painted, and everything is looking clean and neat."

"Yes, all for you, my love." Essie fell backward onto the bed with her feet still planted on the floor. "Come here. Will you please come and join me, honey?

Don't just stand there."

"Sure, honey. There's nothing else I'd rather do right now." He stared at Essie as she slowly undressed, starting with her underwear. "You have a wonderful body." Conroy also started to undress.

"Don't tell me about it. Come and get me. I'm all yours."

"Okay, I will." They both climbed onto the bed and started kissing. He kissed her along the right side of her neck. He moved her hair to one side and kissed her neck and collarbone, licking her smooth, velvety skin all the way down to the tips of her toes and back to her glorious middle section, making Essie moan and groan for more. Conroy knew well how to please a woman in sexual heat. He knew the art of lovemaking. His love was ecstasy. His love was large. His time could never be too long. It slowly opened up her body and blew her mind. Being well endowed, he gave her all that he had, and she loved every minute of it.

When Conroy was in town, he would stay for three or four days at most. He was very happy to have a pretty, sexy woman like Essie to spend the time with. Providing her with an apartment was more than worth it.

After about a year together, Essie got pregnant, and they named the baby girl Lela Levy. Not long after Lela's birth, a relative named Miriam who lived in Mount Salem, a popular district in Montego Bay, offered to help her with the child and support her. Essie took Miriam up on the offer and let her unofficially adopt the baby, with the genuine intention of taking her back at a later time. Miriam had some difficulties having children of her own at that time, so she was happy to care for baby Lela.

Chapter 11

Conroy Levy agreed with the unofficial adoption of Lela by Essie's cousin Miriam. He understood that it would mean less of a financial burden for both Essie and him, though he could have borne that burden. Lela Levy had a strong resemblance to her father, who was in no way a handsome fellow, but he was a relatively rich man. It's often said that a rich man is nothing but a poor man with money. Whatever the case, Mr. Levy was considered a wealthy businessman by all standards.

He gave Essie a used pearl-black Chevrolet even before she had a license to drive. Essie didn't mind not having a license because she was able to employ someone to drive it for her. Whenever she planned to do her errands, she would call her driver and be transported wherever she wanted to go.

Essie started enjoying the high-society lifestyle of being Levy's second lady. She loved it, and for the first time, she felt that life was being fair to her. She even found a way to make extra money when Mr. Levy was away. She used her car as a taxicab, and her driver ran a regular route. The driver would take out a salary for himself and would give Essie the difference from the profits made each week.

This arrangement served Essie well for a long time, until the driver had an accident and the car was a total loss. When Mr. Levy heard about this incident, he became upset with Essie for using the vehicle as a taxi without telling him. He felt betrayed and stopped visiting Essie when he was in the area. He cut her off completely and stopped sending money or child support.

Essie did everything she knew to do to reach him and tried sending him messages and letters, but he would not respond. Luckily, she had had the forethought to put all the extra cash she'd made from her taxi business in the bank. Therefore, she had some money to keep her going for a little while, but it didn't last long. She started looking for employment as a cook in various hotels and private resorts. Due to her excellent recommendation from Round Hill Hotel, she got a job at the Chatham Hotel Resort. She then employed a friend, Vera, to help her with the kids.

By this time, Essie had developed a drinking habit, and her smoking had increased. If anyone asked her why she drank, she would say she had too many thoughts running through her head at night and she drank what it took to put her to sleep. On her way home from work every day, she would stop at the rum bar and order a quarter quart of Jamaican white rum to take with her. Then, just before bedtime, she would drink the full quantity in one sitting.

On her way to the rum bar one night, she met her next love mate, Leonard Williams. He was a frequent visitor there. A scholar and once a highly respected lawyer in Montego Bay, he was a popular figure, although he was not a handsome man. He was very wealthy and had a great personality, and he could get any girl he wanted. He usually chose the prettiest and most desirable ladies in town.

Therefore, when he saw Essie, he decided he would have her. One day he invited her over to his mansion for lunch and sweet-talked Essie into making love to him. "Young lady, I would give the world just to touch that lovely young sexy body of yours."

"Really? Is that so?"

"Sure, there's nothing I wouldn't give to make love to you."

"You really think that I have a wonderful body?"

"Yes, I do." Leonard leaned forward to touch Essie's hips. "Yes, your body is heavenly."

"Oh, you're just saying that to make me feel good."

"Let me feel these lovely boobs." He began touching Essie's perky breasts. "How nice they are."

Essie simply smiled at him, so he continued to touch and caress her. Before long, he had Essie's boobs in his mouth. He played on her most sensitive weak spot, and that was all it took.

Essie's mouth quivered as she sizzled under the romantic manipulation of her body's erogenous zone by Leonard the lady charmer. She couldn't resist his audacious advances and gave in to his charms, allowing him to strip her clothes off as he smoothly caressed her body.

He led her to his bedroom, where she climbed into bed. He took his clothes off and hopped into bed with her. They started exchanging sensuous kisses, and Leonard proceeded to kiss her all over her body.

He charmed Essie and successfully won her over. They had a brief relationship, but when Essie realized he was an out-of-control alcoholic, she broke it off before it got too far. At least, that was what she thought.

63

In reality, she ended the despicable relationship just a little too late. She missed her period the following month and was pregnant by the alcoholic lawyer. Essie was not at all happy with this news, but she would never abort a healthy child. Moreover, because of how difficult it was for her to have her first child, she had promised herself that she would never abort any of her pregnancies. When the baby was born one day after Christmas, December 26, 1957, she named her Myrtle Williams.

Now Essie had five children to feed and care for. With a big assist from her cousin Miriam, who helped with Lela, she started working in two different places. She would work in the mornings at the Chatham Hotel Resort and at night at Verne Hill Resort. She skillfully juggled these two jobs so she could maintain a roof over her kids' heads and give them good food to eat.

On weekends she would do the regular grocery shopping. She had a very tight budget, so she went to the local food market because the food was known to be fresher and less expensive. One day she went to buy yams from a vendor there, and a strange thing happened.

After she chose the yams and some mangoes, the man weighed the food, put it in a bag, and gave it to her. "Here, this is from me to you, my pretty lady."

"Thank you, sir, but what is the cost?"

"Nothing, my pretty lady," the kind vendor replied, as if giving things away was not a big deal to him.

"Thank you. God bless you, sir."

She thought that it was a little strange because no one gave anything away for free, but she just smiled and walked away. The next day, while she was home relaxing and reminiscing on the kind deed that had come her way, it dawned on her that she remembered the face of the vendor. She recognized his eyes and his smile, but she could not for the life of her remember where they had met before. It bothered her all week, so much so that she couldn't wait to go back to the local market on the following weekend to meet this person again and to find out how she knew him.

Saturday morning bright and early, Essie hurried to the market, more to satisfy her curiosity than to purchase groceries. She rushed to the same spot where the kind gentleman had been, but he wasn't there. Baffled, she circled the area several times as she shopped, but couldn't find him. She checked with the nearby vendors, but no one recognized her description. After a whole day of inquiry, she gave up and went home, vowing to return every week until she found out who the kind man was.

Three weekends later, Essie found the vendor whose identity had escaped her. Not knowing what to say, she went up to him and ordered the same things she'd ordered on the previous occasion: yellow yams and a few mangoes.

After weighing the produce, the vendor put it in a bag and gave it to her. "Here, my pretty lady. This is from me to you."

"Thank you, sir, but I want to know why you're giving me this food for free."

"You remind me of a good friend I once had. She was special to me, so giving you this gift is like giving it to her."

"What was her name?"

"Essie Streete." He tossed the name out casually, although it meant the world to him. He didn't expect much reaction. What could it mean to this woman, anyway?

All of a sudden, it came to Essie. *Tim!* Her whole body quivered, and she let out a shrill scream, causing a stir in the market. It all came together: the eyes, the familiar smile. He was her old friend from childhood. She was fourteen again, living back in the countryside of Cascade and barely speaking to anyone in her jealous and abusive family. Tim was her only friend. He would walk her home from school in the evenings and listen to her talk about her unfair treatment by her adopted family.

Tim was sixteen at the time, very black-skinned and rather handsome. He felt privileged to be Essie's friend. He knew he wasn't the brightest child in school and planned on quitting, but Essie convinced him to stay in school. He only agreed because it meant he got to walk her home each day. They became good friends, which helped her cope with being an unwelcome member of her household.

One day during those teenage years, Tim saw her standing at the public pipe in Cascade waiting in line to get her bucket filled with water. He greeted his friend with a warm, happy-to-see-you hug. "Hey Essie, you're out very early this morning, I see."

"Oh yeah," Essie said. "I have to fill the three water drums at home, so I thought I'd get an early start." Her cheerful tone showed she was happy to see her friend. It was always wonderful to meet him on the road.

"Really?"

"Can you believe it?"

"Three huge drums?"

"Three huge drums."

"That small bucket will take forever, Essie. I could take a slow boat to China and back, and you would still be here filling dem drums."

"You can say that again. I'll never finish today. I couldn't find a big bucket, so I just took the first one without a leak in it."

"Essie, I have an idea. Let me run home to fetch a larger bucket so I can help you fill up faster."

"Would you? Thank you, Tim. You're the best."

Tim ran home, eager to help Essie. He considered it a pleasure and couldn't think of anything he'd rather do. He returned shortly with a large bucket in hand.

It was always a joy being around Essie. Aunt Rose wouldn't let him come into their yard, so he would sometimes wait outside the gate, just hoping to get a glimpse of Essie. He didn't try to go in because he believed in the saying, "Never test the water with both feet." He was content to meet Essie on her errands somewhere along the streets or at the shops.

The drums held water for both household and personal use. Because Essie's house had no plumbing, all water needs were satisfied through the drums. On a rainy day or during the wet season, there was less need to get water from the public pipes. The drums, set up in strategic locations outside of the house, collected rainwater through gutters, which were mostly made from bamboo trees and lined the top of the house on all four sides. The residents of Cascade never complained that there was too much rain. Rainwater meant more than a blessing to them; it meant survival.

Another time back in Cascade, Tim saw Essie on her way to the river to wash some of her family's dirty clothes. "Essie, where are you going?" he shouted.

"To the river," Essie shouted back.

Tim was on the other side of the road playing a game of dominoes with his friends. "Which one?"

"Rocky Point River."

"To do what?"

"Tim, stop bothering me. You can see the basket of dirty clothes on my head. If you want to come, just come."

That was all Tim needed to hear. He ran across the street to join Essie. "All the way to Rocky Point

River? That's very far, but I'll come anyway."

"You know you want to come, so don't pretend."

"That's a lot of clothes, Essie. That basket is really big." Tim nodded at the overloaded brown plastic basket, so full of dirty clothes that a variety of items hung over the side.

A well-wrapped piece of clothing provided a buffer between Essie's head and the basket. Essie skillfully leaned the packed container to one side. She looked like a typical country girl. This only made Tim admire her even more.

"Yeah, it is," Essie said. "Are you going to help me with it?"

"No! Are you crazy, Essie?"

"Why not? You're not my friend anymore?"

"Yes, but my friends will laugh at me."

"Laugh? Why?" Essie pretended ignorance, although she knew very well that he was right. Boys can be so brutal to each other when it comes to those types of manly myths. She figured she'd tease him a bit.

"They'll laugh because I'm carrying women's clothes on my head," Tim said.

"So what's wrong with that?"

"You don't know what they say about that kind of thing? It mek yu dung grow," Tim said in a mix of Jamaican patois dialect. "You done know that already, mon. I don't need to have my height retarded because I carry female clothes on my head."

"That's ridiculous, Tim. I've never heard of that before. You're just a male chauvinist piglet who follows silly ideas."

In the end, Tim did help Essie with her load. He helped her all the way to the river. While at the river, he sat on a rock close by while Essie washed her clothes. They talked and made fun of each other until it was soon time to go.

On their way back from the river, Tim again helped Essie with her load, but this time they stopped to rest more often. The wet clothes, much heavier now, slowed them considerably, as did the uphill journey. On one of their many rest stops, they decided to pick some mangoes off a nearby tree. Tim climbed the tree and threw the ripe, delicious fruit to Essie. When they had collected enough, they sat under the tree and enjoyed their treats. Refreshed, they continued on their journey home.

Essie enjoyed their time together, and Tim was delighted to have spent the day with the prettiest girl in the whole town. Tim's friendship back when they were kids was a breath of fresh air to Essie, but she still dreamed of a bigger and better place than the little village of Cascade.

Although Essie had left the countryside of Cascade behind, she always carried a soft spot in her heart for Tim. She'd missed her friend dearly, and sometimes wondered how he was doing. Never in her wildest dreams did she expect to see him in Montego Bay so many years later and, of all places, at the local food market.

She emerged from her flashback and shouted to the kind vendor, "I'm Essie Streete! And your name is Tim, right?"

"Timothy Brown," he said, nodding several times as he gazed into her eyes.

"You're Tim? My best friend, my Tim from back in Cascade?" Essie grinned, her face radiating joy.

"Essie? My sweet Essie? My Lord, I can't believe my eyes."

"Tim, what's happened to you? You look so old, I wouldn't recognize you at all," she said frankly.

They embraced, holding each other in a long and

joyful hug. Thrilled to see each other and know they were both alive and well, they shed sweet tears, oblivious to those around them. They didn't care that people stared at them as they renewed their childhood friendship. For them, a miracle had occurred.

They stepped aside, as they had a lot to talk about. A number of years had passed between them, and they now had a lot to catch up on. As luck would have it, they both had kids, but they were free and single at the time. It was like it was meant to be. They didn't waste any more time hiding their true feelings, but confessed everything to each other. They initiated an intimate relationship that very same day.

Essie brought Tim home to meet her kids, and he spent the night at her place. It was one of the most sensuous and erotic nights of their lives. After Essie prepared a very special dinner for Tim, they spent the rest of the evening locked away in their room.

Essie knew she had a beautiful body. She stripped off her clothes, remaining in the nude for the rest of the night.

Tim stripped down to his boxer shorts and admired his newfound love from head to toe. She looked great to him. He loved a woman with long, sexy legs, and he wholeheartedly loved Essie's legs. He loved her wide, shapely hips and her small waist, her navel, and her big sexy boobs. He loved the coy smile on her face, especially when she got naughty.

"Tim, come over here, honey. It's time to sample your gift." Essie turned toward him and sensuously slapped one side of her naked batti. Essie may have been a shy, naive person in public, but she sure was a big tease in the bedroom.

"What did an old countryman like me do to deserve such a pretty young woman like you, Essie?"

Tim climbed up onto the bed and was about to

say something else when Essie stopped him. "Enough talking, Tim. May I . . . you know?" She looked down at his boxer shorts.

"Sure! Why not? I just took a shower, and I'm as clean as a whistle."

"I only do this for you, Tim, because I really do love you."

They could not have been happier with their emotional and joyful reunion. They discovered they lived in two different worlds and both liked where they were living. However, they promised to meet each other halfway. They would compromise and help to carry each other's relationship baggage, because that's what good friends do.

Tim remained in the parish of Hanover. He lived in Clear Mount of Jericho, a small town not too far away from Cascade. He had become an independent farmer with lots of land and brought produce to Montego Bay once a month to sell at the local market.

Essie decided not to return to the country, but nevertheless, vowed to maintain an intimate relationship with Tim, even if it had to be a long-distance one.

Over a period of ten years, whenever Tim was in town, he would visit Essie and spend the night or a full weekend in Montego Bay. During that time, Essie bore two sons by Tim. The first, born on August 10, 1959, they called Karl Brown. The second, born four years later on June 12, 1963, they named Leonard Brown.

One night when Leonard was two years old, Essie returned home very late from work in a taxicab. The area where she lived had no streetlights, so the headlights of the taxi provided the only light. When the cab was still two blocks away from Essie's home, there, focused in the lights, was a young boy sitting in the middle of the road. As the headlights approached, he started running to the side of the street to avoid the car.

Essie saw the child and began to scream. "Stop! Stop! That's my baby! Stop! Oh my God! What the hell is he doing on the road at this time of night?" She jumped out of the car as soon as it stopped and ran to her son. She couldn't believe her son was out there and wondered what would have happened if she hadn't come home when she did. Surely her son would've been struck by a moving vehicle in the pitch dark.

What had happened? Everyone was asleep, including the babysitter. Moreover, they were not aware that Leonard was able to walk, so they felt sure he was safe in the house.

Essie immediately quit her night job to make sure that something like that never happened again. Many years later, she still remembered this shocking incident and often said that was when she realized Leonard was special. From that night on, she knew in her heart he was born to be a great person, and she hoped to see it happen.

Karl was in much safer hands. When he was two years old, Tim volunteered to keep his first baby boy with him in the country. This he did to help Essie with some of her load as a single parent. Leonard remained with Essie in Montego Bay, and Tim would readily supply the whole family with free produce whenever he was in town.

Chapter 12

O, my love is like a red, red rose
that's newly sprung in June:
O, my love is like the melody
that's sweetly played in tune.

As fair art thou, my bonnie lass,
so deep in love am I;
and I will love thee still, my dear,
Till all the seas go dry.

Till all the seas go dry, my dear,
And the rocks melt with the sun;
And I will love thee still my dear,
While the sands of life shall run.

And fare thee well, my only love!
And fare thee well a while!
And I will come again, my love,
Though it were ten thousand miles!

Robert Burns, 1794

The long-distance relationship between Tim and Essie was blessed, wholesome, and free of major stress. Tim was madly in love with her just as he had been as a young teenager, and he would give Essie anything she asked for, if it was within his means.

The only problem was that his means were not much to a city girl. Tim's wealth was in his country farmland. He had lots of it, over a hundred acres he'd gained through hard labor. Each time he reaped a crop, he would use the profit to purchase more land. In addition to that, the more he farmed, the more land the government would give him as an incentive to increase production.

Though Tim was rich in potential real estate, no one with money would buy the land except to use it for farming. Moreover, a lot of hard work and toil would be required to bring the land up to farmable quality. An average farmer couldn't afford this land, so with few potential buyers, it had little resale value. Tim never minded that, because he was happy being a country farmer. He had never liked having a boss, and he liked the peace of mind that came with living a simple country life.

The best Tim could do for Essie was to supply her with a great deal of fresh food. He would therefore bring box after box of fresh produce that he harvested every month. This was perfect for Essie, because she had more than seven hungry mouths to feed at any one time. Therefore, food was one less thing Essie and her large family had to worry about. Her small salary could take care of everything else.

In addition to being friends first, Tim and Essie were truly in love with each other, so they could understand each other's differences. Although one loved the country with its simple life, and the other loved the big-city lifestyle, they held this relationship together for almost ten years. This was the longest bond that Essie ever had, and it provided her and her children with the most stable period of their lives.

However, the kids were getting older and had needs greater than the need for food. Gena, approaching nineteen, was almost an adult. Essie knew she could reason with Tim and that he would understand, so she went to the country to have a serious heart-to-heart talk with him.

Tim always welcomed her warmly whenever she visited. He treated her like a queen, pampered her, and near worshiped her. Essie didn't have to raise a hand to do anything. He even cooked for her and nicely dressed up his home. It was his pleasure to satisfy Essie in every way. Moreover, he knew deep down in his heart that she was in a class far above him. He knew that he was not worthy of such a beautiful, sophisticated, big-city lady like Essie. He was honored to have her love and attention.

That day, when Essie visited Tim, he rolled out the red carpet as usual. They had a wonderful country-style dinner with their son Karl. The meal was just the way Essie loved it. Afterward, they sent Karl outside to play. Then they went to the bedroom and locked the door.

While Tim undressed and climbed into bed, Essie changed into sexy black silk lingerie for Tim to admire. By now, Essie had gained some weight, but this only made her more attractive to Tim. He loved a woman with a big bottom and large boobs, not to mention sexy legs. She paraded around the room like a model while he admired her intensely. He could see her very large buttons protruding through her fishnet top. He also noticed her long, sexy legs, always one of her best assets.

Though a little surprised by her actions, Tim was

more excited than he had ever been and couldn't wait for Essie to join him in bed. But Essie didn't rush into bed with him that evening. Instead, she told him that she had something very important to say to him.

She sat down beside him on the bed. "Tim, you've been my friend since I was fourteen," she said softly, "and I want you to be my friend until the end. I love you, and I will always love you. You are a very special person in my life." She leaned over closer to him, slowly and tenderly stroking Tim's large manhood with her velvety soft hands. "But I have something very important to tell you, and I would like you to understand my position."

"What is it, my pretty lady? Just tell me, because you know you can tell me anything. I know you better than any other person on this earth, so don't be afraid. I will understand."

"I have a lot of needs, Tim, financial needs you cannot solve. I met a wealthy guy in Montego Bay who promised to help me with my finances, and I'm going to accept his offer."

Tim felt his heart break within him, and for a moment, he forgot how to breathe as he fought the pain in his gut. He remained silent for a long time, and it seemed as if time stood still and the noisy silence lasted at least a lifetime. His heart was pierced, and he was bleeding a heavy flow of internal sorrow. The thing he dreaded most, his biggest fear in life, had come to pass. His beloved was leaving him for a big-time city guy. He had to be strong, strong for Essie, because that was what good friends did for each other. He slowly raised his head and looked her in her eyes. "That's okay, my love. You must do what you must to survive. I'll be right here waiting for you whenever you need me."

"Thank you, Tim, for understanding. I still love you." Essie climbed into bed with him. They made violent, explosive love, yet it was filled with strong, caring affection. They threw caution to the wind, releasing their inner beast. A sea of warm, tingling sensations washed over Essie's body. She was soaked with sweat as spasm after climactic spasm coursed and rippled through her body. They synchronized their moves until they became one.

It was rough sex with deep passion. At the end, they held each other close and cried because they knew it was their last time together. It was a sad day for both of them.

Chapter 13

Mr. Bernard Dun was a self-made wealthy white Jamaican of short stature but large personality. Not only was he short, but he had a petite body structure. Handsome of face, he always dressed casually.

He made his riches from livestock farming in the city. He sold beef and poultry on a commercial scale and also supplied a large sector of his community with milk from his cows and eggs from his hens. He was well established in the town of Montego Bay and had a large but average-looking home on an extensive piece of property in a nice residential area of the city. His farm was at a different location from his place of residence.

Essie and Bernard Dun made an eye-catching pair because they were so physically mismatched. Essie was tall and had a thick body, while Mr. Dun was short and thin. In spite of this, Mr. Dun was infatuated with Essie and pursued her aggressively, offering her clothes, jewelry, money, and free livestock products.

With Tim's blessing, she welcomed Bernard's advances, and from the day Essie returned to Montego Bay, she was all his. She gave herself completely to

Bernard.

Bernard Dun was a strict businessman with a frank and dogmatic attitude. He made it clear to Essie that because she had so many children, they wouldn't live together, but he would wholly support her and her kids. Essie was okay with that, since her relationship with Tim had been the same. In fact, she preferred it that way, having become used to her semi-independent lifestyle.

Although Essie would visit Bernard on a regular basis, his visits to her home were rare. He had one son of his own, but although he could enjoy kids, he did not want to be around a large family. However, he expressed his desire early in their relationship that Essie give him a child because she was such a pretty woman.

That was okay with Essie. She truly loved her kids and believed they would change her life for the better. Every child she bore represented another chance of achieving her hope, the hope that one day, one of them would make her proud by becoming a doctor, lawyer, or a great person in some noticeable manner.

Essie herself dreamed of living a comfortable, worry-free lifestyle, but she didn't need to be rich. If riches came her way, she wouldn't turn them down, but she only wanted the ability to give her kids a better life than she had.

Essie also didn't mind having one more child if she could. Her only concern was whether she could still have healthy children, considering that she was now in her forties. She came to the conclusion that having babies was one of her strongest bargaining tools, and she had brought that belief to all of her prior relationships.

When a man saw a pretty woman like her, the first thing he thought about after sex was having a pretty little baby of his own. It seemed to her that all the men in her life pursued her for her body and her offspring. She even went so far as believing that some men preferred her offspring to her body.

Essie realized that God had blessed her after all, blessed her with the ability to have children, and with this ability, she was able to survive. Having kids was her survival tool, as well as her bargaining tool. So far, it seemed that she was at the losing end of all of her previous bargains, but she still had high hopes. Like an addicted gambler, she kept betting on the future prospects of her kids.

She only hoped that at least one of her bargaining chips would pay off in the long run. Maybe one of her kids would turn out to be a great person in the world.

It was early in their relationship when Essie became pregnant for the last time. Bernard was overjoyed at the birth of a wonderful baby boy, and together they named the child Bunny Dun. Essie felt tremendous relief when she brought the child to full term. She had been afraid that her increasingly bad habits of drinking and smoking, plus her age factor, might prevent her from delivering a healthy baby.

She was very nervous about the consequences of not having a successful delivery, remembering all too well the loss of her first lover, Stedman, due to her lost third pregnancy. She knew that her relationship with Bernard hinged on the successful delivery of a child. Thus, she felt a big weight fall off her shoulders after the birth. With Bunny, she repaid him for all the things he had done and continued to do for her and her large family.

She and Bernard maintained their arrangement for a time, but as Bunny grew older, Bernard cut back on the support payments. He eventually told Essie he was unable to provide for her whole family and could only give enough child support for Bunny. Eventually, he started decreasing that also.

Essie was upset but not at all surprised. She had seen it coming and knew all along that Bernard had only been nice to her because he badly wanted a child from her and would do anything to get one. She was right about him all along.

Essie felt better when she considered that it was not a bad deal. He had something she needed, and she had something he needed. It was a good arrangement while it lasted. Now she had to do what she did best— lean on her single-parent strength and skill to make it from here on.

Essie didn't complain. She braced herself to find a good chef job so she could stay in the two-bedroom apartment that Conroy Levy had initially gotten for her.

Chapter 14

Essie went back to work, and this time she got a job at a large, ten-bedroom private resort in Ironshore, owned by a Dr. McNelly. He was a rich white American, a snowbird who had purchased the large home as a vacation retreat. Dr. McNelly lived in the United States and only returned to Jamaica once or twice a year during the winter months. When he was not in residence, the home doubled as a guest house.

Dr. McNelly hired a local real estate company to manage and maintain the property. The company functioned as a travel agency and residential management group, placing advertisements around the world for tourists to lease the mansion. The company also hired staff to take care of the property: a chambermaid, a butler who was also a gardener, and Essie as the chef.

Essie was excited. She had prayed for this type of work and always dreamed about getting it someday. No disgruntled manager peered over her shoulders or questioned her recipes, making this her ideal job. She was her own boss as long as the guests didn't complain about her service or her cooking. She felt confident about her abilities, and she knew that this was a place where she would be able to take her natural cooking skill to the next level. She began an intense reading and self-education program at the Montego Bay Public Library and went there every chance she got.

While returning from the library one day, Essie met an interesting man named Ruben Malcolm. He was a little older than her, but very handsome and well built, with a strong, muscular body. He asked Essie if she would like to go out with him, stating he was single with no kids. He had just separated from his domestic wife, but he neglected to tell Essie that part of his story.

Essie liked him, and even with as many bad experiences with men as she had already endured, she felt she needed a strong man to lean on. However, after many failures, she knew what she wanted and what she didn't. "Ruben, I have eight kids, and I don't intend to have anymore." Essie was firm about that point.

"Well, lovely lady, you don't have to worry about that. I'm very comfortable not having my own children. Your kids will be mine. I've always dreamed of being a part of a large family."

"I have six kids living with me, so I don't want any overnights. You can visit, but you can't stay. I don't mind meeting at your place or anywhere you want me to meet you."

"Yes, that will be fine with me," Ruben replied.

"I have financial commitments, and I'll need your help. If you don't have any money, I don't want to waste my time. Okay, Ruben? We need to establish these things from the start."

"I work a construction job. Sometimes I have a lot of money when work is good, and sometimes I have very little when it gets scarce."

"Okay then, just as long as we have everything

clear, we can date each other and see where it goes."

"Okay, let's start by having dinner somewhere nice. Is that a deal?"

"Deal," Essie replied.

Essie was proud of herself. It felt good to demand what she wanted. She wished she had had that strength earlier. Maybe her life would have been different. After all, life is just a matter of deals and breaks.

Essie and Ruben had a long, wonderful relationship. It was a complete reversal from Essie's previous experience with men.

Ruben desperately wanted to be a part of Essie's family, to be a real father to her kids. Whenever he was around them, the pride he felt showed in his face. He made himself useful whenever he went to Essie's apartment. He fixed everything that was broken and tried to play a fatherly role for each child.

Ruben believed that kids and a family, in general, needed more than money. He believed they needed fatherly love and attention, something usually missing in a single-female family. He believed that with that fatherly love and personal attention, kids could go far in life because it gave them the kind of confidence a mother couldn't instill by herself.

Ruben also believed that the psychological development of children required 50/50 input from both parents. A single mother, with her best efforts, could only increase her input to 60 percent, at best. Therefore, Ruben believed that the children of single parents never developed to their maximum potential, no matter how much time and money one of their parents gave them.

In Ruben's opinion, kids needed both parents equally, and they should only be denied that basic need if there was no other viable alternative. Moreover, this was Ruben's chance to feel what it would really be like if he had kids and a large family of his own.

Essie was the one who limited Ruben's role. She didn't want him to change the structure or dynamics of her family. Her kids were mostly grown, and she couldn't risk putting a father in their lives just to see him walk away, leaving them brokenhearted. She would shield them from that disaster, instead taking the full brunt of the blow by herself. She considered herself an expert in being brokenhearted. There was no doubt she could deal with it, but not her kids.

Therefore, she never gave Ruben the chance to wholly fill a fatherly role in her family. Skeptical, she kept him at a distance and would call him only when she needed him, or she would visit him at his home. She never let him fully into her family's life.

That arrangement worked well until one day while she was relaxing in his bed, and a seemingly madwoman broke into the house and tried fighting her. Essie had to run for her life. When she found out the madwoman was Ruben's ex- wife, Essie abandoned her relationship with him.

She landed on her feet, started running, and never looked back.

Chapter 15

The horn of the old country bus bellowed as it ripped around the corner. Its face looked tired and overworked as it approached, and grayish-black smoke streamed into the air from its tail. It leaned to one side as if it was about to turn over.

Essie had taken her kids to the countryside to spend a few days of the summer near Tim. They loved it and always looked forward to this annual activity. This time, they had gone by way of the old country bus.

It was overloaded with baskets and bags full of fruit, green bananas, potatoes, and other farm produce. There was no more space left on top of the bus, not even enough for a fly.

The rusty red-and-gray metal caravan pulled up to the bus stop at Jericho Square. The driver, dressed in a full suit of brown shirt and pants, jumped from the bus and jogged alongside it. Still leaning to one side, the vehicle jolted and bucked twice before it came to a complete stop, sinking lower to the ground as it did so. The driver wasted no time getting to the back and climbing on top of the bus in order to unload the needed items carried there.

An elderly lady slowly stepped down off the bus through the front exit, followed by a continuous line of passengers behind her. There was one exit at the front of the bus and another at the back, and the passengers poured out of the two doorways in a somewhat orderly manner.

At the back door, fourteen-year-old Junior leaped out. "Jericho, we're here!" he shouted.

Gena, age sixteen, sprang out right behind him. "Yeah, we're here," she said. "Come on, guys, let's go to the back of the bus to get our stuff." Happy and excited to have reached her destination, she held out her hand to thirteen-year-old Betty to help her down the steps.

"Thank you, Gena," Betty said.

"You're welcome." Gena turned to help Myrtle, who was eleven.

Myrtle accepted Gena's helping hand and safely exited the doorway. "Thank yuh, sis."

"Everybody move out of the way," yelled Leonard, age six. "I'm going to jump!"

"No!" Gena shouted. "You might fall! Don't do it!"

"I'll be okay. Look!" Leonard leaped out of the back door of the bus and landed safely on his feet, though somewhat off-balance. "See, I told you I could do it."

"That was just a lucky jump," Gena said with a frown on her face. "You almost fell."

"Yes, but I didn't. That's what matters, right?"

"Whatever," Gena responded. "Let's head to the back with Junior to get our stuff."

"Where are Momma and Bunny?" Myrtle asked.

"They're at the front of the bus," Gena said to her little sister. "They'll be out soon."

No sooner had the words left Gena's mouth than Essie stepped out of the front door holding two-year-old Bunny in her arms. "Guys, did you get our bags?" Essie asked.

"Not yet, Momma," Gena said, as the kids all rushed to the back of the bus. Junior was already in position to catch the first bag, which the bus driver was about to throw down.

"Boy, can you catch?" the driver asked. He was bravely standing on the mountainous load of luggage on top of the bus, between large baskets, bags, and pans. Before Junior could say a word, the bag was on its way down to him.

"Got it!" Junior caught the bag and quickly passed it on to Gena, who placed it carefully on the roadside beside a two-foot-tall sitting wall made of white stone and concrete.

"Next one! I'm ready." Junior continued to receive their luggage until he had all four bags and two suitcases.

They gathered their belongings and headed to the hills of Clear Mount. Essie led the way, and Gena carried baby Bunny. Soon, the town of Clear Mount came into sight.

"There it is!" Leonard shouted. "We're almost there."

"Yes, I can see the big mango tree!" Myrtle screamed. "There's Mast Tim's gateway." She took off running toward the town's narrow entrance. Leonard followed immediately behind her. They raced ahead to see who would be the first to get there.

"I bet I can beat you both to the mango tree!" Junior shouted. He waited until Myrtle and Leonard were far enough ahead, and then he took off running. Betty also followed. The kids all raced ahead, leaving Essie and Gena behind.

"Be careful, guys. If you keep on running like that, you might fall!" Essie called out to her kids, but they were too excited to listen to her.

Junior ripped past them and was the first to get to the familiar old mango tree. By the time they all got there, they were out of breath. The thick, solid roots of the great tree grew three to four feet above the ground. Panting heavily and gasping for air, the kids took a seat on the roots and rested while they waited for their mom, Gena, and baby Bunny.

In no time, there was a handful of curious little country kids standing along the street in front of Mast Tim's gateway. They stood there to watch the bunch of town folks entering their village.

Ten-year-old Karl heard the noise outside his gate and ran to the door to see what was going on. It was his family from town, who had come to visit him and his dad, Mast Tim. He ran out through the door. "Momma, Momma! You're here!" he yelled, rushing into his mother's open arms.

Essie had stooped down low to Karl's level. "Hello, Karl. How are you, son?" She hugged him and kissed him on the cheek.

"I'm fine, Momma."

"Is your dad home?"

"Yes, Momma. He's cooking in the kitchen."

Karl was happy to see her and all of his brothers and sisters, who had come all the way from Montego Bay to see him. He greeted all of them as well.

After they had all happily greeted each other, they went into Tim's old country house to meet him and set their luggage down. Before long, the kids were all back outside playing with Karl and his friends in the front yard. They played and had fun until suppertime. After they had eaten, Essie instructed the kids to take a bath and change into some clean clothes before night fell.

The water drums were critically low, and the kids ran short on water while taking their baths. Karl decided to rush to the public water pipe to refill the drums. He did this so that the remaining town folks and visiting family could all take baths and prepare for the evening's activities at his home. This night's scheduled activity was what they called "story time by Essie."

Karl made many trips back and forth to the public water pipe. On his last trip, he stopped to pitch a game of marbles with some friends, whom he had met up with at the pipe area. He was also engaged in a game called stone tag. This was a game in which they took turns tossing a particular stone at each other's stones. The first one to hit the opponent's target stone would be the winner. They played for a long time, and Karl lost track of time.

When he finally realized this, it was already getting dark. "Oh my God!" Karl said to his friends. "It's getting late. I must go before night falls." He hastily bid them good-bye and ran off to fetch his last bucket of water.

On his way home, he had a strange encounter. It had just turned from dusk to dark. He was walking with the bucket of water on his head, being led along his pathway by the glowing light of the moon. He made it around a deep corner of the undeveloped road and started up a steep curve. As he made it over the curve, he was led right into the long stretch of straight, narrow dirt road leading to his house. He suddenly realized that he was the only person on the street.

Maybe he was the only person in the entire village who was out at that time of the evening. All activities in the country town of Clear Mount virtually stopped at six o'clock. The village seemed to be asleep by seven-thirty, and it was now eight, give or take a few minutes.

He continued along the road for a while when all of a sudden, a cold, tingling chill blanketed his entire body from his head to his toes. His heart skipped a beat or two. His head felt like it was growing larger and larger, way out of proportion to his body. He turned around, and in the distance, he saw an image bearing the likeness of an animal. However, this was no ordinary animal. It appeared to be a giant cow or ox with an enormous head. It had a long iron chain tied around its neck. The beast raced toward him at full speed, dragging the chain along behind.

Karl's eyes were flooded with panic and his palms were sweating. His whole body shook with fear. Terrified, he took off running. His body felt wobbly and uncoordinated as he ran, and his knees shook like an unbalanced washing machine.

He looked back and saw that the creature was rapidly catching up to him. Realizing he still had the bucket of water on his head, he threw it away quickly, as if he had been hit by an electric shock.

He hit his right big toe on a stone in the road, but kept running and hopping as he tried to make his getaway. He glanced back briefly to see how he was doing. The angry beast continued to close in on him. It was so close he could smell its rotten, rancid breath and see the strange look in its bulging eyes. Its eyes were as red as fire, but the weirdest thing of all was that they looked almost human.

Karl realized that this gigantic creature was not an animal. No, it most definitely was not. It was what they referred to in the countryside of Hanover as a "rolling calf." Karl was being chased by a ghost! He had heard about them, but he personally had never seen one before—well, at least not until now.

A rolling calf was a ghost that often appeared in

the form of an animal. These ghosts had large red eyes like a dragon's. Some even said that they could breathe fire through their mouths. Most people who had had close encounters had reported that they had first heard or detected the rolling calves by their unique, loud chiming and an unnerving clanking noise. This familiar sound was made by the long chain the creatures usually dragged behind them.

Some said that rolling calves were the spirits of evil butchers who had been cruel and mean when they were alive. They said that the best way to get away from these monstrous beasts was to drop various things on the ground. If one dropped things on the ground a little at a time, the rolling calves would have to stop to count each one. Reports of past encounters indicated this getaway method worked every time.

When Karl realized his pursuer was most likely a rolling calf, he forgot about his damaged toe. He forgot about hopping while running. He just ran—at top speed, Carl Lewis or Asafa Powell style. Now all-out sprinting, he shifted into sixth gear and took off blazing a trail for dear life. Neither Usain Bolt nor Michael Johnson nor any other athlete or track and field star could have kept up with Karl that night. He was sure that he must have broken some kind of world record. He could feel the wind rushing by him like a turbulent storm and thought he must be on the verge of flying.

One strange thought came to him while he was running for his life. A voice kept repeating inside his head, *Boy, the country is no place for a coward like you. Why are you here running for your dear life when your family is living nicely and comfortably in the big city of Montego Bay? Boy, you've been grossly neglected and discarded into these bushes, and that's just not right. That's just not right.*

Karl made it home to tell his brothers and sisters

about his frightening story. He burst through the doorway and into the living room, looking frightened and breathing heavily. "Leonard, Myrtle, everybody, you'll never imagine what just happened to me."

"Oh Lord!" Essie cried. "Karl, what happened to you? You look like you've seen a ghost."

All the rest of the kids dashed to the living room to see what the big commotion was about.

"I did, Momma, I did." Karl sank into the couch. He was still trying to catch his breath.

"Boy, don't be ridiculous," she said. "There's no such thing as a ghost. You must be mistaking some shadow or something."

"No, Momma, I saw . . . I saw a rolling calf!" Karl, now in tears, managed to get out. "I saw a rolling calf. It was . . . it was chasing me all the way home."

"Karl, did . . . did you say *rolling calf?*" Betty asked, shaking with fear.

"Yes, it chased me all the way home!"

"I'm never going outside at night, never ever," said Leonard. He was also trembling, and his eyes were bulging with hysteria.

The kids all got nervous and scared that night while they were in the countryside of Clear Mount.

"Calm down, guys. Calm down. Rolling calves are not real. They simply do not exist. There is nothing to fear. Karl must have seen an animal that was loose and was out of control going wild on the streets."

Essie was able to calm her kids down that night, but from that day on, Karl was never the same. He didn't remember how he had gotten home, only that he had lived to tell the tale. However, from then on, he took a real dislike to the countryside of Clear Mount. He would rather do anything or live anywhere than continue living a backward, country lifestyle. Karl decided that he wanted to live in the town of Montego Bay with his brothers and sisters.

Chapter 16

At forty-five, Essie had become a much wiser and stronger person than she had been when she was younger. She now knew exactly what she wanted out of life. She was determined not to let herself be pushed around by any man—not anymore. She was sick and tired of being despicably used and disregarded. She would put a stop to all of the abuse in her life.

Essie finally realized that nothing in life came easily. Therefore, her love and her attention would not be easily obtained, either. All her love and attention would be for her kids and her kids only. If any man wanted it, he would have to be willing to sacrifice a lot.

This was the attitude she had when Dr. McNelly, the owner of the private cottage resort, came on to her. One day in December 1970, Dr. McNelly visited his cottage without his wife. That was unusual, because all the other times when he traveled, he brought his wife along with him, and sometimes even his kids. This time he came alone, and he came to spend a whole three months' vacation. He was able to spend such a long period of time because, now sixty-three, he had retired from his profession as a physician.

Essie was one of his favorite staff members. He loved her cooking dearly. The sensational aromas of her tantalizing meals stimulated his appetite, and he eagerly anticipated her zesty island-style foods. One day, after enjoying a scrumptious lunch, he graciously came into the kitchen to praise her for her outstanding cuisine, as he often did.

The sweet-smelling scent of the island spices still hung in the air. It filled his nostrils and titillated his appetite all over again, but his appetite drove him mad for something more than food. It must have been the horny goat weed that Essie so skillfully added to the aphrodisiacal clam preparation. Or maybe it was the soul-soothing Cajun sauce or the jerk island spices that she used to sauté the lobster. Or possibly it was the teasing amount of caviar that she sprinkled over his meal as a topping. Whatever it was, it was surely working its magic.

He complimented her as usual. However, this time, he embraced her softly, with his hands resting on her buttocks. They hugged for an unusually long time, and then he kissed her on her cheek while still embracing her. She recognized only too well what her boss was trying to do, and she was not about to let this big opportunity pass her by. This man was very, very rich. Maybe this was her ticket to travel to the United States or an opportunity to get a raise or a large sum of money.

She was not going to deny him anything he wanted. Therefore, while still in his embrace, Essie made a very seductive gesture. She turned her head and looked up into his desire-filled eyes, and she smiled. Dr. McNelly was pleased to see her reaction, so he proceeded to kiss her on her lips. Essie kissed him back, and one thing led to another as they basked in the sweet, enticing aroma that lingered in the air. Before they knew it, they were in his bed making love.

This passionate occasion set the stage for regular lovemaking between Essie and her boss. There were two other employees who were around most of the time, so the secret lovers had to be discreet about their affair. It was part of the chef's job to stay overnight or to live in while there was a guest at the cottage. But the other two employees, the chambermaid and the gardener, usually worked standard hours, from nine to five, and then they left. That worked out well for Dr. McNelly and Essie. They simply met after the two employees had left for the day.

The retired doctor had many weird sexual preferences. He requested positions that Essie had never seen or done in her whole life. Essie admitted that this sexual experience with Dr. McNelly was the most challenging she had ever had. She had tried many things in her lifetime, but none so bizarre. Essie kept her mind on the prize, though. Like an order from the food menu, she fulfilled all of his sometimes bizarre requests the best way that she could.

She complied with his requests because she knew that there would be a payoff, and she expected it to be a big one. Many times, while she was making love to the older man, she got caught up in the fantasy of both of them traveling to the United States and doing lots of exciting things together. Sometimes, she would fantasize that, after sex, he would hand her a fistful of American hundred-dollar bills.

Essie thought about all these things, but she did not request anything of him. She knew better. She knew that it took time. At the right time and the right place, she would know what to do.

After about six weeks of this affair, Essie decided that she would have a serious talk with Dr.

McNelly. She figured that this was the right time because he only had two weeks remaining before he left the island.

Essie timed their next sexual encounter carefully. After he went into his room, she slipped in behind him and closed the door. She swiftly changed into some provocative red lingerie. She then enticingly paraded around the room like a Victoria's Secret model while Dr. McNelly lay fully nude in bed, admiring her beautiful body.

He eagerly beckoned her to come closer, but she did not. She continued to flirtatiously model her outfit around the room with her sexy, luscious booty showing slightly and her big, beautiful breasts with her hard buttons protruding through her inviting see-through top. Dr. McNelly was fully ready and was anxious to get down to business.

Essie, discerning his state, said to him, "Doc, you know that I have eight kids to take care of, and I'm both their father and their mother. Did you know that they all live in one bedroom?"

"How can I help, Essie? Just let me know."

"Doc, my kids are all getting big. I need a decent home for them."

"How much is a nice three-bedroom house going for in Jamaica?"

"I don't know, Doc, but I can find out."

"Okay, Essie, do that. Look around and find a nice three-bedroom house, and let me know. I'll take care of you if you'll take care of me."

"Thank you, Doc." She hastily jumped into bed with him, and they made love. Essie was gratified and happy with the deal.

The next day was Essie's day off, and she didn't waste any time getting started on her house-hunting project. She went to the district of Glenworth because she had once overheard rumors that some wonderful houses were on sale there and that it was a fast-growing neighborhood where one could get the most for one's money. There she met a man by the name of Mr. Gibbs, who was selling his spiffy three-bedroom single-family house. It had a nice front patio overlooking the cul-de-sac of a street nearby. The house was made of wood rather than building blocks.

Essie thought that she had a good chance of affording this home. Moreover, it was in an excellent location where one could see the ocean way out in the distance. You could also see the wonderful sunrise in the mornings from the front porch. When she asked how much it cost, Mr. Gibbs told her that the house was significantly underpriced to sell expeditiously. The adorable, spacious three-bedroom house on the slight incline of a hillside close to the road was being sold for only fifty-five thousand US dollars.

The next day at work, Essie excitedly told Dr. McNelly the price of the house, and he immediately reached for his checkbook and wrote a check for twenty-five thousand US dollars. Essie was grateful and happy for the money, but she was befuddled. Had Dr. McNelly misunderstood the price that she had quoted him? She therefore repeated it.

"Essie," he said, "you may take today off. Tomorrow, you and Myrtle can come by for the remaining amount."

Essie was even more bewildered.

It was sobering when it dawned on her that her boss was handing over to her the unbelievable amount of fifty-five thousand US dollars. After all was said and done, it was a huge amount. This was the lump sum of US dollars that she had been fantasizing about. This was bigger and better than hitting the jackpot. This didn't happen every day in an average person's life.

Essie concluded that this one instance of good fortune made up for all of the other misfortunes in her life.

Chapter 17

Everyone now had some elbow room. There was a room for the girls, there was a room for the boys, and there was a room for Essie, the hardworking queen of the family. It was like an instant change in social class and social status. The family felt revived and rescued from the tightly gripping claws of the ghetto. Now they could hold their heads up high with pride and dream big dreams. Owning their own home, free of any mortgage or rent, was a tremendous boost to everyone's confidence.

Essie was happy about the change in her family's lifestyle. She was proud of their new home and the neighborhood in which it was located. However, she still had problems sleeping at night and had doubled her alcohol intake. Her smoking habit, which she had once tried to quit, was now worse. Essie had become a fighter in her own battle to survive. She knew that she had to keep on fighting, because her children needed her now more than ever.

In an attempt to steal her away from her job so

that she could work for them instead, a real estate company handling another private cottage in the same area of Ironshore had made her an offer more than a year earlier. They had offered her a much higher salary because they had heard of her excellent cooking skills. Essie didn't accept it then because of her loyalty to her current boss. She thought that with the fringe benefits, her job was worth more in the long run than what the other realty company was offering. But when they had called a few weeks earlier and raised the offer even higher than before, she decided to accept. At this point it was easy for Essie to leave her current job.

Essie was serious about life now, and she wasn't going to take any second-best job. She knew that she was a first-class chef, and she wasn't going to settle for less. She had a family to feed and clothe, so she reasonably drove a hard bargain.

***

Essie worked very hard while her children developed their own individual identities. Now that the family was securely settled in their own home, Karl separated voluntarily from his father, Timothy Brown, and moved to Glenworth. Now fourteen years old, he had been fed up for some time with the country lifestyle he had led while living with his father. Karl completed his secondary education at Glenworth All-Age School and went on to a trade school to study the science of welding.

At twenty-one years old, Gena, the miracle baby, was now the mother of three boys: Don, Andre, and Breath. Don was the oldest, and prior to this time, he had been living mostly with his father's family. Breath was the youngest of them all, and he was very clingy when it came to his grandmother Essie. Andre fell in the middle; he was the quietest of the boys.

Gena got her big break when she obtained a visa to go to Nassau, in the Bahamas. The day she was leaving, she trustingly left her kids with Essie. She cried and vowed that she was going to make it soon and then pave the way for her family to follow.

Gena quickly obtained a job in the Bahamas and started sending food and clothes for the family every major holiday. Within two years, to everyone's surprise, Gena called to let them know that she had made it safely to the United States. It was not an easy journey. She had stowed away on a large cruise ship, had been repeatedly abused by multiple crew members, and had almost gotten thrown overboard into the open sea.

Through it all, she persevered and lived to tell the story, though for a long time, she didn't tell her family about the gruesome parts of her journey. She only told them about the good news concerning her successful arrival in the United States.

For many years, Gena struggled to survive in New York City, but she still found a way to continue her regular support of the family on major holidays. She had a special closet that she reserved just for her family. After she had successfully filled and sent off a minimum of two barrels—with one of them containing food and the other containing clothes, shoes, and other things— she would immediately start on the preparation for the next major holiday.

The first thing she did was replace the two barrels she had just sent to Jamaica with two empty ones and set them aside in her reserved closet. Each time she went to the supermarket or did some type of shopping, she searched for good two-for-one deals or any other incredible sales. She bought these items with certain family members in mind, and when she got home, she would meticulously put a name on each piece of clothing or pair of shoes.

She also sometimes made little notes concerning an item, such as *For Bunny's birthday*, and pinned them to the item before storing it away. She put food items directly into the food barrel.

She continued this process until both barrels were full or until it was the next holiday and it was time to call the international freight carrier. The carrier picked up the barrels from Gena and delivered them directly to her family in Glenworth.

Holidays for Essie's family meant that barrels were on the way from the United States. There was always excitement in the air, and they all held their breath in anticipation. They never knew what was going to be in the barrel for them. But one thing was for sure: there would definitely be something in the barrel for everyone. Gena never forgot anyone.

Once the barrels arrived, the holiday officially began. There was usually an anxious crowd of family members surrounding the barrels, like children at Christmas who had gotten their nicely wrapped gifts and couldn't wait to rip into them to see what Santa had brought. It was the barrel of clothes and other things that magnetically drew the crowd, more so than the food barrel. Once the cover had been removed, everyone would freely rush to see what was in that barrel for him or her.

The male members of the family logically went for the pants and shirts or anything male-related, and the females, likewise, dove into the barrel to pull out female-related stuff. They then checked to see what names were attached to the items. If a name wasn't the name of the person who was holding the item, then he or she would shout out the name of the person for whom it was intended, and that person would dash forward to joyously collect the item.

Sometimes the barrel ceremony was a lot more organized. A designated distributor would be responsible for opening the barrel, taking out the various items one by one, and calling out the names on each item. But it was hard to find a good distributor, because there was so much excitement in the air that once the designated distributor started the orderly distribution of items and ran into his or her own name, he or she usually stopped to admire or try on the new item. As might be expected, no one was willing to wait around for such time-wasting activities. It therefore led right back to the rowdy pandemonium of everyone diving in and scooping up items. It was like Christmas morning all over again on each holiday, and Gena was like the Santa Claus of the family.

The excitement didn't end with the distribution of new clothes and shoes. After each person had collected his or her share of goods, it was time to try them on and hope that they were the right fit. Gena had a unique skill for figuring out the changing sizes of each member of her family. It was rare that an item didn't fit. However, when that did happen, pandemonium broke out again as everyone attempted to trade the items that didn't fit for ones that did. The scene sometimes resembled the scene in the story of Cinderella where the stepsisters try to force their way-too-big feet into the tiny glass slipper brought by the prince.

After what could be humorously perceived as the opening ceremony and the distribution ceremony, there was the trade show. Everyone tried on their clothes and shoes to see if they fit and to see what they could profitably trade for another item. Sometimes the trade was not only based on fit, but also on likes and dislikes.

Once everyone had obtained the appropriate items, the next step was the display show—probably the best part about the whole barrel activity. Everyone put their items on display by wearing them. The community of Glenworth always knew when the barrel had been received by Essie's family, because all the family members would be out that day roaming the streets in their brand new apparel, thanking God for Essie's miracle baby, Gena.

Essie's children were all grown or growing up and pursuing a variety of interests. At ten years of age, Leonard had vowed to become a doctor one day so he could help the family while healing the world. Everyone in his family laughed at him and called him funny names. They laughed at him because he was the goofy and nerdy kid in the bunch. They called him the Reverence, which was the shortened form of an even longer, more ridiculous nickname: Leonard the Reverence-Ripe-Banana-Junjay. He knew there must be a story behind that name, but he had never quite figured out what it meant or why they called him such a crazy name. He thought it was safe to say that it was a form of mockery to indicate that he was just a fool.

Technically, they were right. Considering all the odds that were stacked against him, he was a fool to think that he could make it to the top of the intellectual hierarchy to become a physician, especially coming so far from the bottom of the pile, with no form of support structure. He had no role model or highly educated person in his family or anywhere around him.

However, Leonard didn't care how impossible it seemed. He didn't much mind if they laughed at him. He was determined to be a doctor someday. He wanted to make a significant contribution to his society and had decided that contribution should be in the medical arena. Moreover, he wanted to be able to help his struggling family someday, and he wanted to help them in a very big way. He got baptized in the Seventh-Day Adventist (SDA) Church at the age of ten. This was shortly after his sister Myrtle had stopped attending that same church.

Myrtle had been attending the SDA church ever since she had been invited by a neighbor, Mr. Mulgrave. She attended church every Sabbath and had almost perfect attendance. She even got baptized one year later. She had to go alone because, at that time, she was the only one in Essie's family who had chosen to follow a religious pathway. Eventually, Leonard started to attend church with her.

However, Myrtle quit church after she found out that she had rheumatic fever and heart disease. She also quit school and started roaming the town, doing lots of rebellious things: fighting, drinking alcohol, and smoking marijuana. She also got pregnant against her doctor's advice and gave birth to a premature baby by the name of Dean Myers seven months into her pregnancy.

Junior, at age nineteen, was also smoking marijuana. He was an apprentice to an electrician and later learned the trade and became a popular electrician in his community.

Though heavyset, Betty was the prettiest child of all Essie's children. After trying her hand at dressmaking, she decided at eighteen years of age to become a beautician. She eventually went on to own her own beauty parlor. She also had one set of twin girls, Kate and Keisha, and later had another pretty little girl named Charlene.

Lela, who was still living with Miriam, was now going to an exclusive SDA private school. She wanted to be a nurse.

Bunny, the handsomest boy in the family, was still young and undecided about what he wanted to be. One thing everyone noticed about him was that he was charming and had a way with words. He was an outstanding speaker and could easily grow up to be a great politician someday.

Chapter 18

It was barely dawn, but Essie couldn't wait a moment longer. "Wake up, wake up! It's Easter Sunday. Everybody get your bathing suits and bathing trunks."

The closest they came to a family trip was when Essie took them to the beach on Easter.

Bunny jumped up and down, clapping his hands. "Great! We're going to the beach."

Myrtle frowned. "I don't have a bathing suit."

"What happened to the one Gena sent you not so long ago?"

"It's too tight now, and it's ripped on both sides."

"Let me see it. Maybe Gena—no, Betty—can fix it on her sewing machine."

"Do we have to come, too, Miss Essie?" asked the twin.

"Yes, I want everybody to come. Is that too much to ask? I know I didn't tell you about it, but I've been planning this for a long time. I want to enjoy this

Easter Sunday with my family, and you're part of my family now. I've already bought lots of spice buns and cheeses for the picnic. On our way, we'll stop by the shop to get one or two crates of sodas to drink."

"Yeah!" Leonard exclaimed, rejoicing over the good news. "We couldn't celebrate Easter Sunday without buns and cheese. We're going to have a good time."

"We should be going to church to celebrate Easter Sunday, not going to the beach," said Karl. "I'm not going with you. I'm going to church instead."

"Junior—I mean, Karl—you don't want to join us at the beach?" Essie said. "It's going to be fun. Everybody will be there except you." There was deep regret in her voice.

"I don't care about everybody. I'm going to church. Easter is a church day, and that's what I feel like doing."

"Okay, you can stay here and go to church if that's what you want."

Essie gave in to his request because she knew how much he resented her for having sent him to live in the severely underdeveloped countryside with his dad. She tried hard to make him happy and comfortable now, but Karl openly swore that he would never forgive her until the day he died. He showed his resentment of her every chance he got.

What Karl didn't understand was that when he treated her badly and with deliberate disrespect, it didn't matter, because nothing he could ever say would make her feel worse than she already did. If only she'd known that he had the same strong anti-country gene as she did, she wouldn't have sent him to live with his father. She shared his pain. She knew what it felt like to be a big-city-minded person trapped in a small country town.

Laden with lots of spice buns and cheeses, as

well as a large delicious fruitcake that Essie had made and a crate of sodas, the rest of the family headed off to Doctor's Cave Beach. They laid out their blankets and towels and placed all their picnic items under the shade of a great almond tree just to the right-hand side of the beach. Like the great Christopher Columbus, they declared this area to be their family picnic spot for the day.

They jumped, splashed, dove, and swam in the ocean until their weary souls filled with satisfaction. They spanned, rolled, and played on the beach, and their bodies glowed with the blazing island heat. They had a nice picnic lunch and a happy afternoon. They roasted in the tropical inferno and worshiped the mean island sun for a day as they frolicked around each other.

Essie's family was filled with the resurrection spirit as they amused themselves on that Easter Sunday. Essie was right: they were all having a wonderful time, and it brought the family a little closer together.

While everyone was having fun, Essie went for a walk alongside the crystal-clear ocean. As she strolled along the tropical playland, the warm ocean water reached for her feet on the sun-heated beach, and the sand tickled her toes. She watched as the gentle tides curled and rolled in toward the shoreline. The waves rocked and changed direction ever so slightly with the wind. Kids and adults alike fulfilled their aquatic hearts' desires as they swam in the warm, soothing water.

Essie stared in front of her at the long stretch of pure white sand. Sun-thirsty bodies were laid out in long rows of white plastic reclining chairs, soaking up the healing rays of the island sun. Near the chairs stood large green-and-yellow or red-and-white umbrellas, in case the sunbathers wanted some shade.

Livelier sun worshipers in barely-there bikinis and bathing trunks rocked to the rhythm of the reggae

111

music beat playing at the tiki bar farther away from the shore. A dance instructor taught the island enthusiasts reggae and soca dance moves while the staff made sure their glasses were never empty. Others sat around small, round white plastic tables watching the sunset as it painted new colors across the sky and sea. Some were enjoying mouthwatering island foods: spicy beef patties, jerk chicken, jerk pork, and deep-fried chicken wings with golden fries. Some simply settled for a snack and a Red Stripe beer.

Doctor's Cave was certainly a picnic and sunbathers' paradise in Montego Bay. Essie gazed out at the spectacular panoramic view of the coastline and the white sailboats and tiny glass-bottom boats floating in the bay. The latter were mostly fishermen searching for their evening meal.

She looked behind her and observed the offshore reefs and warm, shallow waters, ideal for snorkeling and for underwater enthusiasts.

Essie quietly observed everything around her. She smiled at the sheer beauty and serenity of her environment, the uniqueness of the people, and of course, the natural attributes of the tropical island of Jamaica.

"Momma, we should do this more often," Betty said when Essie returned from her stroll on the beach. "I can't tell you how long it's been since I've been to the beach. It's rejuvenated my body and my mind."

"Yes, it's true," Junior said. "We should do this more often. I also need to teach the boys how to swim."

"I can swim," Bunny said.

"I can swim, too," Leonard said, indignant.

"Well, yes, you both can swim," Junior said, "but Don, Andre, and Breath don't know the first thing about swimming. I need to take them to the beach every Sunday to teach them."

"I can swim a little, but not that well," said Don, Gena's oldest son.

"I almost drowned today, trying to swim," Andre said.

"Me too," Breath agreed.

"No!" Essie said. "That's not true, guys. Don't say that, because if your mom hears it, she'll die."

"They're both exaggerating," Junior said. "Nothing happened to them, Momma. I was with them all day, playing with a beach ball at the edge of the water."

Essie summed up the festive day, happily reminiscing about her childhood. "All in all, this has been a great day. It was always my dream to see the whole family come out to have fun at this beach. I used to come here quite often as a young girl. I love this beach so much, it makes my heart glad to spend this day with my family." She reached for Don, Breath, Andre, and whoever else she could grab and gave them all a big hug.

Chapter 19

"Happy birthday, Junior—no—Karl. Hmm . . ."

"Bunny, Momma, I'm Bunny."

"Yes, Bunny. I meant to say Bunny. Today is your birthday."

"I know, Momma." His look said he couldn't forget it if he tried.

Unlike other nurturing parents, Essie hadn't taken her family to the movies or to any major family gatherings lately. They had spent no time on family trips or weekend vacations away from home. She was too busy working to put food on the table and to provide other basics. She was sometimes even too busy to celebrate the kids' birthdays.

"Happy birthday, son. Today you're seven years old."

"I know, Momma," Bunny said, as if it were no big deal.

"Come give your mother a big hug." Essie held out her beckoning arms.

He ran to her as if he could be in for a big surprise.

"Junior—" She struggled again to remember his name.

"Bunny, Momma," he said. He knew she loved him very much, but sometimes she got too busy and confused to remember his name, even after seven years of his being a member of the family.

Actually, she was doing excellent today. Sometimes it took her many attempts to get it right. She usually used the wrong names, starting with the oldest child—the most familiar—and traveling down the line until she got to the right name. The children did their best to help by identifying themselves whenever they sensed her confusion.

"Yes, Bunny, may you live to see many, many more birthdays. May you grow up to be a fine young man and have a wonderful life. And remember your mother when she's old and gray." Essie picked him up, held him inches from her face, and gave him a big kiss on his left cheek.

"Thank you, Momma," he said as she put him back on the floor.

"So sorry I'm not rich. I wish I could give you everything you want, but at least I'll make sure that you don't starve and you always have a roof over your head. Okay, son?"

"Okay, Momma. No problem. So I'm not getting anything for my birthday today?" He tried to understand his mother's words, though they seemed like mumbo jumbo.

"Bunny, don't you remember? Gena sent you your birthday gift on Christmas. Remember, the sneakers she sent you had a written note that said, 'For Bunny's birthday.'"

"Oh, yes," he said. "I forgot about my sneakers.

Gena always remembers my birthday."

"Oh, may God bless her. She's my lovely, God-blessed miracle baby. I don't know what I would've done without her." Essie raised her hands toward the heavens. "Thank you, Father, for my daughter Gena."

"Wow! Gena sent me my birthday gift three months early. That was why I forgot, Momma. That was why I forgot."

"Bunny, I'll also bake a cake at work for you. I'll take it down to you on Friday, okay?"

"Okay, Momma, thank you. I love you, and I love Gena, too."

"We love you too, my son."

"Momma, when is Gena coming back to Jamaica?"

"I don't know. I don't know. Maybe you should write her a letter and ask her yourself. You know how she loves to hear from you kids, so write her a letter, and I'll post it."

"I'm going to write her a letter today."

"That's good. I have to get to work now, and I'm running late. You know what a long walk it is."

Myrtle sat on the front porch steps, listening to Essie and Bunny's conversation. She sat watching the sun rise above the serene ocean way out in the distant view. "Yuh don't have to walk in the burning sun every day, Momma. Yuh know that, right? Why don't yuh take a cab to work today?"

"My dear child, I don't have enough money to take a taxi to work," Essie complained, her voice low. "I have to leave money for you all to have lunch and dinner. But sometimes I get lucky and a car stops for me and gives me a lift to the bus stop. I really hope I get lucky today because I'm tired of walking, especially in the blazing hot sun. In addition to that, when I reach Half Moon, I have to walk over that long hillside to get to work. Oh Lord, I get so tired sometimes."

"Madda," Karl said, "are you coming back home this evening, or are you staying at work all week?"

"I usually only stay overnight if I'm having a guest, but there're no guests, so I'll be back tonight. I might be a little late, but Betty will be cooking dinner, so don't worry."

He snorted. "I'm not worried," he said, his voice boorish and impolite. "I never get worried. I'm a country man, and I eat anything that moves. I know how to survive. Don't you worry about me; worry about yourself."

"Karl, why are you always so nasty? You should know by now how to talk to me. I'm your mother. You know that."

Karl kept walking toward his room, the room he shared with his three brothers, Junior, Leonard, and Bunny, as well as Gena's three sons, Andre, Breath, and Don.

Betty, Pauline, and Myrtle, plus Essie's latest additions to the family, Paulette and Pauline—twin sisters seeking refuge from the street—shared the other bedroom. Since there was already a Pauline in the family, they usually referred to the other Pauline as the "Twin Pauline" or "Pauline-the-twin." Pauline was more like a true sibling in the family, having been there longer, while Pauline-the-twin and Paulette were new arrivals learning to adapt to Essie's large family.

Pauline-the-twin and her sister, Paulette, had joined the family after Essie went to town two weeks earlier to buy fresh meat from the butcher shop. Essie spotted the two young ladies, who were about eighteen, sitting on the same wall downtown where she'd sat twenty years earlier. That's where she met Gena's father, the Reverend Murray. The two young ladies looked worried. On her way back home, Essie noticed them still

117

sitting there. One of them offered comfort to the other, who was in tears.

Essie was sure they needed help, so she went over to introduce herself. "Hello, young ladies. I'm Miss Essie. I noticed you're both looking sad today. What is the problem?"

"We're fine, miss," the one doing the comforting said. "Thank you."

"Is this your sister?" Essie asked.

The girl nodded.

"If everything's all right, why is your sister crying? Why don't you take her home if she's not feeling good?"

No sooner had the words left Essie's mouth than the girl who was crying burst out, "No! We're not okay, miss. We're not okay at all. She's lying."

"What's wrong?"

"I shouldn't have listened to my sister." She attempted to dry her tears with her hand. "Now we don't have anywhere to stay. She brought me all the way here from Savanna-la-Mar in Westmoreland to find a job, but there are no jobs here. I want to go home."

"If you want to go back to that stinking place, you'll have to go alone," her twin said. "I'm not going back."

"Okay, ladies, you don't have to fight each other. You can stay at my place in Glenworth until you find a job or decide what you really want to do. There's plenty of work, but sometimes it takes a while to find a good job. You'll have to check the newspaper daily until you see something that you like, but it won't be long. How old are you?"

They spoke in unison. "We're eighteen years old."

"Okay, you're of age. Come with me and tell me more about yourselves. I have a large family at home,

118

but you can make yourselves comfortable until you find good jobs."

Essie took the twins home with her, where they had remained for the past two weeks. Up to this point, they were still adjusting to the new environment, and while they never talked much to anyone else, they whispered often to each other.

The third bedroom in the Glenworth house was reserved for Essie, but sometimes the younger children like Bunny, or Gena's kids, would sleep with her to balance out the number of people in each bedroom. At other times, when Essie stayed overnight at work, Myrtle would occupy Essie's room until she got back, usually a week or two later.

"Where is Momma? Has she left yet?" Junior crawled out of bed in his boxer shorts, his upper body shirtless.

"She just left," Myrtle replied.

"Where is she?" He rushed to the front door of the house just in time to see Essie slowly make her way down the rocky steps, roughhewn and uneven, that led to the roadside. She walked carefully, making sure each step was well placed before she made the next, as if she'd fallen many times before. It was like she was walking a tightrope in the circus.

"Momma, do you want me to walk with you to the bus stop?" he called.

Essie turned back to speak with him. "No, Junior. Or is it Karl?" She struggled to remember his name.

"Junior, Momma."

"Thank you, but you have to go to work soon, don't you?"

"I finished the job I was working on yesterday, and I'm just waiting to get paid. I might stop by there later during the day. There's a new one that I'm about to start, but that won't be until tomorrow."

"I won't stand a chance of getting a free lift to the bus stop if you're with me, Junior," Essie shouted back.

"Bye, Momma. Take care and walk carefully. Good luck with getting a ride to the bus stop." Junior watched his mother walking with pride and confidence in her nice-fitting outfit. The attractive black handbag matched her stylish black high heels. As she almost disappeared into the distant curve, a red car stopped. After a short conversation with the driver, Essie got in, and Junior turned to reenter the house.

Junior was pleased with the day so far. Essie had gotten her wish and found a free ride to the bus stop. If she was lucky, she'd get a free ride all the way to work.

Myrtle still sat on the front steps. She turned back toward the house and screamed, "Leonard, Leonard, Momma said to make sure yuh eat breakfast before yuh go to school. Okay? Leonard, did yuh hear me? Did yuh hear what I said?"

"Leonard, Myrtle is calling you," Junior said as he poked his head into the boys' room. "Are you just now getting ready?"

"Yes, and I'm running late."

"I heard Momma calling you to get ready hours ago."

"Yes, but I couldn't use the bathroom because Karl was using it first," Leonard explained. "I had to wait for him."

"You need to wake up earlier so you can be the first to use the bathroom."

"Momma has to be the first to use the bathroom," Leonard responded. "Then me, then Karl, and then anyone else can use it after that."

"Boy, you sure like to give back answers," Junior said. "Do you think you're Mr. Wise Guy?"

Yes, I'm Mr. Wise Guy, Leonard thought, *especially when compared to you.* But he dared not say it out loud unless he wanted Junior's wrath to come crashing down upon him that morning. Leonard had learned pretty well how to navigate around trouble in his large, sometimes rowdy and tumultuous family. He knew what to say and when to say it and who to say it to. He had bigger and better plans than they could ever imagine, so he didn't get lost in the day-to-day trivial matters. "Yes, Myrtle, Junior said you were calling for me."

"Yes. Momma said to make sure that yuh eat breakfast before yuh go to school. She also left yuh school fare with Betty." Myrtle knew why her mother refused to leave money in her care. Essie feared she'd buy cigarettes or marijuana.

"Okay, thank you, Myrtle."

"Don't thank me, thank your mother. She was the one who got up early this morning and cooked breakfast for everyone. Karl's and Bunny's breakfast is on the table, and yours is on yuh favorite plate, covered up on the side of the stove. I've already eaten mine. The rest will have to divide theirs for themselves when they're ready."

Leonard rushed to the kitchen and peeped at his plate to see if the meal was worth his time. It was his favorite meal—yummy, tempting ackee and saltfish with cooked green bananas and dumplings. He grabbed his plate and made his way to the table. He was already late for school anyway, so now he'd be late with a full stomach.

Leonard whispered a quick prayer: "Thank the Lord for what I've received, for Christ's sake. Amen." He added to himself, "Thank the Lord and thank the hand." This was a table grace Essie had taught all the kids to say before they partook of their meals. There were two things that she was very strict about. One was to say grace before eating, because that would make a way for the provision of the next meal. She had taught them never to take a meal for granted.

The next thing was that none of her boys should let the sun rise and catch them still lying in their beds. She believed that if this happened too often, they would grow up to be useless, good-for-nothing men. She would have none of that in her family, and went around every morning waking each male child, one after the other.

Almost every morning, Essie made breakfast, prepared for everyone's lunch and dinner, made a list of things for each person to do, and had money distributed to those who would need it that day. The latter was an incredible feat for Essie, who earned only twenty US dollars every two weeks. It was like the Bible story where the Lord used five loaves of bread and two fishes to feed a multitude of people.

Leonard knocked and entered the girls' room. "Betty, Myrtle said that you have my fare and lunch money."

"Yes, there it is on the dresser—eight US dollars. Momma said that it's for the whole week, so don't go finishing it now before time, or you'll have to walk to school and eat your books for lunch, okay?" She looked at the time and shouted frantically, "Oh my God! It's eight-thirty already. I have to get to work. Leonard, you're very late for school."

"Yes, I know, I know. I'm out now. Bye." Leonard rushed through the door.

"Did you say happy birthday to Bunny?" Betty called after him.

"Happy birthday, Bunny," Leonard shouted at the top of his voice. "May you live to see many more." He hoped he had said it loud enough for Bunny to hear, wherever he was.

Karl went into the kitchen to eat the breakfast Essie had made and left nicely covered on the table. "Which one of these plates of food is mine?"

"The larger one is yours, Karl," Myrtle shouted. "There are only two prepared on the table. The other is for Bunny."

Ever since she had dropped out of school and had open-heart surgery, Myrtle's favorite thing to do was to sit on the steps. She often spent the whole morning there, observing those who passed by and waving to her friends. She heard everything that went on in the house and responded as needed, as if she sat in the center of life, directing traffic. "Karl, did yuh find it?" she shouted.

"Yes, Myrtle. You can stop shouting now."

"Yuh ungrateful thing, yuh." *Oh how ungrateful you are,* she thought. *Now that you're full, you don't want to hear from me anymore. Be careful because you might choke on your food for being so ungrateful.* "Mind yuh don't choke."

Karl hurried through his breakfast and rushed toward the door to his welding trade school. "Myrtle, my little sister, why are you so miserable?" He tried to calm her, sensing that she was not too pleased with his last comments.

"Don't touch me. I'm not yuh little sister. I'm older than yuh, yuh country bumpkin." She remembered how rude he had been to Essie earlier and used the opportunity to ask him about it. "Karl, seriously, tell me, why're yuh so rude to yuh mother? Don't yuh know Momma really loves yuh? We all love yuh. Why're yuh still holding grudges against her?"

"Myrtle, why don't you go and live in the country, then, and take my place?"

"Because Mast Tim a nuh mi Puppa, that's why."

"Cool your heels. You don't know how evil that woman is."

"Well, if yuh don't like it here, why don't yuh go back home to the country and leave us alone?" Myrtle said, quite irritated. She was fed up with his rude, sarcastic ways.

"Myrtle, watch your heart. You worry too much about everything, even the things that don't concern you. I love you anyway. I'll see you in the evening. Bye."

"Did yuh remember to tell yuh brother happy birthday?"

"I was the first to tell him this morning. I told him before he even got out of bed."

"I love yuh anyway, Mr. Longelarla, Mr. Light-post Man." Myrtle often teased Karl, indicating he was too tall and skinny.

Karl left feeling a lot better, now that the conversation had ended on a lighter tone. He really didn't like seeing his sister angry; he loved her. As a matter of fact, everyone loved her unconditionally, even though they didn't always agree with her. In their eyes, she could do no wrong, especially since she had gotten sick and had life-threatening surgery.

"Bye, Myrtle," Betty said. "I'm leaving. I have an early appointment today. I'll be back in time to cook dinner this evening." Betty adjusted her dress, twisting it once to the left and then back to the right, and headed out the door to fetch a cab for work.

"Did yuh get your breakfast? Momma left our food in the pot this morning."

"Yes, I shared out a little for myself. Thank you, darling, for reminding me."

"Okay, yuh're welcome, fatty bum-bum."

"Yes, my dear, I know. I need to lose some weight."

"Don't pay me any attention, because yuh look

good, my sister."

"Happy birthday again, Bunny," Betty yelled aimlessly toward the house, as Leonard had.

"Thank you, Betty," a faint voice yelled back at her from some unidentifiable corner of the house.

Betty made her way carefully down the stairs and out onto the sidewalk. She waved as she crossed the street, fetched a cab, and headed off to her beauty salon.

In an attempt to deliver Essie's remaining messages, Myrtle shouted, hoping to wake up the others who still slept. "Pauline, Paulette, and Pauline-the-twin, listen to me. Momma said to wash yuh clothes today. I'll wash the boys' clothes, okay?"

There was no answer.

"Did anybody hear what I said? Pauline and the twins, Momma said to make sure to wash yuh clothes. I'll wash the boys' clothes, okay?"

"Oh no, Myrtle, you can't do any serious washing as yet," said Pauline as she walked out to the front porch. "You just had surgery not too long ago. I don't feel comfortable with you washing clothes right now. I'll wash my clothes and the boys' clothes. Miss Essie knows I don't have any problem washing the boys' clothes. I usually wash Junior's clothes, anyway, so I'll just do everything all together."

"What's wrong with me?" Myrtle frowned in disagreement. "Nothing is wrong with me, and if I want to wash them for myself, then I can. I've washed them before. If I'm going to die, then I would've been dead already."

"Oh no, Myrtle, don't bother yourself," Pauline insisted. "Let me do it this time, okay, my love? Don't worry your little heart. Let me do it."

"Okay, next time I'll do it," Myrtle said. "Are the twins awake yet?"

"Yes, they heard you. They're aware of Miss

Essie's message."

"Please tell Gena's kids that I'll give them their breakfast when they're ready, okay?"

"They're still in their room," Pauline said. "When they're ready to eat, I'll let them call you. Miss Essie made a big breakfast today. She really cooked a lot of food."

"Maybe it was because today is Bunny's birthday. That's one of his favorite meals, and Momma always cooks a little special meal on our birthdays."

Other than the extra amount of cooking that Essie did, this was a typical morning in the life of the large family in Glenworth.

Chapter 20

Essie had a noteworthy ability. Whenever she went to town to shop, she would invariably spot a young woman who looked as if she needed help or shelter. Essie was skillful in spotting such a person in the midst of a crowded plaza; she could seemingly do so with her eyes closed. While the average person wouldn't notice anything strange or different about the girl, Essie would. She could discern all the telltale signs. It was as if she had developed an eye for that particular situation. No matter how busy she was, Essie would walk over to the young woman, talk to her, and astutely figure out what was needed. Whenever possible, Essie would provide the answer to the need from her own resources.

Sometimes all the girl needed was taxi fare to get to where she intended to go. Sometimes she was simply lost and needed directions. Often, however, she was a runaway teenager desperately looking for a place to stay.

Even if Essie couldn't help the girls herself, she

wouldn't leave them until they got what they needed. Many times she brought them home to stay overnight or for a longer period, if necessary, so that they could get to where they had to go or successfully reach the person they needed to reach.

Whenever the young ladies were runaways, Essie took them into her home and had them do light chores for pay. She did this so they would be able to save, get a real job, get an education, or meet a partner so they could move on and live an independent life.

Seemingly every other month or so, another young lady joined Essie's family for one reason or another. Essie's home often appeared to be a rehabilitation center, especially during the runaway teenager season—though there was no real seasonal flow. There could be as few as one per year or as many as six all in the same month. There were no true age restrictions, either. Just as a teenager could need help, a woman at age thirty-nine could need rescue for a few days or more from an abusive husband.

Essie was brilliant at telling when a person truly needed help. If so, she would without a doubt do the best she could to help her.

Among many of those whom Essie took into her home was Pauline Anderson. Pauline was a young runaway girl from the town of May Pen in the parish of Clarendon in Jamaica. Essie first noticed Pauline at a shopping plaza. Pauline had a tattered old shopping bag in her hand with what seemed to be a few groceries in it. Essie noticed her pretentiously walking around as if shopping, like the rest of the crowd. However, Essie saw that the teenager really wasn't buying anything. Rather than look at grocery items, she mostly stared despondently into people's faces.

Essie noticed a familiar destitute look in her eyes and realized instantly that she had to be a runaway teen. So she briskly walked up to the young lady and said in a kind voice, "Hello, young lady, what is your name? May I help you with anything today?"

The young lady looked up at Essie with a bewildered look. "No, ma'am, I'm just shopping," she replied confidently. But for a split second, a sign of irritation crossed her face, as if she were in no mood to deal with any stranger.

"What's in your bag?" Essie asked.

Not any business of yours, the girl thought, with an annoyed frown upon her face as if she would rather be left alone. Instead, she said, "Just some groceries."

"Are you sure I can't help you with anything?" Essie asked one more time.

"Do I look like someone who needs help?" the young lady said, slightly annoyed.

Essie quickly answered, strongly and assertively, "Yes, you do, and this is a very cold, mean place for you to take any chances with your life. Go home to your parents; you'll be better off."

Shocked, the young lady stopped and stared into Essie's eyes. She saw the deep, motherly concern in her face. But she shouted back at Essie, "I'm looking for a nice single man to take me home. Why do you care, anyway?"

"I care because I've been there before, and I know that things don't always work out the way you intend."

"I just got here from May Pen, and I don't intend to go back. I want to start a life for myself."

"I can see that you just got here. Kids are usually very confident in the morning, much more than they are in the evening. What is your name, young lady?"

"My name is Pauline, miss."

"Well, Pauline, my name is Miss Essie. I must tell you the truth; you don't need a young man. What you need is a job. I'm not rich. I can hardly take care of my large family at home, but they have a roof over their heads, and it's all mine. You can join my family and help with the cooking and cleaning when I'm away, and I'll give you a small salary. When you are good and ready, you can get a decent job and help yourself."

"Thank you, Miss Essie."

After shopping together, Essie took Pauline home and introduced her to the family. No one was surprised. They were familiar with Essie bringing new people to join them, so they all welcomed Pauline with open arms, as if she were another sibling who had just been added to their family.

Pauline was amazed to see how friendly and accepting everyone was to her. She noticed that the family didn't have a lot of fancy things, but the house was very clean, and the family was a happy and peaceful one—except for Myrtle. Every now and then, Myrtle got into a fight at her school.

Pauline was somewhat shy at first, but as time went on, she got more comfortable and started opening up to everyone in a friendly way. In no time, she seemed just like one of Essie's own children. Eventually, Pauline gave them the full story of her background, saying that her parents were too strict with her, and she didn't like the town of May Pen. Being curious, she wanted to know what life was like in a bigger city like Montego Bay.

Essie decided to research Pauline's background herself and found out that her parents were good and decent people. The problem was that they had pushed Pauline a little too hard to get the best out of her life, and that was what had driven her away. In general, they meant well, and they really loved and missed her. When Essie first contacted Pauline's parents, they were very happy to know that she was alive and doing well and was in good hands.

They made an appointment to meet Pauline at Essie's house. When they finally saw her, Pauline's whole family shed tears of joy to see how happy, neat, and clean she looked that day. They decided that they would respect Pauline's wishes to remain with Essie's family in Montego Bay.

One day about a year later, Pauline and Junior— Essie's oldest son—were at home alone together. Pauline knew that the best way to a man's heart was through his stomach, as the old proverb said. Now eighteen years old, she offered to prepare a special meal for him. He accepted, so she prepared his favorite meal, spicy fish tea, which is also known as fish soup.

The rich, spicy fish soup did work its magic, because it seemed to stimulate more than Junior's appetite. As if his eyes had been opened, he suddenly began to see Pauline in a different light. She appeared to him as more than an unofficial adopted sister. He noticed Pauline's bigger-than-usual breasts and other parts of her body, especially when she sensuously brushed up against him—intentionally—as she passed by. This particular day, he became vulnerable to all of her flirtatious ways.

Pauline was surely aware of Junior's weakness that day, and she took advantage of it for all it was worth. Seductively dressed in a tank top and sexy red silk underwear, she sat on her bed with her legs wide open and called Junior into her room. He approached her to thank her for the delicious lunch that she had prepared for him.

"Junior, why don't you thank this?" She opened her legs even wider, looking at him with a mischievous grin.

"Are you crazy, girl?"

"Why not?"

"You're like a sister to me!"

"No, I'm not. I've only been living with your

family for less than a year, and I am not your sister, nor am I your adopted sister. You can consider me a long-term guest in your family."

"Okay. Sure, I will thank it with a kiss. How about that?"

"That's a start, but first you should make sure the door is closed."

"Okay." Junior quickly checked the door to make sure that it was securely closed, and then he briskly walked over to Pauline. He knelt down in front of her and gave her a quick kiss on the front of her red silk underwear just below her navel.

"Not there!" Pauline shouted at Junior. "Lower down. You have to kiss me lower down."

"Okay, where?" Junior kissed her a little lower down on her red, tight-fitting silk underwear.

"Lower than that."

"How about here?" Junior kissed Pauline on her red silk underwear squarely between her legs. That day, Junior ended up thanking Pauline for much more than the delicious meal she had prepared. He had to thank her for the wonderful sexual experience that she had given him.

That day was the beginning of their secret rendezvous, which later became public, because soon after that, Pauline became pregnant with Junior's first baby girl. They named her Denise Allen-Browdie.

At this point, Essie was concerned that Pauline would need a real job. Her boss was able to create a position for Pauline in the laundry maintenance department at the private cottage resort. Shortly after that, Junior and Pauline moved out of Essie's house to live in a small two-bedroom house they built at the back of the same property. That was Pauline Anderson's rescue story.

There were many more dynamic stories of young ladies whom Essie saved from the streets of Montego Bay. There was the story of the twins, Pauline and Paulette. There was the story of Joan. There was the story of Evan. There was the story of Marva. There was an avalanche of stories to tell of young girls that Essie took home for temporary—and sometimes even permanent—shelter from the streets.

Essie's children were now teenagers or older, but Essie was still the main breadwinner of the family. This fact hit home when she was in a terrible car accident one night after work. There were five passengers in the taxi when the car spun out of control and hit another vehicle. The taxi was destroyed and everyone was injured, but no one died. Essie's upper teeth were knocked out of her mouth, and she had other injuries, but nothing major.

When they first heard the news of the accident, Essie's family cried frantically. They cried because they loved her, but also because they realized that she was all they had. They could not live without her. That night, Essie's family truly understood that they could not afford to lose their only parent figure. The accident was a wake-up call to all of her kids, who had thought that Essie was immortal and would always be there to meet their every need.

Essie recovered fully, and her kids learned one good lesson: they should not take her for granted. They should tell her every day that they loved her and appreciated her always.

Essie herself also had a wake-up call from that accident. She realized that she should take better care of her body and stop the heavy smoking and drinking habits she had developed over the years. She made many attempts after that accident to stop smoking, though she failed miserably each time. She also tried cutting down on her alcohol intake at night.

Chapter 21

One peculiar thing about Essie was that she enjoyed a good funeral celebration. Oddly, she had fun at funerals, but she wept at weddings.

Once, a young man named Mike was playing behind an ice truck when he was hit by a car. In those days, a truck full of large square blocks of ice visited the community of Glenworth once or twice a week to provide ice to those people without refrigerators. The vehicle was a large, open-back truck—a supersized pickup. The pickup's body was made of wood, and one or two workers usually worked in the back. They used a large, scissorlike ice holder to pick up the individual blocks of ice and slide the blocks to the back of the truck so that they would be easier to divide into smaller pieces. They divided the ice with an ice pick, which was a long, pointed screwdriver-like tool. People had their iceboxes and bucket containers ready to receive their ice for a small fee. These ice trucks would make many stops to effect these humble transactions.

One day, after the truck had made a regular stop, Mike, who was a friend of Leonard and about the same age, decided that he would hop onto the ice truck while it was moving slowly from one neighbor's house to another's. Mike did a good job of holding onto the moving truck until the truck stopped at the next neighbor's gate. He jumped off and immediately ran to the other side of the road without checking for oncoming traffic.

Unfortunately, he didn't make it to the other side. A taxicab was coming at full speed right around the side of the ice truck.

Essie was very sad about her neighbors' unfortunate loss. She went over to their home to give her condolences to the family. However, more than anything else, she went to find out how she could help with the prefuneral celebration, also called a wake, a setup, or a nine-night.

A nine-night was a traditional Jamaican way of cheering up a grieving family that had just lost a loved one. It was an Afro-European-Jamaican traditional ritual that varied in its forms and styles. In all its variations, there were two basic elements that usually remained constant. Those elements were the acknowledgment and showing of respect to the spirit of the deceased, and the cheering up of the grieving relatives. Usually, the nine-night was funded by the family that had encountered the loss, but often, a relative, a good friend, or even a church would step in and donate extra funds for the occasion.

The entire community, although sad and disappointed by the loss of a dear loved one, participated wholeheartedly in this prefuneral celebration. It started out slowly on the first night and picked up momentum over a nine-calendar-night period. By the time it got to the ninth or last night, the occasion was in full swing. Sometimes it turned out to be a big dance party with lots of liquor, food, and loud music.

Only the most committed nine-night followers showed up on the first and second nights. They were the "rumheads" or alcoholics, some would say. Usually they brought their own rum and hard liquor with them, if it was not supplied by the grieving family.

They met at the gate of the deceased's home or in the front yard and formed a circle, where they sang familiar songs that were unique to that occasion. A typical nine-night song was one called "Come We Go Down." It was very Afrocentric, and it went like this:

> Come we go down, gal and boys,
> fi go broke rock stone.
> *Let's get down, girls and boys,*
> *to break rock stones.*
> Broke dem one by one, gal and boys.
> Broke dem two by two, gal and boys.
> We go broke rock stones.
> If you mash yuh finger,
> don't cry, gal and boys.
> We go broke rock stones.

While singing this song, they bent down or sat with two or more stones in their hands, knocking them together and then passing them along to the next person. Each time the stones went completely around, the nine-night participants increased the speed with which they passed them along. Sometimes playing this game while drunk could be a serious challenge.

For other songs, there was usually a leader in the group who read the verses of the song while the other members of the group followed by repeating word for word whatever the leader said. This style of singing was often referred to as a "Sankey."

The leader clearly and loudly spoke the words of

the song: "Amazing grace, how sweet the sound."
Then the group sang that line of verse only, the best way they could. "Amaaazing graaace, how sweet the soound."

"That saved a wretch like me," the leader continued.

"Thaat saaved a wretch like meeee," the group sang and then patiently waited for the leader to read the next verse.

"I once was lost but now am found," the leader said.

"I onnnce was looost but noow am found."

A story was told of a Sankey at a nine-night ritual celebration that was being held in the countryside of the island. A highly respected leader was doing an excellent job of leading the group into the verses of the song. It was a very large group, and all were singing and having fun. It started raining lightly, and the leader decided that it might be time to quit and go inside to get some shelter from the rain, so he told the large group, "I think it's time to quit."

"I thinnnk iiiit's timmme tooo quit," the group sang.

"We must go inside to get some shelter from the rain," the leader warned.

"Weee muuussst goo inside to geeet some shelter from thee rain," the group sang, and waited patiently for the leader to lead them into the next one.

"I don't know about you crazy people, but I'm going inside," the leader said arrogantly.

"I dooonn't knooow about yoouu craaazzy people, but I aam going insiiiide," the group faithfully and naively repeated.

"Enough is enough. I'm getting wet, and I don't find this blasted thing funny at all, so I'm out of here. You can find yourself another leader." He was fed up and upset, so he took off while the group was still singing his last words of warning to them.

Essie loved to have fun at these nine-nights. She usually showed her support by baking a cake for the occasion and donating it to the grieving family. She loved to bake and would bake a cake every chance she got. If someone had a common cold or the flu, Essie offered to bake a cake for him or her. Everyone could rely on her. She brought a cake or two to every occasion that she attended.

However, if you asked her to make cakes for the purpose of selling them, she wouldn't do it. She enjoyed doing it for free. She would take donations to buy the ingredients, but she didn't want to profit from this hobby.

Essie usually attended the last night of the nine-night. That was as much time as she could invest in this occasion with Mike's family. The last night was the big night with Jamaican white rum, oxtail, curried goat, rice and peas, and power water. All the popular ethnic Jamaican foods would be there, plus all types of music, but mainly the most modern reggae music. Sometimes it was like a big block party. If that didn't cheer up the grieving family, nothing else would.

Chapter 22

There was a story once told of a new priest who had to be disciplined by his superior at his second Mass. The new priest was so nervous at his first Mass, he could hardly speak. After Mass, he asked the monsignor how he had done.

The monsignor replied, "When I'm worried about getting in the pulpit, I put a glass of vodka next to the water glass. If I start to get nervous, I take a sip."

So the next Sunday, the priest took the monsignor's advice. At the beginning of the sermon, he got nervous and took a drink. He proceeded to talk up a storm. Upon returning to his office after Mass, he found the following note on his door:

> Sip the vodka; don't gulp. There are ten commandments, not twelve. There are twelve disciples, not ten. Jesus was consecrated, not constipated. We do not refer to Jesus Christ as the late J. C. Jacob wagered his donkey; he did not

"bet his ass." When Jesus broke the bread at the Last Supper, He said, "Take this and eat it, for it is my body." He did not say, "Eat me, for it's my body."

The new priest was disciplined for his lack of judgment and his reckless behavior. In the same way, Essie disciplined her children when she felt they needed it. She did not spare the rod and spoil the child. On the contrary, she didn't hesitate to use the belt. However, she felt she was prudent and knew when to stop. She believed that where parents went wrong with physical punishment was that they sometimes didn't know how far to go or when to stop.

Essie made sure that she got in at least three good strikes at her children when she was administering physical discipline to them. However, she only used physical discipline after two or three verbal warnings had failed. She believed that you should talk to your kids first. Let them understand your concerns. Let them know the danger they face if they don't comply with the rules.

On the topic of obedience and discipline, Essie once told the story of a man and his pony to her children. "Once upon a time, a man and his son set out from the country to town to sell their pony to take care of their immediate finances. They had to go through several villages before they got to the auction. When they entered the first village, they were both riding on the pony.

"The village people were concerned about the pony. They shouted, 'Oh, wicked people you are! How could you put so much weight on the poor pony? You should both walk and let the pony walk freely.'

"The man and his son complied. They got down and let the pony walk free of the load. As they entered another village, the people of that village became concerned about the old man walking. They shouted, 'Poor old man! Why waste the precious use of the pony while the old man suffers? Let the man ride the pony, and the boy can walk.'

"The man and his son again complied. The man rode the pony while his son walked behind. As they entered the next village, the people of that village became concerned about the little boy walking while the strong father rode the pony. They shouted, 'You cruel old man! Let the little boy ride the pony. You are strong enough to walk.'

"Again, the man and his son complied. The man let the son ride on the pony while he walked behind. By the time they had passed through the final village and gotten to the market, both the man and his son, due to the urging of the village people, were now carrying the pony."

Essie always closed with the moral of the story. Her kids had to know what they wanted in life. They couldn't always listen to everything other people said to them, or they would make fools of themselves.

Essie had an astute way of administering discipline at times. She suggested that the child she was about to discipline go outside and choose the switch or belt that she would use for the spanking. She considered this to be a psychological challenge that cleverly forced the child to think really hard, even if it was just for a second, about the bad deed he or she had done and to play an active role in assessing the degree of discipline that fit the behavior that warranted it.

One day, Essie told Bunny to make sure to sweep and clean up the front and backyard before she got back from work in the evening. Bunny, twelve at the time, conveniently ignored her request and went to play soccer. He spent all day with his friends and didn't get back until late in the evening. When Essie came home from work and noticed that Bunny hadn't done what she had told him to do, she got upset and threatened to give him a spanking. "Bunny," she called in a stern voice. "Yes, you Bunny. Where are you? I want to see you right now."

Bunny started explaining as he approached his mother. "Yes, Momma. I forgot to do the yard. I'll do it tomorrow." He felt guilty because he was aware, due to the anger in her voice, that he was in big trouble. He tried to beat Essie to the punch, hoping to change the impending situation that he faced. "I'll do it as soon as I'm up tomorrow, I swear."

"Boy, what did I tell you this morning before I left?" Essie asked her trembling son.

"You said that I should sweep the yard before you got back home, Momma," he nervously responded.

"Did you do as I told you?"

"No, Momma, but I was going to do it as soon as I woke up tomorrow."

"What did you do all day while I was gone?"

"Nothing, Momma—no, I mean I went to play soccer with my friends. Forgive me, Momma. I won't do it again. I swear. I won't do it again."

"When I tell you to do something, I expect that you do it first before you go out and play. I don't mind if you go out and play soccer. What I care about is for you to be a responsible person. You can't make it in life if you aren't responsible. Everyone has duties around here, and today, your duty was to clean the yard. Do you think that was too much to ask?"

"No, Momma. It wasn't too much. It was fair. Momma, you're a fair person. That's why I love you, Momma. God knows, I really love you, Momma. Please forgive me. I'll do whatever you say. If you tell me to jump and touch the moon, Momma, I'll do it."

"Okay, son, jump and touch the moon for

Momma."

"What?" Bunny's jaw dropped to the floor. His poor little heart skipped a beat. Shock and astonishment left his mouth wide open.

"Just trying to prove a point, son. Don't make promises you can't keep." Essie smiled, seeing the confusion on Bunny's face. "Son, I love you, and that's why I want you to grow up to be a fine young man someday and get a nice job and do whatever you are hired or told to do. I'm going to spank you only because I love and care for you. Go outside and get me a switch now so I can give you a good spanking."

"Okay, Momma, I'm going now. I'm going to get you the best switch that I can find." To him, it was like going outside to look for the bullet that would be used in his execution. It was one of his hardest tasks yet.

It didn't take Bunny long to figure out that this task was even harder than the initial task of cleaning up the yard. *Why didn't I just clean up the yard before I went to play soccer?* he thought. *Things would have been so much better if I'd done that; I wouldn't be faced with this difficult task.* After a few minutes of pondering, Bunny had a great idea. *Maybe I can spend the whole time searching for the right switch until it's time for bed. By then, maybe Momma will forget about it, and as soon as I wake up in the morning, I'll take care of it. That way, I won't have to deal with this whole scenario at all.* Half an hour later, he was still in the backyard searching for the right switch to take to his mother.

Essie didn't mind the length of time that it took because she knew that was part of the punishment. It was a twofold disciplinary action. This was the psychological part of it, and the longer Bunny pondered it, the more likely the point had been made that he needed to be responsible. Essie knew that in order for her kids to take her seriously, she had to follow through.

144

It didn't matter how long it might take. After an hour, Essie noticed that Bunny still hadn't returned, so she went outside to get him.

When Bunny saw her coming toward him, he trembled with fear and shouted, "Momma, I'm looking for the best piece of switch I can find. I'm searching for the right size. I want you to be happy with the right size and type of switch, so I'm not going to stop searching until I find the right one. You deserve to get the right one. Momma, I'm not going to give you anything less. So you can go back in and let me take care of this. Please, Momma, go back in. I promise that I'll bring the best switch to you. Don't worry, Momma, I know that I deserve a spanking, and that's why I'm trying to find a good switch."

Essie immediately looked around her in the backyard and noticed that there were many good choices. She could have just as easily grabbed one and started spanking him, but she was curious to see how far Bunny had planned on dragging out this two-minute situation. She was interested in the game that Bunny had going with her. "So you're making sure that you get me the right switch, huh? Okay, son. I'll be inside waiting."

Essie turned away quickly. She couldn't help grinning. The thought of how her little twelve-year-old son was trying to outsmart her made her smile. She rushed inside, lest Bunny notice the amusement on her face. She couldn't help thinking how her son was so bold as to try out an Oscar-worthy acting performance on her.

She thought, *This boy is going to be something special when he grows up.* However, it was her job to make sure that he got there, so she had to follow through, even as humorous as she found this situation to be. She thought that it would have been much easier for him if he had just come forward, taken his punishment,

145

and gotten it over with. But he had decided to take the long route, which meant an even heavier punishment than she had planned.

Bunny continued to wander slowly around the backyard until it was obviously time to go inside. He couldn't believe that his mother had fallen for his simple deceptive plan. *Maybe she's changed her mind,* he thought to himself. *Maybe she's forgiven me, or maybe she just gave up because I've outwaited her, and it wasn't worth her time waiting around for me. Maybe I was the last thing on her mind among a million other things that she had to do.* He felt victorious, although the end of his act had not yet played out. He felt like an athlete who was doing a ten-lap race and was ahead by five laps. He was celebrating his victory even though the race was not yet over. He knew he had to face the music at some point. *What am I going to do now?* he thought. *Should I, after all this long wait, still take a switch to Mother? Then it wouldn't be a victory anymore. No, I can't afford to do that. I've invested too much time and effort in avoiding being spanked.*

Slowly, Bunny realized that he had gotten more punishment just in doing his elaborate and extensive search for a switch than if he had just faced the music. He decided that he would simply go inside and let the chips fall where they may. He went inside and tiptoed silently into bed before anyone noticed him. Before long, he was fast asleep.

Not long after, Essie went to check on him with a strap and found him sleeping. Despite his adorable smile, she couldn't let the other kids feel that this was a smart way of getting around whatever she demanded of them. She had to set an example for them. Although she thought that it was very cute how he had spent so much time trying to outsmart her and avoid being spanked, she had to follow through.

146

She tapped him lightly on the shoulder. When she felt that he was awake, she raised her hands in the air and said, "Boy, I will give you a chance this time, but you must know that you are not smarter than me. Next time, you must do what I say, okay, boy?"

"Okay, Momma. I'll do whatever you say." Bunny was relieved to know that the saga was finally over. It was funny, but he did not feel victorious even for a minute. Instead, he felt bad. He knew that it hadn't been worth it. He went back to bed and had a good night's rest. The first to wake up the next morning, he rushed to clean up the yard.

Essie was committed to administering the proper discipline to her kids because she strongly believed that if she didn't take care of the light punishment, then society or the cops would be doing the heavy punishment later in life. By then, her kids would be totally unredeemable and out of control. She believed that the parents were the ones who made a difference in society, and it was her job to teach her kids how to be good citizens.

**

On his days off from school, Essie's son Leonard used to spend most of his time across the street with his neighbors, the Mulgrave family. That was okay with Essie, because the Mulgraves were a nice, upright, SDA Christian family. Essie thought it was a plus for her son to spend as much time as possible with that family, because by so doing, he could learn more about what it was like to live a true Christian life. Moreover, they had family devotions or prayer services twice a day, and they included him. If Leonard wasn't at home, Essie didn't question his whereabouts; she automatically assumed that he was with the Mulgraves.

Leonard enjoyed spending time with his neighbors for all the same reasons his mother thought he did. However, in addition to that, the Mulgrave family usually included him in their dinner plans and cooked a little extra with him in mind. Sometimes, if he spent the whole day with them, he could expect to have breakfast, lunch, and dinner. It was like a home away from home.

One day, Leonard's friends—who were about the same age as he was, fourteen—encouraged him to follow them to the ocean to go fishing. It was an intriguing idea. He knew that his mother wouldn't approve of him going so far away without her consent, but he refused to risk asking because she might say no. He figured that if he went with his friends, his mother wouldn't have to know. Maybe she would simply assume that he was at the neighbors' house. After a long time pondering his options, he decided to join his friends.

"Sure, let's go," Leonard said to Ben. "I love to fish, but I don't have a fishing rod or line or any fishing tools, for that matter."

"Don't worry about that, mon," Ben said. "We have what you need, and we'll share everything. I even have extra line and hooks for you, but when we get there, we'll have to hunt for our bait."

"What are we going to use for bait?"

"Don't worry about that. You don't have to do anything but come and enjoy yourself. It's going to be lots of fun; I guarantee it. If you don't have lots of fun, you can hit me in the head. Do you think I like being hit in the head? That's how much I'm sure you're going to be happy if you come with us to the beach."

There were three other boys in addition to Ben. If Leonard went, there would be five people in all. The journey wasn't too far because they only lived about five miles from the ocean anyway. Leonard thought it would be fun either way. He couldn't lose, because if the trip turned out to be more trouble than it was worth, there was always Ben's proposition. He could see hitting Ben in the head as being a lot more fun than he had had in a long time.

Leonard had always steered clear of trouble and tried to do the right thing. He had learned most of his lessons from when other kids got in trouble, and he saw the high price they had to pay. Take Ben, for instance. He got in trouble with his parents, the Mulgraves, just about every other day. He was regularly on his parents' most-wanted list. He was always doing something dangerous, risky, or outright bad.

Leonard knew that Ben Mulgrave was the last kid in the world to take any advice from or to be associated with when his parents weren't around, but going fishing wasn't that bad. There were no major dangers involved. It would be just some innocent kids having some fun fishing without their parents' consent. How bad could that be, especially if their parents wouldn't notice that they had gone away on this fishing excursion?

So Leonard held to his decision to go along. The other boys were mostly Ben's friends. Leonard was just tagging along as a new member of the crew. This posse knew that Leonard usually had a clean reputation, so they were more than happy to have him tagging along. They needed to be in a little good company every now and then. Maybe it would help their bad reputations.

Ben freely introduced the boys to Leonard. "Hey, Leonard, these are my friends, Johnny, Dave, and Jasper. I call them 'bad company' because they get me into trouble all the time."

"Yeah, we're the Bad Company Posse," Johnny shouted out gleefully. "That's a good name!" Rather than being offended by Ben's statement, they all seemed happy to be called the Bad Company Posse.

"Yeah, I like it, " Jasper said joyfully. "We're the Bad Company Posse. It has a ring to it. From now on, that will be our name."

"How about the Good Company Posse?" Dave quickly suggested. "That's a good one."

"No, no," Johnny insisted. "That just doesn't sound right. It makes us look like a bunch of disciples heading to church. We couldn't have that."

"Okay, we're the Bad Company Posse," said Johnny. "All in favor say, 'I love fishing.'"

"I love fishing," Jasper said merrily.

"I love fishing," David happily repeated.

"I love fishing," Ben blissfully said.

"I love fishing," Leonard added, timidly joining them in their vote for solidarity.

"Now let's go catch some fish," they shouted in unison and headed off to the ocean.
Leonard eagerly joined the fishing crew as they changed spots and locations hastily, trying to find a place where the fish were biting. They all got a tug or two, but none of them were lucky enough to catch any fish.

Leonard was having fun just trying. He was sincerely happy that he had decided to follow the Bad Company Posse to the ocean. There was no need to hit Ben in the head after all.

The crew began to get a little restless. It wasn't a good day for fishing; they all seemed to be down on their luck. However, it was always a good day to take a swim in the ocean. Johnny decided to change into his bathing trunks, and without any hesitation, he jumped into the water and swam over to a desolate houseboat that was always unattended and fairly close to the seashore. They all could swim to it with ease, but the rest of them wanted to keep trying their luck at fishing. Johnny climbed up to the top of the two-level houseboat and skillfully dove off the balcony into the water. He repeated this action many times, as if trying to entice his friends.

Eventually, it worked. Before long, they all threw down their fishing tools and joined him in the water. They briskly climbed onto the houseboat and made several different expert dives.

Leonard was having the time of his life. But then, suddenly, he remembered that it would be best if he got back home before his mother returned from work. It was time to pack up and leave while everything was still going well. Leonard knew that even though it was fun, what they were doing was dangerous. Moreover, they had no adult supervision. He started pleading with his new friends: "Guys, it's time to go home, don't you think?" He hoped someone would agree with him.

"Aren't you having fun, Leonard?" Ben asked.

"Yes, I am, but now it's getting late, and I don't want my mother to get home from work before I get back."

"Okay, we're leaving in a few minutes. I'll do just one more dive, and then we can all leave."

"Okay. I'll swim over to the other side and start getting myself ready to go. You can follow when you're done."

As Leonard swiftly started swimming toward the seashore from the houseboat, he heard the other boys shout at him.

"Hey, Leonard, where're you going? Are you leaving already? Why so soon? We just started having fun."

He didn't respond to their taunting cries. He simply kept on swimming toward the beach. As he continued to swim, he heard a big bang behind him. He quickly looked back and noticed that the railing from the upper level, which they had been using as their diving platform, had broken off and fallen into the water. Ben was holding the side of his head with one hand and grimacing in pain.

"Are you okay, Ben?" Leonard asked with genuine concern.

"Yes, I'm fine, just a little bump on my head. I was lucky, because it could've been much worse."

"You've been asking for a hit in your head all day. I hope you're happy now."

"Yeah, I've been asking for it, haven't I?"

"Come on. I told you it was time to go."

"Yes," Ben said, "I was taking my last dive when it happened. I'm ready to go now, Leonard."

"Okay, let's go before something worse happens."

Ben called out to his other friends while he was still in the water: "Everybody, let's go. I'm going home. You all should, too."

"No, we're not ready yet. You can go ahead."

"Okay, Leonard and I are leaving because it's getting late."

"Okay, bye," they said. "We'll see you later."

Ben swam over to shore, got his fishing gear together, and bid his friends good-bye once more. He pointed out to Leonard why he referred to his friends as bad company. They never knew when to stop and didn't until they got in some kind of trouble. Ben and Leonard walked home slowly, weary and tired, planning their explanatory story.

"Hey, Ben, remember, if my mother asks you where I was, you must say that I was at your house all day. Okay?"

"Okay," Ben said as they separated to go to their respective homes. "But if my parents ask you where I was, you can say I was at your house so I don't get in any trouble either."

Unfortunately, Essie was at the door waiting when Leonard got home. She had been searching for him all evening since she had gotten home from work.

"Where were you, Bunny—I mean, Leonard?" she asked.

"Momma, I was at the same place where I always stay." Leonard lied to his mother with a straight face, not knowing that she had already checked with the Mulgrave family and realized that he was not there.

"Where is that place that you always stay?

"At the Mulgraves' house, Momma."

"Come in here, boy. Let me teach not to lie to me ever again. I was going to let it slide today if you'd told me the truth. But now that you're lying to me, I have to teach you a good lesson."

"Okay, Momma, I was going to tell you. I was really with Ben and his friends at the beach. We went fishing, but we didn't catch any fish. I was hoping to catch some fish to take home to make dinner." Leonard nervously told the truth, but he was too late. Essie was ready to discipline him both for leaving without her consent and for lying on top of it all.

"Boy, go get me a piece of switch and come back to me. Let me teach you not to be deceitful."

"Okay, Momma." Leonard, just like the rest of Essie's kids, had learned a lesson from Bunny's experience. It made more sense to go straight for a switch and get it over and done. He rushed to the backyard and picked a small but reasonable switch and brought it to his mother. She took it from him and told him to hold out his hands. She gave him three hard strokes on his palms and warned him never to do that again.

***

Karl was the only child who had never really been disciplined by his mother. Essie was lenient with him because she always felt guilty for letting him grow up in the country with his father. To make her feel even guiltier, he held it over her head and would remind her about it every chance he got.

Other than his very bad behavior toward Essie, he was a surprisingly well-disciplined child. He never got in any major trouble or fights, except with his mother. He was focused on becoming a successful person when he grew up and always bragged about how he was going to be a millionaire. A self-motivated person, he read many mind-empowerment books. One of his favorite was entitled *The Road to Becoming a Millionaire*.

If he hadn't carried such a strong grudge against his mother, he could have been considered the perfect child. But his resentment was so strong, it consumed his very being and overshadowed any good that he had inside of him.

Myrtle was a firecracker, the "bad kid" in the family. Nevertheless, everyone loved her dearly. Essie had a special love for her also, but she wasn't afraid to discipline her when it was necessary. Essie knew that when she did, she would have to be ready for a big fight. Most of the time, she allocated the power to discipline to Junior, because he was her oldest son. She allowed him to deal with Myrtle and most of the other younger kids when it was really necessary.

Essie seldom had to administer discipline to her oldest kids, Gena, Betty, and Junior. She did sometimes have to discipline Junior when he was a young child in order to get him to go to school; he never really liked going. But he was a well-behaved child, as were Gena and Betty.

Chapter 23

Baking was Essie's favorite hobby, and she made all types of cakes as needed for various occasions. She especially loved to make her favorite cake—the delectable, mouthwatering Jamaican fruitcake.

Long before the occasion, she would start getting the various bits of dried fruits and other individual components ready. She would have the fruits soaking in rum for days, and then, when it was close to the time needed, she would bake the cake.

If it was for the kids, she would omit the rum but would add a sweet, finger-licking glaze of icing after the cake was baked. If it was for the grownups, then she would go all the way with the dark Jamaican rum and raisins—the whole shebang.

Essie baked her own delightful birthday cakes for all of her kids' birthdays. They could absolutely depend on the fact that there would be a nice yummy cake baked by their mother with their name on it and a wish from her to them. Most of the time, she wasn't able to buy her kids a big gift, but she was able to make them an appetizing, to-die-for cake.

When Betty turned eighteen years old, she woke up to a joyous chorus of the famous birthday song sung by her brothers and sisters.

"Happy birthday to you. Happy birthday to you. Happy birthday, dear Betty. Happy birthday to you!" they all sang to her while she lay in bed. She was half asleep and half awake, but she recognized them all.

"Thank you, guys. Thank you so much."

"You're welcome," they said together.

Betty noticed that her mother was the only one missing from the gathering. "Where is Momma?"

"Momma is still at work. She stayed over because she got held up while preparing a surprise for your birthday." Junior lied to cover for Essie, who was in the kitchen putting the finishing touches on the cake.

"Hope you live to see many more wonderful birthdays," Bunny said with a big, gleaming smile.

"I wish you the same," Karl said.

"May you have a wonderful year," Leonard added.

"I wish you lots of prosperity," Myrtle said.

"I wish you good luck," Andre and Don said to their aunt.

"I wish you good luck, too," said Breath, just in time before Essie burst into the room with a large, luscious, sweet-smelling fruitcake that she had baked the day before at her job and finished off minutes ago.

"Surprise! Here is your cake that I baked for you. Happy eighteenth birthday, my daughter." She rushed into the room with the enticing white fruitcake decorated with letters that read, *Happy Birthday, Betty. We wish U luck & prosperity. Mom and family.* It had one candle in the middle.

"Oh my God!" Betty shouted. "My birthday

157

cake. You guys lied to me. It's a wonderful cake. I love it, Momma. Thank you so much. A birthday is not a birthday without one of your special cakes!" She sprang out of bed to blow out her candle.

"Make a wish," Essie said.

Betty paused and closed her eyes. With one big blow, she extinguished the candle. She was very happy, although she hadn't received any other gift from her mother. She knew that Essie's cake, made especially for her, was the best gift that she could have gotten on her eighteenth birthday. Essie once again had made Betty's special day a delightful one. She gave her the best of what she could afford, and she gave it with the deep, caring love that came directly from a mother's heart. What more could anyone ask for?

Essie also baked cakes for Leonard's church harvest or for any major occasion or celebration at his church. She would bake several cakes and give them to Leonard to take with him. The church members all looked forward to Essie's contribution.

"Hey, Leonard, are you coming to this year's church harvest celebration?" a church sister asked him.

"Sure, I'm looking forward to it."

"Does that mean you'll be bringing one of those lovely, titillating fruitcakes that your mother usually makes?"

"I don't know yet. I'll have to ask her."

"Oh, please do! Don't forget to ask her to make a cake for harvest. You know how much we love her cake."

"Okay, I must remember to ask her about it."

"It wouldn't be a harvest without your mother's oh-so-delicious fruitcake. Mmm . . . makes me hungry just thinking about it. Remember now, don't forget, or else I'll have to go and ask her myself." Leaving Leonard with that threat, the church sister walked away.

Leonard told his mother about the church harvest celebration that was scheduled for three weeks away, and Essie gladly baked two large fruitcakes for him to take.

Essie also baked for school and community occasions. Once Bunny's class was having a school party, and the students were all told to bring any kind of food they liked. Bunny's teacher was familiar with Essie's delightful fruitcakes from a previous occasion, and she specifically instructed him to bring one of them. "Bunny, don't forget to tell your mother to send a cake for the class party," she reminded him. It was no secret that the teacher was more interested in the cake for herself than for her class. At the previous party, she had taken two-thirds of it home with her.

As a matter of fact, the whole neighborhood knew and loved Essie for her fruitcakes. In order to get a big turnout to a community event, one just had to advertise that Essie's fruitcakes would be available there, and that event would be a guaranteed hit. It goes without saying, Essie was famous for her fruitcakes.

159

Chapter 24

After being baptized, Leonard became a strict member of the Glenworth Seventh-day Adventist Church. He had taught himself to play the guitar after his sister Gena sent him a little toy-like guitar from the United States. He often used it to comfort himself when he got moody and sad.

He became sad when he thought of the odds that he would make it out of his limited situation, which were slim to none. He considered his situation limited because he wanted to be a physician so badly when he grew up, but his family was too wretchedly poor to even consider it seriously.

He didn't quite know what it took to be a physician, but he knew he wanted to be one. His chances of making his ambitious dream come true in Jamaica at this time were poor—about as good as a Haitian refugee heading off to the Miami shores with only a lifeboat, a broomstick, two paddles, and some extra swimming gear.

He often thought of the truth in one of his favorite songs, "Many Rivers to Cross," by a well-known singer named Jimmy Cliff.

> Many rivers to cross
> But I can't seem to find my way over . . .
> And it's only my will that keeps me alive . . .
> And I merely survive because of my pride . . .

Strangely, it was another one of Jimmy Cliff's songs, "You Can Get It If You Really Want," that helped to motivate him.

> You can get it if you really want
> But you must try, try and try
> Try and try, you'll succeed at last . . .

Leonard made a vow to himself that he would be a physician or nothing at all. Surprisingly, he came to this decision when he was only ten years old.

He also promised Essie that he would one day write a book about her life so the world would know her true story. Leonard was very young, but he could remember bits and pieces of some of the disasters that had happened in the family's earlier years.

In one particular flashback, he was in the back of a pickup truck with some of his brothers and sisters. He was sitting on a pile of furniture and was on some obscure journey. He figured no one knew where they were heading, because everyone in the truck was clearly flustered. They were crying and reassuring each other that they would find a place to stay.

He never asked many questions about that

incident, but each time he had that flashback, he thought ambitiously of writing the full story of his mother's life. *Maybe I'll name that book* Essie, he thought to himself, *as a shortened form of my mother's real name, Estelle.*

Essie loved to hear Leonard's big dreams. She was the only one who took him seriously. She knew that her life was noteworthy, to say the least, so she prayed that Leonard's dream would come true one day.

She always hoped that at least one of the seeds that she had planted on this earth would become a great, influential figure in this world. When times were unbearably hard, during her various pregnancies, these were some of the thoughts that helped her to make it through those tough times.

It was therefore easy for Leonard to convince her to send him to an SDA private school, Harrison Memorial High School. Essie didn't have the money to pay private-school tuition, but she knew it was necessary to at least try to make it happen, so she signed him up. She struggled tremendously with the various costs, but she did everything she could to meet his tuition each semester. Sometimes she even had to borrow money from her neighbors to meet his school expenses.

Leonard was now the only one in his family who attended church regularly; Myrtle had fully dropped out. One day, he invited his mother to a crusade meeting that his church was conducting, and Essie went with him to that church for the first time. At the end of the service, the minister gave an altar call and requested those who might need him to pray for them to come forward.

Essie reflected on one particular thing that the minister had said in his sermon. "God knows that we are only human, and in a lifetime of temptations, we are bound to sin. That is why He sent His son, Jesus. Jesus has died for us all so that all our sins may be forgiven. If you accept Christ in your heart, all your sins will be forgiven."

Essie kept hearing the last phrase repeatedly ringing in her ears and in her head: *All your sins will be forgiven.* She went to the altar for the minister to pray for her. As he prayed, tears ran down her cheeks. For the first time in her life, it dawned on her that Jesus was the only man she really needed. If she had Jesus in her life, everything else would fall into place. Essie was pounded in the head with salvation. She fell to the ground under mercy and forgiveness. She woke up to a brand new life of Christianity.

Essie left the church a fully changed person. She told Leonard that she was going to quit smoking and drinking that night. She told him that she was going to give her heart to the Lord. Essie's words were simple, but they were bafflingly true. She never smoked another cigarette again in her life. She never took another sip of alcohol again in her life. Essie quit cold turkey.

She was baptized within two months of the night she had astonishingly found God. The only reason she wasn't baptized sooner was because she wanted to do one more thing first. She needed to do it so she could start a new, respectable life. She needed to get married to the man she really loved, the man God kept putting in her life every time she needed him most, the man who had been in her life from when she was a teenager, the man who was, right now, waiting patiently for her. Essie decided that she was going to ask for Tim's hand in marriage before she got baptized.

"Timothy Brown, the true love of my life, will you marry me?" Essie went down on both knees with her hands clasped in a prayerful position in front of her face, as if she were pleading for his forgiveness if she had done him any unforgivable wrong in the past. Pitifully, she looked up at Tim as she asked him this life-changing question. She knew in her heart that she had done him wrong.

Tim didn't say a word. He was as silent as the day Essie had left him for a big-time city guy. He stood still for a moment, then looked down at her, swallowed up into her wanting stare. He looked up to the heavens, on the verge of breaking down. "Thank you, Lord," he said, his body shaking as only a grown man shakes when he cries.

He took Essie by the hand and gracefully raised her up from her knees. He was thankful to God for answering his pleading during many lonely nights. He hugged her like the father hugged his son in the story of the returning prodigal. "Essie, my pretty lady, we started it, so it's only right that we end it together. That's what good friends do; we wait for each other to catch up in life. I'm glad you came back to the arms that were always longing for you. Having you as my wife will make me a happy man. You make my life complete. I can go to my grave in peace and with dignity."

"Tim, I'll love you until the day I die," Essie promised him. "You know I wouldn't have it any other way. I love you. I've always loved you."

After she married Tim, Essie was baptized and became a true Christian. She insisted that everyone should call her by her new married name, Mrs. Essie Brown. She no longer had repeated thoughts of suicide. She now knew God understood all things. She knew that God had forgiven her for all her sins and made her into a new person.

The more Mrs. Essie Brown understood the Bible and the ways of God, the happier she became. Eventually, Mrs. Essie Brown became such a strict Christian, she was almost like a religious fanatic.

She prayed to God twice a day. She sang songs from the hymnal, read her Bible, and prayed from thirty minutes to as much as two hours early every morning for the rest of her life, and did the same thing in the evenings. Mrs. Essie Brown praised God so much that it seemed as if she was trying to make up for lost time in her earlier life, for the time when she was not a Christian. She just could not get enough of serving God. When Mrs. Essie Brown found God, it was irrefutably the happiest time in her life.

Her husband, Tim, remained in the country, and she remained in the big city. Just like old times, Tim rolled out the red carpet for his adorable, gracefully aging Christian wife every time she came to see him.

Mrs. Essie Brown would do the same for her warm, humble, country farmer husband whenever he came home to her in the big city. Some people were made to be different. But that didn't mean they weren't meant to be together.

Chapter 25

Mrs. Essie Brown's life took a significant upswing after she perspicaciously found herself. She had made the first major change in her life with her own two hands. She had lived her life as a strong single mother until she married Mr. Timothy Brown. Now she officially and proudly was no longer a single parent.

This much-needed change came a little late in her life, reminiscent of the ironies mentioned in the lyrics of a song titled "Ironic" by Alanis Morissette:

It's a death row pardon two minutes too
late . . .
It's a free ride when you've already
paid . . .
A traffic jam when you're already
late . . .
It's meeting the man of my dreams
And then meeting his beautiful wife . . .

In Mrs. Essie Brown's case, it was a woman

who had gotten married after living her whole damn life as a single mother, and who finally got a good father or stepfather for her kids after her kids were already grown. Though late, the change was significant for Essie. Her kids could say they had a stepdad for the first time, and no one can ever be too old to have a stepdad.

Also, for the first time, there was someone other than Essie who was responsible for both her social and her financial well-being. For the first time in her life, she had someone who swore that he would be there for her to lean on, for better or for worse, for the rest of their lives, for however long that would be.

These were pretty simple things, but they were huge in Mrs. Essie Brown's eyes. These things were significant for natural and psychological closure in the long, wild, single-female and single-motherhood period of her life. It was as if she had been brokenhearted ever since Stedman and her best friend betrayed her more than twenty-five years earlier. She had been carrying her broken heart in her hands like a cracked egg this entire time. As she went from relationship to relationship, it crumbled a little more each time.

But now the buck stopped here. She could feel her heart heal as each crack fused back together to make one uncluttered, trusting, whole, beautiful organ. She could exhale and breathe easily again. Instead of a gloomy, colorless world, she could now see and enjoy the wonderful array of colors in the rainbow and in the fresh dew roses along the way. Mrs. Essie Brown, at age fifty-four, felt complete again. She was ready to live, trust in love, and dream big dreams once more.

***

The next significant change in Mrs. Essie Brown's life was made possible by her miracle child,

Gena. Gena providentially got married to a wonderful, humble, down-to-earth American citizen named Mr. Wesley Dobson. Soon after that, she was able to obtain her permanent resident status, which propelled her into the legal, working, taxpaying society of the United States. This also allowed her to travel back and forth to Jamaica.

Her trips gave her the opportunity to see firsthand any problems that her family had and to try to solve them, if possible. When she visited, she brought lots of goods with her, and she continued to send barrels of food and goods as well. Gena invested lots of money in her mother's home in Glenworth so that her mother and her three kids, as well as the rest of the family, could live more comfortably.

In addition to helping with goods and food and helping to fix her mother's house, Gena helped with domestic affairs. She encouraged and financed Karl's wedding to his wife, Marva, and helped to pay Leonard's private-school tuition fees so Mrs. Essie Brown wouldn't have to worry about them anymore.

Gena did so much for her family at the time when Mrs. Essie Brown had banished her past and opened her heart to a wonderful new way of life that it appeared as if God had started blessing Essie indirectly through her daughter Gena. It was like a cycle of blessings. The more God blessed Gina, the more she returned the blessings to her family.

One of the most significant things Gena did that helped to change Mrs. Essie Brown's life was to fulfill a promise she had made to her, a promise that she would someday pave the way for the whole family to travel to the United States, where everyone could have a better and brighter future.

The miracle baby couldn't make miracles. She couldn't fulfill her promise all at once, but she could and would keep chipping away at it. She would do whatever it took to get each person from Jamaica to the United States, one at a time.

***

The first person Gena brought from Jamaica to live with her in the United States was her younger brother Leonard. One day, while she was passing by a private SDA high school in New York, it suddenly dawned on her that there was a special type of visa called a student visa that was designed specifically for someone like Leonard, who desperately wanted to become a doctor someday. She thought this would be the perfect means of getting him started on the right track. He could leave his private SDA high school in Jamaica to go to another private SDA high school in the United States.

When the thought popped into her head, she stopped at the school to find out what was required to get her brother admitted. After she had all the information she needed, she then got all the required documents from the immigration office and mailed everything to Leonard to fill out, sign, and take to the US embassy in Jamaica to obtain a student visa. Leonard was super excited. He had wanted to travel to the United States but hadn't thought it possible.

Leonard was the spitting image of his father, Tim. Reserved, skinny, tall, and relatively handsome, he dressed neatly at all times. At Harrison Memorial High School, he had much better than average grades. For three years in a row, he was ranked seventh in his class of more than thirty students, and he was third or fourth among the boys in his class of more than twelve.

Leonard was very organized in everything he did. While all of the other students carried knapsacks and regular school bags, Leonard carried a business-like briefcase as if he were the teacher rather than the student—or a young Wall Street executive. It was a secondhand briefcase that had been given to Essie by one of her bosses, Dr. McNelly. Leonard was more than happy to make good use of it. He knew that he stood out and was mocked by the crowd, but he was proud to be different.

Once Leonard made an unusual book stand in his woodworking class. It had the appearance of a pulpit stand made in the shape of the stone tablets of the Ten Commandments, but in addition, it had a place to hold and keep a book open while reading. Leonard nailed the hands-free book-holder stand permanently to his student desk. Whenever anyone entered the classroom, they could immediately spot Leonard's desk—the only one in the classroom like it. At the end of the school year, he took his special desk to his new classroom.

Another time, Leonard made a special gift for his mother in woodworking class: a wooden frame with a heart carved out in the middle and an arrow running through it like the Cupid sign. He was proud of his handiwork. When he took it home and gave it to his mother, she loved it and decided to hang it in the family room. The next day when he came home from school, he noticed that it had been chopped into many fine pieces with a knife or machete. The culprit turned out to be his younger brother Bunny.

Leonard was very upset, but he understood the nature of sibling jealousy. Therefore, he forgave his younger brother for being only human. Leonard knew that there were many more untapped ideas in his mind that no one could destroy so easily.

When Leonard was fourteen, he and a neighborhood friend named Joseph attempted to stow away on a cruise ship going to the US. It began when

Leonard, being a very close friend, listened to Joseph's big plans and dreams and tried to support his friend's idea as much as he could. Eventually, his support went a little too far.

He was now not only a supporter, but a possible partner with Joseph in his ambitious plan. The plan was that they both would stow away on a ship to the United States and find a relative who would come and get them at the US port or somewhere close by. Leonard was comfortable living his life as a high school student with a bright future. He strongly believed in a good education. He believed that a mind really was a terrible thing to waste. His favorite quote was from the great Bob Marley, who said, "Emancipate yourself from mental slavery. None but ourselves can free our minds." However, if it was a real possibility that he could be transported to the United States safely, Leonard certainly would go for it.

When the time came, Joseph and Leonard excitedly packed their knapsacks with some of the basic things that they naively judged they would need to survive on their expedition. That night they confidently headed down to the Montego Bay pier, where a US cruise ship was docked. Once they got there, however, the reality of the danger involved became obvious. He denounced the audacious but premature plan and canceled his support of Joseph's big idea.

Joseph was angry because he was intent on following through with his plan. But when Leonard left and headed back toward home, Joseph reluctantly followed him. They both decided that there had to be a better way.

Thus, when Leonard received the immigration package from his sister for obtaining his student visa, he was delighted and realized that this was the better way that he had been wishing for all along. The whole family was excited to see that one of them was about to set foot on US soil, where impossible dreams came true. They realized, for the first time, that Leonard might make it to become a doctor after all. Everyone cheered him on.

Mrs. Essie Brown and Leonard got up early one morning and went on a four-hour drive to the US embassy in Kingston. They had high hopes, but when they received a negative response, they were in despair. The embassy gave no explanation. They simply stamped Leonard's passport with a denial stamp and returned it to them.

Leonard felt like it was the day of reckoning, and he had fallen short of making it through heaven's gate because his papers were stamped for condemnation. Both he and his mother returned home from the four-hour journey back to Glenworth sad and depressed, and Leonard sank into a despairing and melancholy mood. It seemed like the deluded dream was dying that day.

But Leonard's dream wouldn't die so easily. His determination was much too strong for the door to be miraculously opened and then suddenly shut on him just like that. It would not happen without a fight.

Leonard encouraged his mother to take him back to the embassy the following week and to get an additional referral from his school, although it wasn't a requirement. Mrs. Essie Brown did obtain the referral from Leonard's school, and they both returned the following week. They presented their documents to the embassy, but were rejected once again.

Leonard, though dejected, pleaded with his heavyhearted mother to take him back to the embassy the following week. That week, they obtained a referral letter from the Honorable Howard Cook, the minister of education in Montego Bay.

They again returned to the US embassy, but they were rejected once more. Even though he kept getting knocked down, Leonard would not stay down. He would not give up. He believed that if he gave up, he would be giving up on his dreams and letting down his sister Gena, who had faithfully done her part. He pleaded with Mrs. Essie Brown to take him one last time.

Although his mother was exhausted, she attempted the trying journey once more. This time, they had obtained a letter of referral from a local politician. Unfortunately, it didn't make any difference. They were turned down again.

Leonard refused to let go; he was like a dog holding on to a bone. He begged his poor, tired, and exhausted mother to try one more time. Mrs. Essie Brown reluctantly and cheerlessly gave in to her desperate son's plea. She didn't know how much longer she could go on with this failing venture. She thought he was like a dog barking up the wrong tree. However, she mustered up enough energy to go one last time. They gathered another referral from a different local politician and headed to the US embassy.

Essie decided that this time, everything was in the Lord's hands, and whatever the outcome, it was what the Lord wanted for her son at that time. She prayed a long, deep prayer, and then she said, "Lord, if it's thy will, let it be done. Amen."

They went inside the US embassy and waited their turn. When they were called to the window, they presented all of the required documents, but sadly, the immigration officer simply opened the passport book, noticed the many previous rejection stamps, quickly added another one, and returned the seemingly condemned documents to them.

They were very sad because they both knew that they had done all that they could do, and this must be the will of God at that particular time.

Mrs. Essie Brown was fully convinced that if the

Lord had wanted her son to travel to the United States, it would have happened on the first attempt. She even blamed herself somewhat for questioning the will of God.

However, Leonard was also a strong Christian, and he still believed that it was the will of God for him to travel to the United States and get started on his journey to becoming a doctor who could do mighty things for the sick and the needy. Why would God not want another pair of healing hands on earth? Leonard believed that it was God who had given him the unyielding drive and intense appetite to become a physician.

He also believed that his mother was right. It was not the will of God for him to get a US student visa at that particular time. "That particular time" was the key phrase that separated Leonard's belief from his mother's. Leonard believed that although it was clearly not the will of God when they had gone to the embassy a week earlier, the following week, it surely would be the will of God.

Leonard convinced himself that where they had gone wrong was attempting to get a student visa one and a half months too soon. They could now see that it was incontrovertibly not the will of God. The will of God was for them to go to the embassy three weeks before the SDA school in New York reopened for the spring semester.

He tried to convince his mother of his logic, but, totally burned out over this situation, she didn't buy it. She did, however, ask her oldest son, Junior, to accompany Leonard one more time to the embassy.

That week, Leonard did the old routine and got an additional reference from another reputable official. Then he and Junior headed to the embassy, but it was like an excruciating curse was upon them. They were

174

appalled to be turned down once more.

Leonard could not believe what was happening to him. He knew this had to be the big break that he needed to realistically move in the direction of his dreams. He believed that God wanted him to be a doctor to help save lives and be an important contributor to this world.

For the first time, his eyes became truly opened, and it dawned on him that his dreams could be delusional. At that time only the richest and the best of the best got admitted to do medicine at the University of the West Indies. He was not in that category at all. He didn't consider himself a top scholar, but he'd always believed that, with hard work, he could do anything that a great man could do.

His motto in life was reflected in one of his favorite poems by Henry Wadsworth Longfellow:

The heights by great men reached and kept
Were not attained by sudden flight,
But they, while their companions slept, Were
toiling upward in the night.

Only sons of doctors, professors, and popular politicians got accepted, because, in Jamaica, the spaces for medical students in those days were very few and highly competitive. Leonard knew that realistically he had no chance of fulfilling his dreams on the island of Jamaica.

Leonard could not accept defeat. He asked his big brother to take him back the following week, but Junior refused to waste his time fruitlessly traveling four hours to and four hours back from the US embassy, just to be turned down again. Leonard pleaded with everyone to take him to the embassy again, but they all refused. They all sadly encouraged their brother to face the fact

175

that his dream was not going to happen.

That week, Leonard went to his school library and did some research. He found out that dentistry was one profession that could not be studied in Jamaica at that time. There was currently no dental program available on the whole island.

Leonard now knew what he would have to do to circumvent the system. He would have to let the immigration officer know that he wanted to do dentistry instead of medicine. Leonard was ready to go to the embassy the next week, but no one wanted to go with him. No one wanted to waste their precious time.

Being sixteen and a half years old, Leonard decided that he would go all by himself. After having gone six times, he was not afraid. He understood the route and the procedure. Therefore, on the appointed day, he got up at 3:00 to walk to the main bus stop and catch the bus that would take him to Kingston.

Although he was the only one on the dark, desolate street, he was not afraid. He remembered what his mother had told him one day when he was ten years old: "Son, all great men will pass away sooner or later, and the new great man is still a child at your age even as we speak. At some point, the society will be looking to your younger generation to fill major roles. It's to your advantage to choose your roles now and choose wisely. They will need prisoners to fill jails just as they will need doctors to fill hospitals and care for the wounded, and lawyers to fight for the weak and the innocent, and presidents or prime ministers to lead the country and the world. Son, the earlier you choose for or against a future role, the better will be your chances."

Ever since then, after praying to God to help him, Leonard made his choice and sincerely believed that God wanted him to live to be a productive man in this world, and he would not die until the job was done.

Because God had chosen him to be of service to mankind, he had no reason to be afraid. The only serious fear Leonard had was that the immigration officer wouldn't deal with him because he was a minor.

When Leonard got to the embassy, he repeated all of the steps that his mother and big brother had previously taken. Eventually, it was his turn to approach the window to speak with the seemingly disgruntled immigration officer. Leonard was ready to put it all on the line. This was his final attempt, and if he was going down, he was going down swinging.

He stepped forward, handed the interviewer his documents, and said in a firm but polite tone, "Sir, I don't know what the problem is. I have all of the required documents and more. I intend to study dentistry in the future, and studies for this profession are not available in any schools in Jamaica. The high school that accepted me in the US is waiting on me. Classes are about to start soon, and I'm still here in Jamaica."

As Leonard spoke, he noticed that the interviewer was no longer listening. Instead, the officer went over to the other side of the counter, shuffled some papers, and signed and stamped some documents. In each of Leonard's previous attempts, the interviewer simply took his documents, read them, and then stamped a rejection notice right there without moving to the other side of the counter. Leonard was dumbfounded. Although he liked what he saw, he was much too afraid that the immigration officer would still reject his documents.

He therefore kept talking, although it seemed as if he was talking to himself. He acted as if this was his judgment day and he was at the pearly gates, nervously pleading for his dear life. "I don't know what the problem is. The school is calling me to find out what's going on. They are expecting me to join the class early. I have books to buy and school-related preparations to make."

While Leonard was still talking, the immigration officer stepped back to the interview window and told him to go through the side door. Leonard was stunned. The officer did not return the documents to him, as the others had, so that was a good sign. Also, he had never been told to go through that particular door before, so that was another good sign.

Leonard was thrilled but bewildered. He couldn't believe what was happening right in front of his eyes. He was about to get his student visa after all, after being rejected so many times in a row. He was amused to be getting it now, after everyone had absolutely given up on him.

The story was once told of a man who was traveling up a snowy mountain and stopped to rest for a minute. It was now night, and it was very dark. Suddenly he fell and started tumbling down the side of the mountain. Luckily, the hiker grabbed a branch as he was rapidly falling. He hung onto the branch for dear life.

He prayed to God to save him, and God answered and told the man to let go. The man was shocked and severely disappointed to hear that his beloved God, the one he had always trusted, wanted him to let go and die. The hiker was not ready to die, so he held on even tighter.

The next day, a crowd of people gathered on the road below. They were amazed at the strange sight of a man who had frozen to death clutching a tree branch. Everyone was puzzled, wondering why the poor man didn't let go of the branch. The road was only three feet below him.

The moral of the story is that you have to trust and believe, but more than anything else, you have to do your part so God can do His. Leonard surely did his part and more.

That day at the embassy, he did receive the long-awaited student visa. Within two weeks, he emigrated to the United States to live with his sister Gena. He was now on his way to pursuing his medical career.

Mrs. Essie Brown was very happy, because she knew that she had a son who was a determined fighter just like herself. It reminded her of the incident when he was two years old and had run frantically out of the street so he wouldn't get hurt by the taxi. From then on, she knew that Leonard was a special person. She believed that Leonard was blessed by God.

***

That was how Gena got Leonard to live with her in the United States. One down, but she had almost a dozen more to go.

After trying a few strategies to get her family members to the United States, some successful, some not, Gena was finally able to file for her mother, Mrs. Essie Brown. It took a little longer than she would have liked. However, Mrs. Essie Brown's papers came through five years after Gena became a US citizen.

By this time, Mrs. Essie Brown's husband, Tim, had unfortunately died from renal complications. Therefore, Mrs. Essie Brown traveled to the United States alone. She then became a US citizen, which allowed her to file for all the rest of her children, and they were all approved.

Finally Gena could say that she had fulfilled her promise to her mother. The miracle baby was able to make a way for herself and then paved the way, against all odds, for the rest of her family. Gena was indisputably the unsung hero of Essie's family. She single-handedly effected a major upswing in the statistical graph of Essie's life.

Chapter 26

Essie often called Bunny her "wash belly," a term indicating that he was her last child. By the time Bunny had come of age, he was doing very well for himself. He lived with Joyce, his committed girlfriend of more than twelve years. The leather business they had started together was growing rapidly and turning over good profits, the way Rumpelstiltskin turned straw into gold.

They also had two wonderful young boys, Fern and Neil. They had long since moved out of Essie's house and had built a huge, splendid home of their own. They had everything that a young, striving couple should have except the blissful matrimonial title of man and wife.

One day Bunny was doing some work in his workshop, which was located at the back of the house, when Joyce came in. "When was the last time you called your sister?" she asked.

"Who? Gena?" Bunny asked.

"Yes, Gena. Who else would I be talking about? I don't care about anybody else. Don't get me wrong. I love all of your family, but I only care if you call your big sister Gena." Joyce clarified what she had said, lest there be any misunderstanding, and Lord knows, there was plenty of that to go around.

"Does that mean that you care for Betty, too?"

"I don't dislike her. It's just that we don't see eye to eye. I don't have a problem with anyone in your family. It's you who have problems with them. After all, Betty is your sister, not mine. You're the one who has problems with her. I'm staying out of it, my dear love."

"So does that mean that I was the only one she kicked out of Momma's house?"

Joyce began to get a little irritated at Bunny's round-the-woods evasion of her question. "Bunny, as I said, I'm staying out of it. I only wanted to know if you called Gena in New York anytime recently. That was all I asked. Why yuh chose to give me a hard time, I don't know. It's just a simple question, with a simple answer: yes or no."

"No, if recently means yesterday, and yes, if recently means in the past six months. You see, my dear love, it depends." Bunny continued to dance around Joyce's question.

"I told yuh that yuh should go into politics. I swear, that's where you belong." Joyce was now convinced that Bunny was hiding something and that was the reason he was avoiding giving her a straightforward answer. She knew him too well. "Why yuh don't want to call yuh sister Gena? She's always so good to you."

"I got tired of her saying the same old thing every time I called," Bunny confessed.

"And what is that?" Joyce asked, as if she didn't already know the answer.

"You know, the same old thing." Bunny refused to say what exactly it was that he considered to be "the same old thing."

"So what's wrong with that?" Joyce asked. "I don't see anything wrong with that."

"Wrong with what? I didn't say what the same old thing was, so now I don't know what you're talking about."

Joyce was tired of the games, so she spoke clearly about what was on her mind. "Don't play Mr. Wise Guy with me, Bunny. Let's just lay it all out on the table. What's wrong with us getting married?"

"Haaaw! See, that's why you're so concerned about me calling Gena. You know that every time I call, she asks when we're getting married. She always says that it's time to make it official and that it's never too late. She always insists that we do it soon. She keeps saying that she'll help us with the wedding, and so on and so on. I'm tired of hearing that. Our life is perfect the way it is; we don't need a ring or any certificate to seal our love for each other."

"Speak for yourself. My life is not perfect. I do, and I repeat, I do. As a matter of fact, it sounds so good, I'll repeat it again: I do need a ring and a certificate to seal this love." Joyce was very firm on the topic of marriage for the first time in the twelve years they had been together.

He stopped what he was doing, put his tools away, and looked up into Joyce's face. "You sound fired up. When was the last time you called my sister Gena? Now I'm concerned."

She grinned from ear to ear.

"Oh! That's what this whole thing is about? Gena's on my case again? I see. When did she call?"

"Yesterday," Joyce confessed, with a big sigh of relief. A bucketload of stress fell from her shoulders, now that it was all out there in the open. The release of tension could be seen on her face. "She said that she'll help us with the wedding expenses if we need her help. She already has a lovely wedding gift for us."

"We don't need her help with any wedding expenses, but we'll be happy to accept her wedding gift—"

Joyce interrupted him. "What are you saying?" she asked, holding her breath, with both hands over her mouth. She felt lightheaded, as if about to faint. She hardly felt her feet on the ground and was barely holding up against the cruel force of gravity. Her two feet were not enough to keep her standing in an upright position. She needed at least two more pairs.

"We have to get married in order to get the gift that Gena has already bought for us," Bunny said in an ironic manner. "Besides, I got away with twelve years already, and our kids are now seven and eight years old. You guys have backed me into a corner, and I have nowhere left to run."

Joyce ran and jumped into his arms with a loud scream. "So that's a yes?" she asked. Without waiting for an answer, she started shouting for joy.

"Wait a minute! If I'm going to do this, I have to do it right." Bunny hurriedly cleared away all the miscellaneous, stray pieces of junk that were in front of him on the floor. Then he quickly climbed up onto his worktable and hastily swept the vertical column that lined the inside of the roof of the workshop. With his hands stretched high, he retrieved a small black ring container, which he had secretly bought a few weeks back after speaking to Gena. He had conveniently left it there waiting for the right time to propose to his loyal lover and the loving mother of his two handsome boys, whom he loved so much. He was sure that he would know when it was the right time to propose to her.

Today, the time was perfect.

He swiftly but carefully climbed down from his worktable and called out to his sons and to all of his six workers to stop whatever they were doing so they could hear what he had to say. Then he clumsily went down on one knee on the dirty industrial floor. "Joyce, my love, I'm so sorry that I've been such a pig-headed, stubborn person. I should've done this twelve years ago when I met you. Thank you for staying with me and loving me regardless during all these years. Joyce, will you marry me?"

Joyce was overcome with emotion. "Yes, my love," she said through her tears. "Thank you, you stubborn fool. You know that I deserve this and that I've been very patient. We both know it was time to do this. Thank you." Joyce shed more tears of joy as she embraced her fiancé and dreamed of an even brighter future together.

Joyce was an active member of the Glenworth SDA Church, so making arrangements for a wedding was not difficult for her. Strangely, she had organized countless weddings before, but had never gotten the opportunity to organize her own—until now. She jumped right into the flow of preparing for a medium-sized wedding. The very next day, she called all of her friends and family to let them know the good news. She and Bunny were getting married on May 21 of that same year, 1994.

"Hello, Christine, will you be my maid of honor?" Joyce asked her best friend in Canada, whom she hadn't seen in more than five years.

"Noooo! Say what? Noooo! I can't believe it. Wait a minute. I have to take a seat for this one. Are you kidding me, Joyce?"

"Would I kid you? Well, I kid you not. Bunny asked me to marry him—finally!"

"Finally! Oh my God! I don't believe it. I gave up on him years ago. I thought that he would never do such a thing." Christine bubbled with excitement.

"Well, you know what they say: 'What nuh dead, nuh call doppy.' If he's not dead, don't call him a ghost."

"You can say that again, child," Christine said. "Never give up on a person as long as he or she is alive. Congratulations! I wouldn't miss the wedding for the world. Let me have the date, dear Joyce, so I can make a request for my vacation at work. I'll be there for sure."

"So that's a yes? You will be my maid of honor?"

"Well, let me put it this way. If you didn't make me your maid of honor, there would be a big fight at your wedding. I would personally come to Jamaica to rip off the dress of anybody else who would even try to take my place, anybody who thinks they're more bad than I am or that they've known you longer than I have. How long have we been friends? From when our eyes were at our knees? Child, just pencil me—no, make that pen— just pen me into your lineup as your maid of honor before I have to perform badly at your wedding."

"Thank you, Christine. I knew that I could depend on you. I'll send you an official wedding invitation in the mail."

"You better do that, girl, if you know what's best for you."

"I'll also fill you in on all of the major happenings as time progresses."

"Congratulations to you again, my friend. You deserve the honor. It's about time Bunny realized what a good woman he has by his side. Keep me posted, okay, Joyce?"

"I will, mon. I will. As soon as we put everything together, I'll let you know more, all right, girlfriend?"

"Already, you've made my day," Christine said. "Bye."

Joyce hung up the phone and turned to Bunny. "Who will be your best man?"

"Well, at least we know it won't be Mickey. We broke up our business partnership after he stole my client, and you know the whole story after that. It just wouldn't seem right to have him as my best man. But he used to be a good friend, so maybe he could emcee the whole program. You know how he loves to talk. He would be a great host."

"So who is left for best man?"

"Well, weddings are about the showcase, so it's a matter of who has the best showmanship, as far as I'm concerned."

"You're right, Bunny. I'm with you on that one. That's a great idea. We need to call him early so he can get enough time to apply for his vacation and make all the necessary preparations."

"So I see that you got where I'm going with this one."

"Yes, man, I got you long time. I was also thinking about him as the best option."

"I'll give him a call now while we're contemplating it." Bunny picked up the phone immediately and called his brother in Florida, Dr. Leonard Brown. "Hello, Doc. How's it going?"

"Good so far. I can't complain. Who's going to listen anyway? I'm just here giving thanks for life and good health. How about you, Bunny?"

"I'm doing good. As you said, just giving thanks for life and good health. How is the family?"

"My wife is doing great. However, all we're doing is working the shirt and blouse off our backs, and we still can't really get our heads above water. I told you about the invention that I recently got a patent pending for. I sent it out to lots of companies, but it's still not looking too good. None of them accepted my idea for a disposable dental floss holder. I was sure that it was the next big explosion on the market, but none of the companies are taking the bait."

"Well, you just have to keep knocking on doors. One day, one will open for you. Just keep trying, my brother."

"Thank you, bro. So what's the latest? What's going on?"

"Well, I have some bad news... Haa! That hurts."

"What's that?" Dr. Leonard asked. "Are you okay, bro?" It sounded as if Bunny had gotten hurt while talking to him on the phone.

"No, it's Joyce here slapping me silly because I said that I have bad news."

"What's the bad news, bro?"

"I'm getting married."

"Wow! Wow! Woooow! I'm sooo sorry to hear that, bro. How did you let that happen?"

"Long story, my brother, but your sister had a lot to do with it."

"No, not Gena again," Dr. Leonard joked. "I feel for you, my bro. I believe Gena is receiving some kind of commission for getting us all married. Obviously, she enjoys playing Cupid without wings. I remember introducing Dolcina to her, and before you know it, we were married. I'm sure she had something to do with it also. We've been married now for four years, and I must tell you, bro, it's not as bad as it sounds. But I really expected you to talk your way out of tragic things like these. What happened?"

"I've been talking my way out of it for twelve years. Time has just caught up with me, my brother. I'm

188

tired of running. I happily turned myself in for the penalty, whatever it may be."

"Well, there's nothing we can do about that now other than to warn your two boys not to take their girlfriends around Gena when they grow up, because the same thing could happen to them. What can I do to help in this dilemma?"

"Brother, I would love for you to be my best man. If you don't mind."

"Hey, I'll be there, but only if you're going to have bulla cake and pear and soda water. Just kidding, my bro. I wouldn't miss it for the world. My little brother's finally getting married after umpteen years. Even if I didn't do it for you, I would have to do it for Joyce's sake. I would be honored to be your best man. I'm going to start working on my speech. By the way, when is the wedding again?"

"May twenty-first of this year."

"Let me jot it down so I can know what days to ask for at work. Don't worry yourself, bro, my wife and I will be there. You know that we'll use any excuse for a vacation."

"Thank you, my brother."

"It's my pleasure. I'm very happy my little brother is stepping up to the plate. It's about time."

"It's long overdue, if I say so myself."

"Congratulations, and may you have a wonderful married life."

"Thank you, my brother. I'll talk with you soon."

Bunny then decided that he would also call Gena in New York while he was at it and tell her the good news.

Gena answered the phone. "Hello, who is this?"

"It's your brother Bunny. How are you doing today, my sister?"

189

"Hey, Bunny! You have good news for me? Believe it or not, I had a dream last night about you. I dreamed that you were crazy happy, and you called me to tell me that you were getting married to Joyce. I was so happy, but the funny thing was, I was the one in the white wedding dress—a pretty, fitted white dress. It looked so beautiful. Oh, the wedding was wonderful! Bunny, you know that I don't dream all the time, but when I do, that means something is up. You know that."

"My sister, did you have that dream before or after Joyce called you yesterday and told you that we were getting married?"

"No, no, Joyce didn't call me yesterday. I did not speak to Joyce yesterday, I swear. I dreamed it. I dreamed it." She laughed. "Oh my God! I can't believe it. My little brother is finally getting married. Congratulations, congratulations, my brother. I don't know why it took you so long, but better now than never. Oh my Lord! That is good news. So when is the wedding?"

"It will be on May twenty-first of this year."

"Good, get it over and done. I'll be there. I have my outfit that I'm wearing down to Jamaica, but I have to go and shop for something for the wedding. I have to talk to Joyce to see how the planning is going. I want you guys to have a wonderful wedding. I know that it's going to be good. Just leave it up to Joyce and me. I have to buy Momma a nice dress to wear. I know Leonard will pay her fare to go to Jamaica. Maybe he could pay Myrtle's fare also. I'm going to speak with him as soon as I get off the phone with you. Did you tell him about it yet?"

"Yes, I asked him to be my best man, and he said yes."

"Good choice. We have to be proud of our doctor brother. Let people know that we have a doctor in

190

our family. Don't be afraid to list him in your program as a doctor, because we have something we can show off about. Our family is coming from afar, and we have to be proud of each other."

"Yes, we do. I don't travel to the United States much, but I did attend his graduation, so I know his credentials are authentic. Why would I not use them? I'm very proud of him."

"I'm proud of you, too, my little brother. You're doing well with your business, and you have a nice big house to enjoy with your family. You have a lot of reasons to be proud. Congratulations, again. I'll be dancing at your wedding in May."

"Thank you. I must make some more calls to let everybody know about the date. It's kind of short notice, but it was the best time for us to do it."

"Don't worry yourself. Do what's best for you. I'll let you go so you can call everyone. Don't forget to call Junior in Los Angeles to see if he can get time off from his job. Okay, bye, my dear brother. Love you." Gena ended the long-distance telephone call.

She was happy to see that her constant urging of the young couple had finally paid off and they'd be getting married soon. It pleased her heart to see couples take that vow. The good news that Bunny gave her really made her day.

Bunny then decided to call Junior in Los Angeles to see if he would be able to attend his wedding. "Hello Junior. This is Bunny. How are you and the family?"

"Hey, my brother, what's going on? I was talking about you the other day, man. I was telling a friend that I have a brother still living in Jamaica, and he is doing much better than everyone I know here in L.A. Ya, man. It is a true thing. He couldn't believe the story. Jah knows."

191

"Really, which brother is that?" Bunny asked jokingly. "Do I know him?"

"You, man. Is you I'm talking about."

"Okay, thank you for those kind words, although they're not altogether true. I have your back on that one. If anybody calls me to double-check on your facts, I'll cover for you."

"Man, Bunny, you don't know how good you're doing compared to other friends that I have here in L.A. who're suffering."

"Well, that may be true. I must thank the Lord, as my brother Leonard would say, for keeping my head above the waters. I thank the Lord for being alive and well."

"Yes, man."

"Junior, your brother is getting married on May twenty-first of this year. Will you be able to come?"

"Which brother is that?" Junior asked. "You and I are the only lucky ones who aren't married, that I know about. So who is getting married?"

"Well, if it's not you, then it must be me."

"Oh my God! I'm so sorry to hear that. Don't tell me. Gena caused it? I knew one day they were going to gang up on you. You should have called me earlier. Maybe I could have helped. You know what they say about marriage, right? It's a three-ring circus: engagement ring, wedding ring, and suffering. No, my brother, I'm just kidding. You did the right thing. To be honest, I found a nice lady here in L.A., and as soon as I can, I'm going to make her my wife. Things are still kind of tough, so I can't do it just yet. But soon, I might be doing a little private thing myself."

"Great! I now believe that when you find the right woman in your life, you should give her the honor and respect that is due to her."

"When did you find that out? Yesterday?"

"You got me there. But it's never too late to do the right thing, as Gena would say."

"True. Congratulations. I wish you lots of luck and prosperity. I only wished that I could attend, but this job is a new job, and I'm not taking any chances with it."

"That was what I wanted to find out. I'm calling everyone early so they can request time off from their jobs. I know that it will be kind of difficult to make it happen."

"No, man. I have to be honest with you. I'm very happy for you, but I won't be able to make it. I'm so sorry, my brother."

"No problem, Junior. As I said, I understand. I have to run. I'm still making calls to everyone to let them know. So, bye for now. Love you, my brother."

"One love, my brother. Jah bless. Seen? You done know. Ya, man." Junior spoke like a Rastafarian, but he had never been a dreadlocks. He always said he was a true Rasta man in his heart, but he didn't have to wear natty hair or long dreadlocks to prove it. Only Jah knew his heart.

After they had hung up, Bunny proceeded to call Karl in Florida. "Hello, Karl, this is Bunny. How're you and the family?"

"Hello, young man. How're you? Thank you for asking. My family was doing good the last time I spoke to them. Remember, they're still right there in Jamaica. I'm the only one here. I see them every six months or so. And you, young man? How're you doing?"

"I'm fine, my brother. I just called to see if you would be able to attend my wedding on May twenty-first of this year."

"Let's see, today is January twelfth. That means you gave everyone less than five months to hurry and get themselves rearranged so they can drop everything to attend your wedding? Who came up with that date? I'm sure it wasn't you, because I know that you know better than that."

"Maybe I got you at a bad time, my brother, but I just wanted to know if you would be able to come to the wedding."

"I'm sorry, nothing personal, but I'm stuck here in Florida. It has nothing to do with work or the short time that you gave. I have some things I have to take care of before I do anything else. It's just one of those things. However, I wish you lots of luck with your wedding celebration. Have a good time, okay, brother? Sorry I can't make it."

"Okay, brother, I understand—more or less. Life throws us these curveballs every now and then. Say hello to the wife and kids for me. Bye." Bunny hung up.

Bunny started realizing that this calling thing wasn't easy. He thought of calling Lela in Washington, but the last call with Karl had drained him of all his energy. He would have to call Lela another time. Besides, Lela—like Karl—was most likely tied up and wouldn't be able to attend. She hadn't returned to Jamaica since she left ten years earlier. What made him think that a poor man's wedding was going to make her revisit Jamaica at this time?

***

The story was once told of a groom who took his wedding vows very seriously, so to speak. At a wedding rehearsal, he approached the clergyman with an unusual offer. "Look, I'll give you one hundred US dollars to change the wedding vows. When you get to me and the part where I am to promise to 'love, honor and obey' and 'forsaking all others, be faithful to her forever,' I'd appreciate it if you'd just leave that part out." He passed the clergyman the cash and walked away very satisfied.

It was the day of the wedding, and the bride and groom had reached the part of the ceremony where the vows were exchanged. When it came time for the groom's vows, the clergyman looked the young man in the eyes and said, "Will you promise to prostrate yourself before her, obey her every command and wish, serve her breakfast in bed every morning of your life, and swear eternally before God and your lovely, beautiful wife that you will not ever even so much as look at another woman, as long as you both shall live?"

The groom gulped, looked around, and said in a tiny voice, "Yes." The groom then leaned toward the clergyman and hissed, "I thought we had a deal."

The clergyman put the hundred dollars into the groom's hand and whispered, "She made me a much better offer."

***

The big day that Bunny and Joyce had been preparing for had come. It was May 21 at 4:00 p.m., and the Montego Bay Seventh-day Adventist Church, one of the largest SDA churches in the area, was packed with wedding guests and regular church members. As many of Bunny's family members as could make it were there, including Essie, Gena and her children, Myrtle, Dr. Leonard and his wife, a coworker of Dr. Leonard, and his female friend from Florida.

Everything was going in order as scheduled. Dr. Leonard stood in the back or vestry of the church, trying to keep Bunny calm. He seemed to be overcompensating for his years of not seeing or spending time with his younger brother. Every time Leonard spied a little bead of sweat on Bunny's face, he pulled out a white handkerchief and nobly wiped it away. He overplayed his role on purpose in order to properly measure up to the honored role of best man. He wanted to be the *best* best man that his little brother could have ever asked or wished for.

When he and Bunny stepped out into the front of the church from the vestry, they could see the cheerful faces of Essie's family, but more than anything else, they could see the tears flowing down Mrs. Essie Brown's face. She was crying tears of joy to see her last little wash belly giving his vows to his own family.

Mrs. Essie Brown always cried at weddings. Most mothers cry occasionally at weddings, but Mrs. Essie Brown was unique in that once she started crying, she never really stopped until the wedding ceremony was over. Sometimes even during the happy reception party, she still had tracks of tears running down her face. Anyone who didn't know her would think that she was sad and was not enjoying the occasion.

When the piano began to play the "Wedding March," she started sobbing openly. As the bride began walking down the aisle in her beautiful, flowing white wedding dress, one like Gena had dreamed about, Mrs. Essie Brown stood up to admire the bride even with her obvious tracks of tears. Gena tugged on her dress and told her that it was best if she took a seat because her teary eyes were not appropriate at this time, along with the fact that she was the only one standing.

After a brief marriage ceremony, the minister said, "By the power vested in me, I now pronounce you man and wife. You may kiss your bride."

Mrs. Essie Brown, still in tears, stood up and began clapping her hands enthusiastically. Half the congregation followed her lead, and they, too, stood up and started clapping their hands in celebration of the newly married couple. Mrs. Essie Brown was very emotional at her kids' weddings, and she was not afraid to show it. She couldn't control the heavy tears that displayed her high level of joy.

***

Essie had displayed the same manner of affection and emotion at Leonard and Dolcina's wedding, which was held two years after Leonard and Dolcina graduated from St. John's University. They were still living in New York at the time, so they elected to conduct their wedding at St. Luke's Episcopal Church of God in the White Plains area of the Bronx. The church was fairly full with guests of the bride and groom.

Most of the guests who had traveled a long distance to get to the wedding were members of the bride's family. They came from London, England, as well as Kingston, Jamaica. Dolcina's mother, Mrs. Garwood, had lived in Battersea, London, for most of her life. Comfortably retired, she lived in a nice flat in one of the newer developments in that area. The oldest of her two daughters, nicknamed Tat, but whose true name was Claudine Garwood, also lived in Battersea with her husband, Grant. Tat's daughter, Paulette, and grandson, Jonathan, also lived with Tat in Battersea. They all traveled to the United States for the first time to attend Leonard and Dolcina's wedding.

Dolcina's cousin, Novia McDonald-White, nicknamed Dawn, also attended the wedding. She lived in Jamaica and was an Air Jamaica air hostess. She traveled from Jamaica to New York for the wedding with her husband, Gerald, and daughter, Grace.

Leonard's family in attendance consisted of all those who were already living in New York at the time: Gena, Lela, Myrtle, Mrs. Essie Brown, and most of Essie's grandchildren. Both the bride's and the groom's families were sitting all together on the right side of the church in the front row.

Leonard and his best man, Andre White, were in a private room of the vestry of the church. Upon hearing their cue, they both entered the front of the church to stand beside the pulpit, where they were expected to wait patiently for the bride to walk up to the front through the main central aisle.

As soon as they reached the center of the podium, where they stopped and faced the audience, Mrs. Essie Brown stood up and started sobbing. "Oh, my son is getting married. May God bless and keep them . . ." But Myrtle, soon thereafter, grabbed onto Mrs. Essie Brown's dress and gave it a gentle tug, indicating that her mother should sit down and not draw so much attention to herself.

She sat down at the gentle urging of her daughter, but she continued crying softly while whispering to herself. "May God bless him and his soon-to-be wife so they may have many, many children and grandchildren. Lord, you know that they can afford it. Lord, bless her womb, so they may give me many, many grandchildren, I pray, Lord."

Then the bridal song started to play, and Dolcina entered the church and began walking down the aisle. Mrs. Essie Brown sprang to her feet again, this time to admire the bride in her lovely, flowing white gown. Myrtle tugged on her mother's dress once again, and Mrs. Essie Brown complied and sat back down in her seat. After a somewhat long ceremony, the minister said, "With the power vested in me, I now pronounce you man and wife. You may kiss the bride."

As if on cue, Mrs. Essie Brown sprang to her feet and started clapping her hands vigorously. Almost the entire church stood up and followed her lead, clapping and cheering. Myrtle tugged on her dress once again, indicating to her that maybe it was time for her to take her seat, but this time Mrs. Essie Brown was in no mood to comply with Myrtle's or anybody's wishes. She wasn't willing to entertain any restrictions at all at this point. She was happy, although still in tears, and she wasn't going to contain herself any longer. With a joy like this, the world should know how she really felt. She was ready to let it all out, like a BP offshore oil well that will not stop pouring it out—at least, not by any simple means. It would stop flowing when it was good and ready. Mrs. Essie Brown was letting all her emotions out that day right there in the church, and no one was going to stop her—at least, not by any simple means.

She was letting the world know how she felt about her son, who had grown up to be a pharmacist and was now about to start his own family. She was crying tears of joy, and she would only sit down when she was ready. Long after everyone else had sat down, Mrs. Essie Brown was still standing, clapping, cheering, and praising God for her son and new daughter-in-law.

***

Mrs. Essie Brown had a soft spot in her heart for weddings. When Karl elected to have a small private ceremony after Gena insisted that he should get married, Mrs. Essie Brown cried heavily at his wedding also. There was only a handful of guests at the small church in Rose Hall. It was mostly family members and a few close friends present—just the way Karl wanted it.

However, when the minister said, "You may kiss the bride," Mrs. Essie Brown burst into tears of joy. Mrs. Essie Brown loved to see her children take that matrimonial vow. It meant that there would be more grandchildren on the way, and it pleased her heart to have lots of grandchildren. It was either that, or there was something much deeper that had to be explained psychologically from other elements in her past.

Chapter 27

The day before Mrs. Essie Brown emigrated to the United States, she called all of her children and grandchildren and set up a clan meeting. She was like an ordained African tribal chief holding a mysterious ancestral clan meeting about the passing of the torch and telling secret, cryptic traditional narratives of their forefathers and predecessors.

They all met together at her home in Glenworth to discuss some issues that were important to her. Among other directives, she wanted everyone to be aware of the fact that, although Myrtle was already away in the United States, the house in Glenworth was hers.

Essie made it clear that she didn't have a will yet, but if she should die on that same day, the house and everything within it would automatically be owned by Myrtle. She also made it clear that if she should die and leave a will behind, she would like for it to be read in the open over her dead body. She wanted to make sure there would be no confusion over her dying wishes.

Mrs. Essie Brown also pledged to everyone that

she would be enlarging the house in Glenworth. She would construct a second level on the top, and it would look beautiful. She promised in her family briefing to do this the first chance she got while living in the United States. This meant that fixing up the house and taking it to another level, literally, was at the top of her agenda as she left for the US the following day.

Living in the United States was more exciting than she had ever dreamed. Mrs. Essie Brown gave thanks for her life in the concrete jungle, New York City, where the coldest day of the year—in January—averaged 32.1 degrees Fahrenheit, and the hottest day—any given summer day—was greater than 90 degrees Fahrenheit.

Mrs. Essie Brown was very happy with her life. She felt that living in the United States justified her uphill, hard-knock life and the tiresome work she had done. She also reflected on the fact that her daughter Gena was truly a miracle baby.

She was very happy that she had heeded Reverend Paul Murray that day when she was sitting on the wall in downtown Montego Bay. Many decades later, Mrs. Essie Brown believed Reverend Paul Murray was truly sent by God to solve her sterility, and ultimately all of her other problems. Mrs. Essie Brown thought that God sure had a funny sense of humor. She believed God's ways were not always typical, but God was always right.

***

Just like Karl, who inarguably got the anti-country gene from his mother, so too, Gena categorically got her gift for cooking from her mother. The only problem was that she only cooked once a year, and that was on Thanksgiving Day. Ever since Gena had made it to the United States, she never took the Thanksgiving holiday tradition for granted.

Thanksgiving Day made her reflect on her past and remember with gratitude how far she had come. She thought about the uncanny story that Essie had told her about her father, the Reverend Paul Murray. She thought about how her mother had struggled with her to survive.

She thought about the time when a vicious tyrant of a girl who lived in her apartment complex used to terrorize Myrtle, Betty, and her every day when they had to pass through the gate to go to school. She thought about the endless mishaps in her life that had made her believe that she would not live to see a brighter day.

She also thought about the different homes the family had lived in and how many times they had to move. They were often forced out because some disgruntled, selfish man didn't need her mother's love or relationship anymore. She thought about the time when someone rudely threw a container of urine in her mother's face because he wanted her to leave the home where they had been staying.

It happened when Gena was sixteen years old. Because of financial hardship, her mother was considering giving up her apartment and moving in with Mr. Livingston. She had given her landlord notice, indicating that she would be moving out within three months.

Essie later shared some of the details of the relationship with Gena, although she didn't know all of them at the time. While Essie and Mr. Livingston were dating, Essie used to visit his home quite often. They had a good relationship, but it was a relatively new relationship, so they spent most of their time getting to know each other. He knew that Essie had eight children, but he never really paid any attention to that part of her life. He had never visited her apartment, but he had met a few of her kids at different times and different places.

Since Essie was living on a very small salary and an even smaller savings account, which was rapidly dwindling, she started getting worried that eventually, she might not be able to pay her rent and take care of the kids' basic daily needs. Therefore, she went to Mr. Livingston to ask him a bold question. But before she did so, Essie made sure that she satisfied his sexual appetite.

She dressed up in sexy white short pants, which just barely covered her feminine assets. She also wore a matching white spaghetti-strap blouse that was so thin, her breasts stuck out prominently. She took Mr. Livingston by his hand, led him into his bedroom, and securely locked the door behind them. She slowly undressed him item by item until he was totally nude. She then instructed him to lie on the bed while she paraded around the room like a Victoria's Secret model.

She took off her blouse and continued to strut around the room while he watched her with lustful eyes. The sight of Essie's big, sexy breasts and sexy body was more than Mr. Livingston could bear. His body was pulsating to the beat of his heart. He beckoned to Essie to come and join him in bed, but she didn't.

Instead, she continued to parade around the room. Then she walked up to him and kissed him lightly on the top of his head. When he moaned for more, she sat beside him. "My dear love, life is getting so hard on me. I was wondering if I could stay here a while until I can get myself together."

"This is a big, three-bedroom house. I don't see why not, my love."

"I'll give up my apartment, because I can't afford to pay the rent any longer. You won't have to give us anything other than shelter. I'll be able to provide everything else that my family needs. Moreover, I'll be able to cook for you and the kids every day, so in a sense, it should save you time and money."

"I'm divorced and have no kids. This is a large house for just one person. I said it was fine as long as you keep the house clean, and your kids don't tear my place apart."

"Are you sure, my dear?" She wanted there to be no misunderstanding between them before she went ahead and gave up her apartment. "I'll have to give up my apartment, so I have to be sure that you don't mind sharing your home with me and my kids."

"It will be fine."

"I never thought that I would have to do this, but sometimes life forces you to do what you have to do. I know that it will be a little inconvenient for you, but I'll make it up to you." Essie said this with a big wink-wink smile on her face.

"Now we're talking. I like the sound of that." He was not a man of many words. He was tall and handsome, with a light complexion and curly black hair. His humble personality and his good looks were what had attracted Essie to him in the first place. She had liked him a lot and was very happy to know that she had found someone with a relatively large house who was willing to take in both her and her large family.

"Thank you, Mr. Livingston," Essie said as she kissed him softly on his lips. "You won't regret it." It goes without saying that they made mad, passionate love that day, and they were both satisfied with the deal.

She started making plans right away to leave her apartment. She packed all of her clothes, as well as the kids' belongings, and started moving her furniture and miscellaneous items over to Mr. Livingston's home. Since she still had three months left on her apartment contract, she was able to move her things slowly, a little at a time. Within a month, she had moved everything.

However, the first time the family spent the night there, Mr. Livingston woke up the next morning like a man possessed with demons. To say he was in a bad mood would be a big understatement. It dawned on him overnight that a large family like this was too much for him to handle. He cared for Essie, but not enough to give up his tranquil lifestyle.

"What is the problem, Mr. Livingston?" Essie asked. "You don't seem too pleased this morning."

"Yes, you're right," he said in a sudden rage. "I want my privacy back. This whole thing is too much for me. I want you all to get out of my house."

"Oh, Mr. Livingston, you don't mean that, do you?" Essie asked in utter surprise. She had hoped that he was not another smooth-talking man who comforted her with empty, futile words. When these men were hit with the reality of the first storm, they dropped her like a plate of hot potatoes coming from an overheated microwave oven and ran away like cowards, leaving her terrified and standing all alone holding the bag of useless promises.

"I don't mean that? Really? See if I'm not dead serious." He ran for a container that was usually stored by the bedside or under the bed. The large basin looked like an oversized cup with a handle and was used for urination during the night because the bathroom was on the outside of the house.

Mr. Livingston daringly reached with one hand under his bed, grabbed the container by the handle, and threw the repugnant, stinking contents into Essie's face. As if that weren't bad enough, he went to the kids' room and tossed the rest of the stale, rancid-smelling urine at them. Most of it got on Gena's clothes, and they were all frantically crying as he began yelling, "Get out of my house now, I say. I want you all out now." Mr. Livingston was raging mad and wanted everyone to know that he was as serious as an ischemic heart attack. He wanted them out of his house immediately.

They all ran outside, hysterical, and watched as he angrily tossed their clothes and furniture out the door. Essie was humiliated in front of her kids. They were all sad and disappointed to see that a man who had gone to bed calm and collected woke up like a raging maniac the next morning. It was as if he had mysteriously turned into a werewolf overnight, and there wasn't even a full moon.

That was by far one of the worst days of Essie's life, but luckily for her, she hadn't totally lost her previous apartment. She still had two months' time remaining on the lease, so she slowly moved all of her belongings back that day.

The experience shattered Essie's family, but it also made them stronger and produced a bond of solidarity. They all became determined that they would make it in life and change things drastically for their mother. No one spoke about that incident ever again, but it haunted Gena all her life.

When she celebrated Thanksgiving, these were some of the things she gave thanks for overcoming. The list was endless. That was one of the reasons why she was so passionate about Thanksgiving. That was why—though she seldom cooked during the year—on Thanksgiving, she went all out. She never dared take that holiday for granted.

Gena, anxious but exhilarated, started getting ready for Thanksgiving about a week before. She was as anxious about Thanksgiving as a little kid was about Christmas morning and what Santa had in store for him. The only difference was that Gena was the Santa Claus of Thanksgiving.

She started by buying the nonperishable items such as seasonings. She also started counting the number of people that she would be providing dinner for. To do this, she would call around to see who in her immediate family had other plans and who was planning on sharing Thanksgiving with her.

After that, she would call her friends and distant relatives and invite them to dinner. No one ever turned down an offer for Thanksgiving dinner by Gena, because they knew that she went all out when she put on a Thanksgiving celebration.

"Hello, Jenifer, what plans do you have for TG this year?" Gena asked her cousin and good friend in New Jersey.

"No plans," Jenifer said. "I've no plans at all for Thanksgiving. My kids will have to pretend that they're eating turkey this year, because I have no money and I have no time to do any big cooking." She giggled a bit. "But I know that you're going to be doing your thing, and I accept. You don't even need to ask. I have already invited myself."

"That's true, Jenifer. You're right. I am doing Thanksgiving this year, and I want you to bring the whole family."

"Thank you, Gena, but did you know that my mother is here with me, too?"

"Shame on you. You have to bring your mother and, as I said, your whole family. I'm just getting ready to do my Thanksgiving grocery shopping, and that's why I'm calling you now. I just wanted to make sure that I know who is coming and who is not."

"Count me in—no, count us in. We'll be there bright and early, or on time."

"Great! I'm happy to hear that."

"What should I bring?"

"Your appetite. Bring a big appetite, because you know me. I make a big dinner when I'm doing this thing."

"I know. Lord, I can't wait, Gena. I'll see you at your big TG."

"Please make sure that you do come, because I'm looking forward to having you in New York. It will be a lovely holiday get-together, because I haven't seen you in a while."

"Yes, mon, no doubt, we'll be there."

"Okay, thank you. Bye for now." Gena hung up.

Jenifer's family almost always joined Gena for Thanksgiving. Jenifer was related to Miriam in Mount Salem. She was close in age to Gena, and they had kept up with each other over the years since they were little girls.

Gena knew that she was a great cook, just like her mother, so she was confident about the quality of the food she prepared. She also loved to impress her friends and family with her presentation. She would reach for the most expensive plates and glasses that she had stored away all year. Thanksgiving Day was when she pulled out all of her best stuff—from dinnerware to clothes.

Gena's style of dress was as fascinatingly bold and flamboyant as a banner with a vivid message that said a lot about nothing in particular—as bold as a banner waving high in the skies, saying, *Let me be myself, and you be yourself.* The bottom line was that she was not afraid to wear bright colors and over-the-top hairstyles.

One special thing that Gena always did on Thanksgiving was to make sure that she invited some poor or needy person from the neighborhood to join the family for dinner. Sometimes she would see someone standing on the street corner on or around the week of Thanksgiving and approach that person to ask if he or she had plans for Thanksgiving.

This year Gena noticed one young black girl who lived in the same building. She had a somewhat dirty, ragged look, like a person in need of some attention. Gena saw her sitting on the front steps of her building and approached her. "Hello, young lady. I'm Gena. We live in the same building. Did you know that?"

"Yes, I see you all the time."

"I see you, too, and I noticed that you're not working, it seems. What plans do you have for Thanksgiving?"

"None."

"Oh, well, that's okay, because I'll be having a large dinner on Thanksgiving Day, and I would love for you to join us."

"Where is your apartment? On the second floor, right?"

"Yes, I live on the second floor in apartment 2G."

"Okay, okay." She slowly nodded her head as she acknowledged the information.

"My name is Gena, as I said earlier. What is your name?"

"My name is Teshana."

"So, Teshana, can I expect you to join us on Thanksgiving?"

"Maybe. I'm a little afraid."

"There's nothing to be afraid of, because my family would love to have you join us for Thanksgiving. So please come by. I'm expecting you, okay?"

"Okay, I'll stop by," Teshana promised.

Gena, just like her mother, could spot a person who was truly in need, and when she did, she was not afraid to approach that person. Also like Mrs. Essie Brown, Gena would run her errands and often bring some stranger home to rescue her from trouble.

One time she brought home a young lady with a two-year-old baby. The lady's name was Ann Marie, and her baby was Sade. Gena saw Ann Marie walking downtown with tears in her eyes, so she stopped to find out what the problem was. Ann Marie told Gena that her mother had been taken to a mental institution. As a result, Ann Marie had been abruptly kicked out of their apartment by the landlord. She sobbed as she explained that she had no other family in New York and didn't know where the baby's father was.

"Where are your clothes and stuff?" Gena asked.

"They're at the apartment. The landlord changed the lock on the door, and I'm not able to retrieve them." She explained that she didn't have so much as a diaper for the child, much less clothes for herself. Gena believed her story. Moreover, it was easy to smell the strong odor that was coming from the baby, as if the child hadn't been changed for days.

"Okay, come with me to Conway. I can get you some basic stuff until you get your things from the apartment."

"Thank you. I've been trying to get in touch with that guy, but he won't answer his phone."

Gena took the young mother and child to the Conway department store, located in downtown Manhattan, and bought them some clothes and other basic necessities. She then took them home to stay in her apartment and to sleep on the couch until they could rectify the landlord issue and eventually find the baby's father so he could aid in the support of his child.

It turned out that such a matter was not that easy to resolve, and therefore, Ann Marie and her baby, Sade, spent a longer time living with Gena than expected. As a matter of fact, even Ann Marie's mother was released from the hospital into Gena's care, and they all lived in Gena's apartment for a considerable time.

Gena never minded helping whenever she could. She was a special, concerned citizen of the human society like her mother. There were very few people like Gena and her mother, who really and truly cared about other people in need. Gena lived a fairly simple life, so she could use the excess to help someone else who was worse off than she was. She had a unique way of caring for other people's problems, like no other could. Gena was the Mother Teresa of her own little world.

On the night before Thanksgiving, Gena was all fired up. She went through her checklist to make sure she had enough of whatever she needed for the big day. If she didn't have enough of something, she would run and get it from the supermarket herself. It was like the one-woman machine had been turned on, and she was about to put it into gear. When she had everything together, she started cooking. She seasoned the meats and made all of the cold side items, such as the potato salads and fruit salad, and whatever little things could be made ahead of time.

The one-woman machine never needed help, not even from her mother. Gena believed that, in order for the dinner to have her special stamp on it, everything had to be made completely by her. Moreover, she enjoyed knowing that she could do all the kitchen work while her mother sat down and was waited on for a change. She never allowed her mother to lift as much as a finger.

Mrs. Essie Brown never complained, because she was now getting tired of kitchen work, since she had done nothing but that all her life.

Gena made sure that all of the pre-Thanksgiving preparations were completed and everything was in place for the next day. Then she turned in early to bed, because she knew that she had to get an early start in the morning.

While everyone else was asleep at 3:00 a.m. on Thanksgiving, Gena was up bright, alert, and ready with excitement in her eyes. It was Thanksgiving Day, and she was about to work her magic. She fired up all of the kitchen aids and appliances: the burners on top of the stove, the oven, the microwave, and the pressure cooker.

She enjoyed being the fairy godmother of early Thanksgiving morning, and she started working like crazy on her tiptoes, making sure not to wake anyone before the right time.

By the time everyone was up, Gena was well on her way to completing the Thanksgiving dinner. Most of the items were already cooked, and what was not cooked was very much on schedule. Gena had everything on timers. That day, she was fully dedicated to the kitchen, moving from one thing to the other. She was like an orchestra conductor directing the pots and appliances to produce great musical flavors. She moved flawlessly as she conducted the Thanksgiving meal all day in the small, semimodern, four-by-four-foot kitchen.

By evening, all of the dishes were done and were being kept warm for the big dinner presentation. As the friends and family and other guests slowly began to arrive, they were greeted with the wonderful, tantalizing aromas of various delightful foods waiting to be appreciatively consumed. Everyone made their way to the living room to socialize and catch up on the holiday happenings, but with a hungry, watchful eye on the kitchen activity.

By 5:00 p.m., the house was full of people, and Gena rolled out her Thanksgiving presentation kit. Using all of her best dinnerware to serve her guests, she explained where each piece had been obtained, and the cost and story behind it. The guests had most likely heard the explanation a thousand times before, but they lent a listening ear anyway. They knew it went with the fine, exquisite meal at hand. Gena went all out to impress everyone with her personalized service.

213

They all loved her delectable, delightful Thanksgiving dinner and chatted up a storm as they ate. Everyone—men, women, and children—was having fun. This was what a good Thanksgiving was made of: friends and family all enjoying themselves, appreciating a good meal, and giving thanks for a good year of health and wealth. It pleased Gena to see everyone taking pleasure in her handiwork.

Moreover, she particularly enjoyed the sight of her family, who had struggled over the years in Jamaica, now getting the opportunity to indulge in one of America's finest holiday celebrations and to enjoy a worry-free good time and good food—all made possible, in more ways than one, by Gena herself.

This was what she had dreamed of as a child when she fantasized about a better place and a better way of life for her and her family. She didn't notice that it was a lot of work. It was more fun than it was work. She didn't mind it anyway, because she only did it once a year.

Mrs. Essie Brown also enjoyed her daughter's handiwork. She knew how cooking a good meal made one feel inside. She had been there and had done that over and over again many times in her life. After all, Gena had gotten her natural cooking skills from her, and she knew that it was a great feeling to see how much others appreciated your cooking.

"My daughter, the dinner was great," Essie told Gena after her first Thanksgiving dinner in the United States of America. "I especially enjoyed the turkey. You are a wonderful chef, just like your mother. I'm proud of you—proud of you in every way."

"Thank you, Mom. I'm glad you enjoyed it."

"Can I help with the cleaning up? There are lots of dishes and things to take care of. I would like to help you now, if you don't mind."

"Yes, I do mind. I don't want you or anyone in the kitchen. I'll take care of all this myself. I've been cleaning as I go along. I have my own system of doing things. Thanks for the offer, Mom, but I'll do it myself."

Gena would clean up the kitchen after she bade everyone good night one by one.

"Thank you, Gena," Jenifer said. "The food was excellent. I enjoyed everything, especially the tasty, uniquely cooked collard greens and stuffing. I must let you show me one day how your stuffing is done. Thanks again, but we have to go."

"You're welcome, my cousin. It was fun having you and your family for Thanksgiving. Thank you for coming. We'll talk on the phone. Drive carefully and be good." Gena bade Jenifer and her family good-bye and good night.

"Bye, Gena," Teshana said. "Thanks for having me."

"My pleasure. Did you enjoy the dinner?"

"Yes, I enjoyed everything. I especially loved your sweet-tasting pumpkin pie and your to-die-for baked macaroni and cheese. I also loved your soft, succulent oxtail. I loved everything. Now I'm as stuffed as a turkey. Thank you for inviting me."

"You're welcome."

Mrs. Essie Brown had a lot to be thankful for. She was thankful to be alive and to experience her first Thanksgiving Day in the United States, and especially thankful to be able to share the holiday with her daughter and the rest of the family in New York City. She was also thankful to have previously experienced her first Independence Day on July 4 in the pleasantly hot and humid Big Apple.

Chapter 28

Mrs. Essie Brown thoroughly enjoyed her first Independence Day holiday in New York City, finding it a sight to behold. She couldn't believe what was happening in front of her eyes and was truly awestruck by the miraculous, starlike formations of the fireworks and the vibrations from the powerful blasting of the hidden cannons. She gazed in awe at the blossoming of the flaming rosebuds. She gasped at the rainbow-colored rays of light spitting fire and creating patterns of all shapes and sizes in the sky. She was amazed at the geniuses at work and the inventiveness of mankind.

Essie was in the middle of hot, muggy, humid Central Park, with her Bible in hand. She was astonished by the breathtaking fireworks display, but even more astonished by the hundreds and hundreds of people who were gathered together in one common location. Mrs. Essie Brown had never been in any one place that had so many people all together, and she had a serious case of culture shock. She was overwhelmed, but very happy to be a part of this huge, worthy Independence Day celebration.

It dawned on her that she now shared the same goals and aspirations as every one of those sightseers. She shared the same appreciation of American history. She was, after all, an American now at heart, and in just a few years, she would be a true American by naturalization. The thought brought tears of joy to her eyes.

Although there were thousands of people in Central Park, Essie felt as if the fireworks display was being performed just for her. It was as if it was her first birthday, and she was being reborn in the United States. This was both her birthday party and her welcome party, and all the other people were just there to share in her celebration.

The fireworks represented everything that Mrs. Essie Brown believed in, including the right to freedom and the right to a better life. She now had a brand new life and a clean slate in the United States. The sky was the limit, as far as she was concerned.

That night, Mrs. Essie Brown saw more than fancy high-tech lights and fireworks. She saw what it meant to be an American. It meant the God-given right to be—to be left alone, to be loved, to be one's true self, to be free, to be treated fairly, to be respected, to be strong, to be proud, and most of all, to be all that one could be.

When Mrs. Essie Brown looked around her and saw how the kids were having fun and how the grown-ups were gracefully celebrating a great country that stood up and fought for what it believed in, it brought tears to her eyes. Whenever Mrs. Essie Brown got very happy, she cried tears of joy.

Mrs. Essie Brown celebrated her first Christmas in the United States by attending the tree-lighting ceremony—a tradition that started back in 1933—at

Rockefeller Center a few weeks before the holiday. Impressed by the large crowd that had turned out, she stood in the midst of downtown Manhattan with her Bible in her hand to witness the spectacular event.

Christmas had always been special for Mrs. Essie Brown, but now it meant even more. They say that when you're in love, everything looks brighter and better. Mrs. Essie Brown was in love with life in New York City, and Christmas seemed better than it had ever been. As the tree was lit and the various groups sang touching Christmas carols, tears of joy again came to Mrs. Essie Brown's eyes.

On December 31, Mrs. Essie Brown attended Dick Clark's New Year's Rockin' Eve and enjoyed it tremendously, although it was very cold. She didn't stay long, but it was important to her to experience this great Big Apple tradition. Again, she was amazed by the turnout of the large crowd.

Mrs. Essie Brown was truly happy and proud to be living in New York City. After all, she was now in the city that boasted the distinctive landmark that greeted millions of immigrants from the late nineteenth century to today. The Statue of Liberty was every woman, like Mrs. Essie Brown.

Mrs. Essie Brown took the time to admire her new homeland. One day she went for a walk with Myrtle in downtown Manhattan. They strolled through the brightly illuminated hub of the Broadway Theater District, the major center of the world's entertainment industry.

They stood at one of the world's busiest pedestrian intersections and admired the famous Times Square that had been referred to as the mother of all crossroads and the ultimate crossroad of the world. Mrs. Essie Brown smiled as she thought about the time when she stood at the T-shaped crossroad in her tiny village of

Cascade and wished to fly away to a larger and better place. She was thinking then of a big city, but never in a million years would she have thought that she would be here standing in the midst of Times Square.

Mrs. Essie Brown observed the Manhattan skyline with its many universally recognized skyscrapers and nodded her head. *It's true,* she said to herself as her eyes caught the Empire State Building. *New York City is truly home to some of the tallest buildings in the world.*

She saw a large, colorful sign on the side of a building that read, *Be bullish when you're on Wall Street.* Her mind drifted to a piece in the newspaper she had seen earlier that day about the New York Stock Exchange. She thought about the fact that God had spared her life and had given her the wonderful opportunity to roam the busy streets of Manhattan, the financial capital of the world and the home of the New York Stock Exchange. She wasn't sure what that all meant, but she was sure that it had something to do with lots of money flowing in and out of the Big Apple.

Mrs. Essie Brown had no regrets. She had seen it all, and it was all worth it.

***

At first, Mrs. Essie Brown lived with Gena in Gena's apartment in New York City. She enjoyed it, but even better, she eventually got her own apartment next door. When Gena did her regular supermarket shopping, just before she headed into her own apartment, she would often knock on her mother's door first to drop off some groceries or just to stop in to make sure that she was doing well. For Mrs. Essie Brown, having an apartment next door to her daughter on the same floor in the same building was the most convenient situation a mother and daughter could've had.

This was all made possible by Gena, who was able to apply for an apartment for her mother because Mrs. Essie Brown was now a US citizen. Mrs. Essie Brown was doing so well that she was able to start helping all of her kids and grandkids who needed her help financially.

Mrs. Essie Brown still could be called a Christian fanatic. She attended the Ephesus Seventh-day Adventist Church, which was located relatively close to her. She learned the route to her church well. She knew which bus or train to take to get her there, and she attended every church service, both the weekend Sabbath service and the midweek Bible study. In addition to that, she still conducted her regular one-hour early morning devotions and regular one-hour evening devotions at home, with or without company.

One difference between her Jamaican and her American devotions was that she sang her hymns louder and with more confidence, although she was now more painfully off-key than ever. Just like a self-ordained minister, she also read more verses from her Bible. Her prayers were significantly longer as she prayed for all of her kids and grandkids. She deliberately prayed for each person individually, and sometimes she even included the president of the United States and people involved in the latest current event of the day.

Anyone who thought that Mrs. Essie Brown used to praise the Lord a little too much while living in Jamaica would have been shocked to know that she joyously and unapologetically praised God even more while living in the United States. Before, she praised God because she thanked Him for forgiving her for all her sins. Now, Mrs. Essie Brown praised God for blessing her so abundantly.

Mrs. Essie Brown felt that she had been blessed abundantly because she was living so comfortably.

Along with getting the opportunity to praise God and go to church regularly, she was able to take better care of her health, since she now went to the medical clinic monthly and more often, if necessary.

Before this time, she had been too busy working and worrying about other people's problems and concerns to take proper care of herself. Her philosophy used to be that she was old and could die at any time, so her kids' and grandkids' concerns took precedence.

Now, she still thought that her family's concerns were primary, but she believed that she was really not that old, and she wanted to live a long and healthy life. In other words, Mrs. Essie Brown now realized that life was worth living and that she had a lot to live for in her remaining years.

Her health care became a serious part of her daily concerns. She never missed a doctor's appointment and would be at least one or two hours early. She was aggressive and persistent when it came to anything that had to do with her health.

When she first arrived in New York, although only in her late fifties, she looked like an old woman who was frail and sickly and on her way to her grave. She was bent over and walked very slowly, using a walking cane.

Now, in her sixties, she looked twenty years younger. She walked briskly and exuded spunk and energy. Mrs. Essie Brown made it clear that she had a lot of reasons to live, and she felt for the first time in her life that she was really living. At age sixty-five, she even considered getting her driver's license so she could purchase a car and drive herself to church. It was like Mrs. Essie Brown had come alive in New York City.

***

At Mrs. Essie Brown's Ephesus SDA Church in Manhattan, she found a church buddy named Ms. Julia Gomez, who had been born in Honduras but grew up in Puerto Rico. She moved to the United States when she was in her early twenties. She had been a member of the church for more than thirty years. The two met one Sabbath after church services and introduced themselves.

"I'm Julia Gomez, but everyone calls me Tia."

"I'm Mrs. Essie Brown. You can call me Sister Brown."

"I noticed that we always walk to the train station together after church, but I jewsally take the number two to downtown, and I think that jer route is somewhere uptown because jew jewsally go to the uptown side."

"I do live in the uptown direction, but only one stop on the train from here," Mrs. Essie Brown replied with a smile.

"I see jew every Sabbath walking to the train. Haf jew ever noticed that we always go that way after church?"

"No."

"Really?"

"I usually don't pay any attention to the people around me when I'm walking. There're just too many people on the streets of New York. If I paid attention to them, I'd trip and fall, and I don't want that to happen to me again. It happened once before when I was crossing the driveway of a Catholic church uptown."

"I wouldn't like that to happen to jew either, Sister," Tia said with genuine concern for Mrs. Essie Brown. "Anyway, let's wolk and tolk as we head to the train station, jes?" Tia's Latin accent became stronger as she got more comfortable with Mrs. Essie Brown.

"Yes, okay. Let's walk," Mrs. Essie Brown said, and the two elderly Christian ladies started toward the

222

subway. Tia was short with a medium frame. She was not too fat, but she was definitely not skinny. She had a typically pretty Puerto Rican look, with a light complexion and long black hair. She had a Spanish accent, but she spoke very clearly.

As they walked together, Mrs. Essie Brown seemed almost twice as tall as Tia because she loved to wear her high-heeled shoes when she went to church. Today, she was dressed very nicely in an off-white two-piece suit, with a jacket and skirt, and white high-heeled, closed-toe shoes. She carried a small black purse in her hand. Mrs. Essie Brown also wore a simple but sophisticated white hat, with her hair tucked neatly inside it. She and Tia walked slowly as they got to know each other.

"Sister Brown, how long haf jew been in New Jork City?" Tia asked as they walked along the busy sidewalk toward the 125th Street train station.

"I've been here for more than five or six years now. I don't know exactly how long. My sister, this head of mine isn't the same as it used to be. I can't remember anything."

"That's all right, Sister Brown. We're at that age where nothing is the same anymore. Sometimes I don't even remember my address and phone number. It takes me a while to collect myself and think real hard before it comes to me. Nothing comes easy at this stage."

"We're old birds. We have to get used to it. How long have you been in New York, Sister Tia?"

"I've been here for more than thirty jears. I jews to live in the Bronx by East Tremont Avenue. That area was getting too bad for me, so I moved to Upper Manhattan, an area they call Spanish Harlem."

"I've heard about Spanish Harlem. How is it living there?"

"It's okay," Tia said. "It's much better than East

223

Tremont Avenue. I live in one of the newer buildings. It's a very nice place, clean and semigated. Jew should join me for lunch one of these days."

"Oh, I'd love that, Sister Tia."

"I live alone now that my three kids are grown and are living in different places."

"What happened to your husband?"

"I don't haf one anymore, Sister. We've been divorced for more than fifteen jears. I caught him in bed with my best friend. I never talked to him ever again. I was so hurt that I never got around to dating again, either. Sometimes I wished that I had a man in my life to help me when things got rough, but I've passed those days now. I just serve my God. He makes me happy. God's the man in my life now."

"My husband passed away years ago," Essie said, "but I live with my daughter Myrtle. I share an apartment with her and her son, Dean. I also have six grandkids living with us. It's a lucky thing that we have such a large apartment to comfortably accommodate everyone. I wouldn't have it any other way. I love living with my grandkids. They make me feel alive."

"How do jew like living in this city, Sister Brown?"

"Oh, I love it. I'm a big-city gal at heart. I love everything. I love the people. I love the food. I love the senior citizens' services everywhere. I love my church. I sometimes don't like the long walk to the subway and back, but I love everything else. I like how everything is close by; for example, the supermarkets and shops are just across the street. God has blessed me with lovely kids and a good life."

"Praise the Lord, Sister! Praise the Lord! I love it, too. I love everything. I can't complain. Sometimes the weather gets too cold, but I just make sure I dress warm before I come outside."

"Me, too."

"How are jer kids, Sister Brown?"

"God has blessed me with eight kids. They're doing very well. I have my beloved daughter Gena, who I call my miracle baby. She was the one who filed for me so that my family and I could leave Jamaica to live here. I'm so proud of her. She lives next door to me, and she has her own hairdressing parlor, which is doing very well.

"I also have a son who is a doctor. He lives in Florida. I go and visit him sometimes. He pays my fare anytime I want to travel anywhere, and he sends me money from time to time. All of my kids stay in touch with me. Thank God. I have a son in Los Angeles doing well and going to church. I have a daughter in Washington who has her own nursing home, and I have a son and a daughter in Jamaica. My son has a very big house there. It's a long story about his house, and someday, we'll sit down and talk about that. He also has his own leather craft business that's doing very well. My daughter in Jamaica has her own beauty parlor business." Mrs. Essie Brown raised her hands high in the air. "Thank you, God! You've blessed me and all my kids. Sister Tia, it wasn't easy, as it was me alone, but thank God He was by my side. He saw me through it all."

"Praise God, Sister Brown. God is good, and He is mighty. I know because I also had to call upon Him many times to help me. I was a single mother for three kids. I got absolutely no help from their father, who is a big-time journalist now living in England. But now they're doing very well."

"Where are you from, Sister Tia?"

"I was born in a place called Tegucigalpa in Honduras. When I was five jears old, my parents emigrated to Puerto Rico because of a business opportunity. I grew up in Puerto Rico and finished my schooling there. I worked in a major hotel as a manager for many jears before I came to live in New Jork for a better income so I could take better care of my kids. I did some home-care nursing assistance until I retired. Now that my kids are grown, I'm just taking it easy and serving my Lord."

"Sister, they say 'many rivers to cross,' but we found our way over. We are both women of substance. Don't ever forget that. What we did, just so that our kids could have a better life, no one can ever imagine."

"Jes! *Es verdad*, that is true, my sister. That is so true."

"Have you ever been back to Honduras?"

"Jes, I've been back a few times. However, when I go, I don't jewsally stay very long. I jews to visit my grandparents there, but they haf both passed away, so I hafn't been back since."

"Do you love Jamaican food, Sister Tia?"

"Jes! I love the jerk chicken, and I like how they do the oxtail, and I love the ackee and saltfish."

"I can make you some Jamaican recipes one of these days. Did you know that I was a personal chef for some very high-profile celebrities, including Roger Moore from the James Bond movies? He stayed at my private cottage resort twice in Jamaica, and he loved my cooking."

"Really? Jew must be a great cook, Sister Brown. I tell jew what. We will trade dinner treats. One day, jew could cook jer Jamaican food for me, and then I'll cook a Honduran Latino special that my grandmother taught me for jew."

"Okay, we'll do that real soon, Sister Tia," Mrs. Essie Brown concluded.

By this time, they were standing at the mouth of the subway. They continued trading stories with each other. When they heard the loud rumbling of an approaching underground train, they realized that they had been in the same spot for a long time, so they decided to bid each other good-bye until next time.

"Okay, Sister Tia. Travel safely and take care of yourself until we meet next week."

"Okay, Sister Brown, here is my number. Jew can call me anytime if jew want to talk. I'll be here."

"Yes, that's a good idea. Take mine also." Mrs. Essie Brown and Ms. Julia Gomez, friends and church buddies, continued a rich, frequent communication from that day on.

Chapter 29

In addition to enjoying her induction into New York City, Mrs. Essie Brown also enjoyed traveling to different areas in the United States and Jamaica. She traveled frequently to Washington, DC, particularly on special occasions, to see her daughter Lela. Lela, now married and the mother of another child, Shana, had her own nursing-home business.

Mrs. Essie Brown didn't play a major motherly role in Lela's life, but Lela grew up in a wonderful family. She stayed with Miriam, Mrs. Essie Brown's cousin, who lived in Mount Salem. Miriam and Mrs. Essie Brown were like sisters and kept an open communication with each other over the years.

Mrs. Essie Brown had promised herself that as soon as she could, she would request that Lela be returned to her. Or, if for any reason Miriam could no longer care for Lela, Essie wouldn't hesitate to take her back home where she belonged. Mrs. Essie Brown always spoke of her eight children, as if Lela was living with her. She did that so she would keep her foremost in her mind and so that her kids would realize that they did have another sister. Lela might not have been living with them, but she was in every way a part of them.

The undeniable fact was that Miriam was able to provide, at almost all stages of Lela's growth, a much better life than Mrs. Essie Brown had to offer. Therefore, there was no need to worry much about Lela's well-being. She was clearly in good hands.

Lela had a great childhood growing up with Miriam's two children, Donna and Mavis. They grew up close, like biological siblings or best friends. Nevertheless, whenever Lela felt like reaching out to her biological family unit, she knew she would always be welcome. From time to time, she dropped by her biological mother's house to pay her a brief visit. Lela knew that she had the best of both worlds. More than that, she knew that she was fortunate to be living with the family that could better care for her.

Miriam lived in a more affluent neighborhood than Essie's family, so Lela's friends were of a higher social class than would be expected if she had been living with Essie. She went to Harrison Memorial High School, an affluent private high school. It was the same SDA school that her brother Leonard had attended.

Lela wanted to become a registered nurse for a private medical center or a local doctor's office. She was steadfastly pursuing such a goal until she met a wealthy businessman who was a butcher and who owned a large, lucrative butcher shop in the center of downtown Montego Bay. She fell madly in love with him and eventually got pregnant and bore her first of two girls by him. Luckily, she was still able to graduate from high school, but she halted her nursing career plans to help run the butcher's shop.

Lela was not completely satisfied with her life.

The relationship was rocky because of this man's constant infidelities. Moreover, he refused to commit solely to her in the form of marriage so that they could build a solid future together. Feeling insecure and doubtful about the direction of her life, she welcomed Gena's offer to travel to the United States to have a brighter future.

Once she got to the United States, Lela tried many different jobs and different career moves, but nothing worked out well for her. She also tried a few short-term relationships, but none were substantial until she met Damian, a black American ex-Army officer. They dated for a while and eventually moved in with each other.

They later got married and had a lovely baby girl named Shana. They started a home-based nursing home business that could accommodate up to eight patients. Funny how life is. Lela, who always wanted to be a nurse, was now working like one for her own business. She and Damian bought a lovely house in Washington as soon as their business began turning over profits.

Her two oldest daughters, who were left behind in Jamaica, grew up to be successful young ladies. Their father emigrated to Pennsylvania and filed for them to come and join him. One became a registered nurse, and the other became a hotel manager.

Lela's youngest daughter was also doing well. She was at the top of her high school class and proving herself to be a true scholar.

Lela's life was wonderful and, some would say, successful. However, not everything was well.

At the time Essie became a US citizen and began filing for all of her kids, Lela was already married to Damian and had one child with him. It was naturally assumed that Damian, an American citizen, would do the right thing and file for his wife and baby's mother to become a permanent legal resident. Therefore, Essie didn't file for her.

But Damian had a unique philosophy. He felt that he had been used and badly hurt by a former lover, and he vowed to himself that he would not let that happen to him again. This time, he would stay in control of his relationship instead of letting the relationship control him. He genuinely loved Lela, but he believed that if he supplied her with everything she needed, except for permanent United States resident status, then he would be in full control of his relationship this time around.

If only Essie had known Damian's philosophy, she would have advised Lela to allow her to play this one vital motherly role in her life by filing for her along with the rest of her family. If she had realized his position, she might have called him another name she deemed more appropriate than Damian.

As it stood, it seemed as if due to Damian's philosophy—Lela was stuck in paradise.

***

Mrs. Essie Brown also enjoyed traveling to Florida to visit her son Leonard, who was married to a pharmacist, Dolcina, and who was a pharmacist himself. Soon after they both successfully graduated from the pharmacy school at St. John's University in Queens, New York, they got married and relocated to Florida to practice their profession and to start a life together.

Leonard had always wanted to have a significant impact on the world. He bragged that he was one of the most ingenious inventors the world had never met. About three or four years after he had graduated from St. John's, he stumbled upon a simple but rather visionary idea at the time. One morning after brushing his teeth, he lazily thought of skipping the next step, which was to floss. It was such a cumbersome activity—forcing one or both hands into one's mouth with a floss string. But as a pharmacist and a promoter of good, healthy living, he knew that it was a necessary means to a healthy, cavity-free mouth. *Why is it so unpleasant to floss one's teeth?* he asked himself.

He knew that if he found it unpleasant, then half the world at least must be experiencing the same problem. *Shouldn't it be a more streamlined process? Shouldn't there be a convenient tool for flossing, just like the toothbrush is a convenient tool for brushing?*

Why, in 1993, were people still using their bare hands in their mouths for the purpose of flossing their teeth? No wonder there were so many kids and adults alike who were refusing to floss on a daily basis.

Leonard thought about a motivational book he had once read in New York about ten years before. The book made mention of the popular saying, "Build a better mousetrap, and the world will beat a path to your door." It dawned on him that he had stumbled upon one of the most overlooked frontiers: finding a way to floss without the caveman-style method of using one's bare hands with a flossing string.

He was excited about his newly awakened idea. He knew that it would only be a matter of time before this oversight was realized by the rapidly growing health-care product industries, and he knew he had to jump on it fast. He sat down to create a tool that he believed could make better use of the flossing string than was then currently on the market.

He quickly mapped out a disposable dental floss holder and made a call to Inventors of Florida, a company that advertised its services heavily on TV. He set up an appointment to see the consultant of new inventions, and then he told Dolcina. "Duls, I have an invention idea. Check it out." Leonard showed his wife his first-grade-level drawing of a disposable dental floss holder. "What do you think?" he asked with pure excitement in his voice.

"Lord, Leonard, get rich quick so we can travel the world."

"Yes, that will come afterward, but I want to know what you think about my idea."

"Well, I'd use it, so I'd guess many other people would want to use it, also."

"Are you saying you like it?"

"Sure, why not? It's an excellent idea."

"Well, is it good enough to pay more than three thousand dollars to get it started? I've already called the Inventors of Florida, and they explained to me about their fees and the general procedures. I have an appointment already set with them. I'm very serious about getting it done."

"Lord, more spending again," she said. "I hope you can make some good money out of it." Then she thought of a dim possibility. "What if someone has already done it, and it's already on the market?"

"Good question. We can ask the consultant when we get there on Monday."

"What time is the appointment?"

"It's at ten a.m."

On Monday morning, both Leonard and Dolcina attended the appointed meeting with the Inventors of Florida. The consultant was excited. He thought it was a wonderful, ingenious idea.

Leonard asked his wife's question. "What if someone has already invented it and it's already on the market somewhere out there?"

"That's an excellent question," the consultant said, "and it has a simple answer." He explained what he meant. "Before we even get started on anything, we first have to do a complete, thorough patent search. The patent search will confirm or deny if you are the inventor of this idea. We do an outstanding job here at the Inventors of Florida. When we say you're the inventor or not the inventor, we back it up with proof."

The excited couple readily made a down payment on the process and initiated all of the paperwork that was necessary. They had to wait a few weeks for the patent search to be completed. Luckily, the search brought good news. There was no existing patent for this product on the market at that time.

Leonard was very excited. He knew that it was the greatest overlooked opportunity of its time, and he was overjoyed to have been the one to realize it.

He knew that he was about to change the world into a better place, even if it was only in the small area of flossing. Imagine millions and millions of boys and girls using his disposable dental floss device in the United States and all over the world. He knew that he was born to be a great human being, and he had done it. He had cleverly discovered a better, more acceptable, and easier way to do dental flossing, and he was now going to allow the experts at the Inventors of Florida to show him how to bring his original idea to life.

Within a month, the Inventors of Florida got engineers to make an artistic and detailed official drawing of the prototype of the product. An application for patent-pending status was filed and obtained. It was suggested by the experts that a patent-pending status was the way to go instead of a patent. It was the expected thing to do if you needed the company to build and market your invention for you.

Inventors of Florida put together a neat introduction package that described the product and marketed it to twenty-five large companies. These included Johnson & Johnson, Procter & Gamble, and

Pfizer, along with a few other popular companies. At least fifteen of the twenty-five companies returned a response of noninterest. The other ten held on to the idea and gave it serious attention for a few months. They kept up constant communication with Leonard, letting him know the progress of their board meetings and follow-up decisions. They also kept him abreast of the method of assessment of his product to see how it might benefit their company. One particularly interested company took his idea all the way to the top level of their evaluation system before they finally came to a sudden denial decision.

It was heartbreaking for Leonard to learn that none of the twenty-five companies had chosen to accept his imaginative idea. Most of the companies concluded that it wasn't worth their time and effort because they were involved in bigger and better things at the time.

Leonard decided that his shot at greatness was not in the invention department, so he decided to sign up at Nova Southeastern University to do a postgraduate PharmD program. A PharmD is a doctor of pharmacy degree. By doing this, he felt that he had a better chance of significantly impacting the world with his enhanced medical skills and knowledge.

Exactly one year later, Leonard walked into a Walgreens pharmacy and was shocked to see the very same product he had invented, with a little improvement, on the store shelf. How ironic was that? When he had marketed his idea to some of the largest companies in the United States, no one thought it was worth their time. Yet, one year later, a product that was not in existence was now a new item all over the country. Someone must have stolen his original idea—giving him no credit, not to mention a reward—for his great vision.

Burning with fury, Leonard took his case to a patent lawyer, who agreed that it was too much of a coincidence not to consider that his idea had been stolen. The lawyer advised that it would take lots of time and money to fight the case in a regular lawsuit. He suggested that Leonard fight his case for much less expense by taking each company that was now producing and marketing the product to small-claims court.

Dr. Leonard, for whatever reason, didn't follow through on the fight to restore credit for his ingenious, well-timed, and inventive idea. After that, whenever he saw a dental floss holder, it still infuriated him. It hurt him to know that he was the bona fide inventor of that idea but he hadn't gotten his due credit.

Still, his mother was correct when she said that her son was going to grow up to be a great man someday. Dr. Leonard did impact the world in a big way; the only problem was that the world hadn't recognized him for his great idea. At least he had impacted the world by improving on a basic hygienic habit.

Immediately after the completion of his doctor of pharmacy degree, Dr. Leonard went on to publish a few medical articles in a popular, internationally distributed pharmacy news magazine. He wanted to reach a wide range of people with his newly acquired health-care knowledge. This activity still couldn't heal his pain and disappointment. He had wanted to make his mother proud, and he knew that his invention of the disposable dental floss device would have been just the thing to do it.

However, Mrs. Essie Brown was quite proud of her son and was very happy every time she visited him and his wife in Florida.

***

Mrs. Essie Brown enjoyed visiting her oldest son, Junior, in Los Angeles. He was married, not to Pauline, but to Patricia. Junior worked at a Kodak firm fixing Kodak machines and was doing well for himself. He had also started going to church regularly. He had dropped the Rastafarian mentality and now truly believed in Christ.

***

Mrs. Essie Brown enjoyed traveling back and forth to Jamaica to visit her daughter Betty. Betty had been living with her in New York, but she decided that she wanted to return to Jamaica to attend to her beauty parlor business.

***

When Mrs. Essie Brown was in Jamaica, she also visited her son Bunny, who was married to Joyce and had three children: Fern, Neil, and a sweet little girl named Zena. They also had an adopted daughter named Brenda. Bunny was content to stay in Jamaica and refused to emigrate with the family to the United States because his leather business was doing very well. He and his wife traveled to the United States every now and then. He had obtained his permanent resident card, as had his two sons, Neil and Fern, just like the rest of Essie's family.

He later became a local politician and a respectable notary of the public of Jamaica.

***

When in Jamaica, Mrs. Essie Brown also visited her son Karl, who was a popular manager in the food and beverage department at the Holiday Inn Beach Resort in Montego Bay. He was still married to Marva, and they had two wonderful girls, Samantha and Sue Helen. Unfortunately, Karl had never forgiven his mother for leaving him with his dad, Tim, in the country while the rest of the family flourished in a modern city like Montego Bay.

He hated Mrs. Essie Brown for all of her shortcomings as a single mother, and he was vocal about it. Mrs. Essie Brown loved him anyway and tried many times to ask for his forgiveness, but Karl couldn't find it in his heart to forgive her.

Karl was an honest and upright Christian in the Glenworth SDA Church, and it was because of his honesty and truthfulness that he couldn't hide his feelings. He loved God. He loved his kids. He loved his father. He loved all mankind. But he hated Mrs. Essie Brown.

He hated his mother like a rat hated a dose of poison. It hurt him deeply every time he thought about the life he'd had as a boy growing up in the country. No one ever knew his full story because he never said much about why he so strongly despised his early days. They just assumed that a country life spoke for itself.

Karl didn't attend his parents' wedding, and he turned down Mrs. Essie Brown's offer to file for him to emigrate to the United States with all of his siblings. She sent him the immigration form anyway, but he tore it to pieces. He refused to take anything from his mother and often called her a "dirty whore." However, he obtained for himself a ten-year US visitor visa so he could travel whenever he wished. For the time being, he wanted to stay in Jamaica and take care of his family. After all, he had a great job at a large, popular hotel. Nevertheless, many years later Karl traveled on his own to Florida and then to New York to live temporarily.

***

When Mrs. Essie Brown was not at home in New York with Gena and Myrtle, she enjoyed visiting other nearby states such as New Jersey and Connecticut where other family members, such as her cousins Jenifer and Junior, who were brother and sister, lived.

It was undeniable that Mrs. Essie Brown was having the time of her life as an honorable, genuine resident of New York City, the ultimate big city. However, she never forgot her striving family, which was now dispersed all over the globe.

Chapter 30

At seventy-six years old and counting, Mrs. Essie Brown, the naive little girl from the countryside of Cascade, relished her life in the ultimate big city of New York. To say that she was enjoying herself would be an understatement.

She was as happy as a frolicking, zealous New Yorker at the Labor Day Parade in Brooklyn, or at the Macy's Thanksgiving Day Parade in Manhattan. She was getting a kick out of living high on life, and she made no more dull, balky, unenthusiastic comments about life. She never let anything get her down, but with a prayer or two, shook off any problems that came her way. She luxuriated in the enjoyment of her grandkids and great-grandkids. She wanted to live forever.

However, Mrs. Essie Brown knew better. She knew that we all have to relinquish life at some point. We can hope for a long, happy, productive life, but sooner or later, we all must pass on.

By this time, she had been diagnosed with diabetes, Parkinson's disease, rheumatoid arthritis, osteoarthritis, generalized hypertension, heart disease, glaucoma, peripheral neuralgia—specifically, peripheral neuropathy—and two mild, silent heart attacks.

She fought her ailments aggressively. She complied with all health-care directives and took all her medications. But although Mrs. Essie Brown wanted to live forever, she began having a strange feeling that the end was near, because her health continued to rapidly and acutely decline. She decided that if she should die anytime soon, she would like for it to happen while she was in her own home in Glenworth, Jamaica. She therefore called her daughter Gena and said, "My dear child, I want to go home to expire in my rocking chair on my veranda in Glenworth."

"But Mom, don't you remember that you lost your passport and all of your major traveling documents on your last trip to Jamaica? Don't you remember that you had a difficult time coming back? We'll have to take care of those things at the immigration office downtown so you can travel again."

"Okay then, try and get them for me. Please hurry, because I'm not feeling too good in my body, and I want to go home to Jamaica."

"Why do you have to go to Jamaica? What's wrong with being right here in New York? There's no one there to help you as much as here, and remember, Mom, health care is not that great there."

"Well, Gena, I don't care. I want to die in my home that I worked so hard for."

Gena got busy trying to regain her mother's travel documents, but a year later, the processing was still unfinished. Mrs. Essie Brown pleaded with Gena to try harder with the US embassy to see if they could speed up the process.

Mrs. Essie Brown now got anxious and irritated because she wanted to go home at any cost. She was as anxious as a kid on Christmas Eve who couldn't wait until the next day to ravish his nicely packaged gift lying ever so neatly under the Christmas tree. She was tired of waiting. The one year that she had waited on her travel documents could have been spent in her home in Glenworth.

Unfortunately, Mrs. Essie Brown—the orphan child, the city girl, the single mother, the religious fanatic wife—did not make it home to Glenworth. In November 1999, she regrettably had a stroke at the age of seventy-seven. This stroke left her partially paralyzed in a large New York hospital.

After three weeks of unsuccessful medical intervention, she had a second, disastrous stroke that left her totally paralyzed and unable to speak. Mrs. Essie Brown, although she was in a fragile condition, resisted the hands of death—or, as some would say, giving up the ghost—for almost one and a half years.

Maybe she was still holding on for the time when her travel documents would be successfully processed by the US embassy. Maybe she still wanted to go back to Jamaica to depart in a peaceful manner in her home in Glenworth, the home that she had worked so hard to obtain and maintain.

Mrs. Essie Brown's home in Glenworth—whether it was her breaking point or her breakthrough point—truly defined her life.

Mrs. Essie Brown spent one and a half years in a nursing home in New York City, paralyzed and unable to speak. She had one and a half peaceful years to reflect back on her whole life. She had time to reflect on all of her successes and all of her failures. She had succeeded in taking care of her kids the best way that she could. She had succeeded in finding a good man to be her husband. She had succeeded in making it in a tough, rough city like Montego Bay. But she had failed in giving all her kids the best life that they could get. She had failed in giving all her kids a father or stepfather early in their lives, when they needed him most. She had failed to make it big time in the big city of Montego Bay.

The grim reality, according to the pessimist, was that she had failed in all of the same areas where she had succeeded. However, according to the optimist, she had succeeded in all of the areas where she had failed.

Mrs. Essie Brown had one and a half calm, tranquil years lying immobilized to think about her mother. She thought about what her life would have been like, or could have been like, growing up with Doris Lynn, the mother she had never met. She often wondered why God took her so early and so young. Her mother never had the chance even to see her face. If her mother had been alive, would she have been proud of the way Essie had lived her life?

Essie had a long time to think about the father that she had never met. She thought about the man who had raped her mother and produced an orphan child. Yes, the perverse fact was that her father had raped her mother. That was the big secret that her mother, Doris Lynn, had died with. That was the reason why her mother refused to discuss any information about the mysterious father of her expected child. Doris Lynn was ashamed and embarrassed because she had been violated by her first cousin.

Doris Lynn was unyieldingly and unkindly violated at the back of a church by one of her visiting cousins from Kingston, by the name of Lester Brown. Mrs. Essie Brown, by mere chance, found out about it from Miriam, her cousin in Mount Salem. Miriam told her the story long after Lester Brown had died in a car accident in Kingston.

Miriam confessed to Mrs. Essie Brown that it

was due to the pure sorrow, guilt, and pity that she felt within her that she was compelled to help her with her baby Lela. Lela was born around the same time Miriam first found out about the rape. Miriam asked Mrs. Essie Brown to keep it a secret to protect the integrity of the family.

Mrs. Essie Brown also had nothing but undisturbed time to reflect on her kids, who had broken through thick, seemingly impenetrable barriers to get to where they were going. Gena, for instance, had made a simple promise from her heart to go and prepare a place for the family in the United States, and she did so like a soldier bushwhacking her way against all odds.

Essie also had undisturbed time to reflect on how Leonard, at age ten, had envisioned himself being a doctor. She wondered how he was able to fight his way to the top in such an astounding way to become a doctor. She couldn't have been any happier, although he was not a physician as promised. She was still very proud of him because he had achieved the status of a doctor, and that was more than what she—a plain, simple, naive country girl—could have asked for from one of the seeds that she had planted on this earth.

She thought of how very proud she was when she attended his graduation at Nova Southeastern University in Florida. That was categorically one of her proudest moments by far. She remembered that her son Dr. Leonard had also promised to write a book about her life before she died.

She remembered sitting down and spilling her guts to him on one of her vacations at his home in Florida. He had videotaped her for hours as she spoke about the ups and downs in her life. She thought that it would have been good to see that accomplishment so she could happily check it off her bucket list, but she was still very proud of him without it.

Mrs. Essie Brown had serene time to reflect on the lawsuit that she had won against the Catholic church across the street from her building in New York City. One day while crossing the church's driveway, she fell in front of the church gate and sprained her feet. She was unable to walk for months. Eventually, she was encouraged to file a lawsuit against the church. She did file a case against them and won ten thousand dollars.

After winning that grand sum, she remembered that she had made a promise to put a second level on her home in Glenworth at the first chance she got. So that was what she did with the award from the court. She sent it to her son Bunny in Jamaica to do the construction on her home.

As a Christian, Mrs. Essie Brown wondered with much guilt if she had done the right thing by suing the church. Was that why the house in Glenworth stood, even today, as an incomplete monument of her desire?

Mrs. Essie Brown had nothing but quiet time to reflect on the means by which she had obtained her home in Glenworth. She knew that if there was a crossroad in her life, it certainly would be the point where she'd had to choose, for or against, obtaining a permanent roof over her kids' heads.

Chapter 31

Maybe the title of this story should have been *Essie's House in Glenworth*.

Junior was one of the first direct beneficiaries of that house. The whole family benefited instantaneously when they moved into their new home, but Junior was the first to benefit solely from the land. When he had his first baby girl with Pauline, the runaway teen, they moved out of the house and built a cozy two-bedroom house in the backyard of Essie's property.

This meant that he did not have to buy land to build his house. He did not have to get any special permission to build his house. He did not have to pay any related fees, such as taxes. The only permission he needed was Essie's, and she was more than happy to see the young couple blossom into a loving, independent family with a lovely home of their own.

Junior and Pauline had two more kids after Denise emigrated to the United States: a girl named Paula and a boy named Caple. The name Caple derived from the name of a well-known reggae singer called Capleton, also known as the Fireman or the Prophet. He was famous for coining the phrase "Fire a go bun them." One of his biggest hit songs was a song called "Tour."

Pauline occasionally hustled as a vendor for tourists, as well as for local citizens, and Junior increased his clientele as he marketed his skill as an electrician. No one interfered with them, and they would have enjoyed a peaceful life in Essie's backyard if they hadn't been their own worst enemies. There were times when they broke out into a serious argument that eventually led into a fistfight.

Junior usually started the arguments, mostly because of jealousy, but it was Pauline who was the first and only one doing the hitting. Poor Junior simply ducked or dodged her blows. He never once retaliated. Instead, he tried to contain her by holding her two hands as long as he could to stop her vicious punches.

It was always the same story. Junior, who in principle didn't believe in laying a hand on a female because Essie had taught him well, was the jealous guy who started the argument and ended up being physically abused by his domestic lover. When the scuffle was all over, Pauline was the person crying the loudest and the most desperately; Junior was the one with the proud victory walk and the swollen face or black eye.

Despite his wounds, he was the person everyone wrongfully blamed and screamed at. Everyone automatically ran to Pauline's rescue because she was crying so hard. No one understood that she was crying so hard because she couldn't get as many punches in as she would have liked. Pauline had a sharp temper like Mike Tyson and a right hand like Mohammed Ali. She was opinionated and did not take kindly to anyone telling her what to do. By nature, she enjoyed a good fight.

Because of Pauline's hostile attitude, Junior was glad when his mother filed for him and his children to emigrate to the United States. Pauline, not knowing that Junior was on the verge of receiving his immigration approval, had moved out of Junior's house two months before he traveled to the United States. One day, she just packed her bags and left Junior and all her kids behind. She went to live with a man who was doing very well in Jamaica, certainly much better than Junior. He had a big, fancy house and lots of money to go around. Pauline had finally found the man that she had been looking for the day she ran away from her parents in May Pen. That she was now much older and had three kids didn't stand in her way.

Mrs. Essie Brown's filing process was right on time. Junior emigrated with Caple to Florida, where he lived with Dr. Leonard and his family for a month. He left Paula behind to stay at his house in Jamaica to watch over it while she took care of some health issues. When Florida proved a little too slow for him in terms of job opportunities, he moved on to New York City.

Unfortunately, Caple died from a grand mal epileptic seizure shortly after arriving in New York. He died at the tender, gone-too-soon age of twelve.

Even after her health issues were cleared up, Paula refused to travel. Instead, she decided to stay and enjoy the peace of mind she got by living on her own in the family home located in the backyard of Essie's house in Glenworth.

***

Betty's story was very different from Junior's. She was independent and easygoing. As long as her beauty parlor was open for business and clients were available, she was a happy camper. She invested all of her time and effort into her beauty parlor business but, unfortunately, with little financial return.

Although she was very good at the art and craft of hairdressing, she was awful as a businesswoman. It was often said that she was too kindhearted—and some would even say too silly—to recoup a profit from her business. She gave away more free services to her clients than the Salvation Army gave away in a lifetime. She made many vain attempts to move out of Essie's house in Glenworth, but when business or her relationship got bad, she moved right back in with her mother. She had her first kids, twins, in Essie's house.

She also had her other children in the Glenworth home. She had six kids altogether, and they all stayed mostly with their grandmother while Betty worked day and night in her salon. The most significant point in Betty's life came about when Mrs. Essie Brown emigrated to the United States and then filed for her and her kids to follow. They all went to live in Mrs. Essie Brown's apartment in New York City.

Betty was not happy in New York, so she decided to leave her kids with their grandmother and return to Jamaica to attend to her beauty salon business. When she went back to live in the house in Glenworth, her youngest brother, Bunny, was also living there with his wife and kids. The rest of the family had emigrated to the United States.

Bunny wasn't too happy to share the house with Betty; he and Betty were cut from two different cloths. Betty was not all that domesticated around the house when it came to house duties or chores, while Bunny and his family were neat, tidy, and well organized. They just could not get along, and eventually—after Essie's intervention—Bunny moved his family out and left the house in Glenworth to Betty. Betty lived happily in the house for the rest of her life, which, unfortunately, was not very long.

Betty fell madly in love with a new boyfriend named Kenneth, who was initially good to her. He bought a new refrigerator, a stove, and some furniture for the Glenworth house. He and Betty lived a good life there together until one day, seemingly for no reason at all, Kenneth coldheartedly decided to leave Betty and find a place of his own. He moved out all of the fancy kitchen accoutrements and new furniture he had bought and boldly went to live with a new girlfriend across the street, about a block away.

Betty couldn't deal with the sudden and shocking breakup. Distressed, she experienced significant weight loss because of excess worry and depression. Within six months of Kenneth breaking up with her, she had two brain aneurisms that eventually ruptured in her head. Doctors tried to save her at the hospital, but she died after three days there. She was only forty-nine.

After Betty's untimely death, the house was left to Lance, Betty's youngest son, and Dean, Myrtle's only son. Lance eventually moved out and put his room up for rent. Dean was now the only family member of Essie's who remained in the house. It was ironic that it was the sole son of Myrtle who was now rightfully inheriting Essie's house in Glenworth.

***

Essie's house in Glenworth didn't have any effect on Lela, since Lela had grown up with Miriam Bertha Streete, her cousin. The only time Lela came in contact with the house was when she occasionally popped into Glenworth to see how her biological family was doing.

Karl, on the other hand, benefited greatly from living at Essie's house in Glenworth. He had moved from the country when he was fourteen years old, but before that, he had visited his family in the city at least once or twice every year.

The family always looked forward to his visits. Karl had a knack for catching on to the latest fashions or behaviors, and it was fun to see the new styles or actions that were arising in the country town of Clear Mount or Jericho. One time, he came to visit the family with a new style of walking that the family called "the country walk." When he walked, he would use one foot to hit the heel of the other foot, therefore creating a dance-like walking or hopping motion.

On the following visit, he introduced the latest style, which was to suck on his inner bicep with his arm thrown across his shoulder while he was walking. This action made it look as if he were hiding his face with one of his hands across his mouth and resting on his shoulder.

On another visit, Karl combined the two styles, the foot hitting and the bicep sucking, as he walked. The younger kids especially enjoyed Karl's displays.

On his last visit at age fourteen, Karl brought all of his few belongings from the country. He had decided that he wanted to live with his family in the Glenworth house, and he demanded that he be allowed to stay.

Karl spent the rest of his teenage years with his family in the city. He joined the Glenworth SDA Church, where he fortuitously discovered a new talent he didn't know he had: he was an excellent singer. Together with two friends, Rodney and Paul, he started a male singing trio. They became so popular that they visited churches to perform at various concerts.

Karl eventually met his wife, Marva, at the church. They got married and built a nice three-bedroom house in a newly developed district of Rose Hall called The Little Spot. They had two wonderful girls, Samantha and Sue Helen. Samantha grew up to be a teacher like her mother, and like her uncle Leonard, Sue Helen wanted to attend medical school to become a doctor.

Although he was a great person and a wonderful Christian, Karl showed open resentment to Mrs. Essie Brown for leaving him behind in the country with his father. His resentment grew stronger and stronger with time. However, he did not deny that her house in Glenworth was a refuge for him, as it allowed him to escape the country lifestyle at an early age so he could redeem himself as a valuable member of the big-city society.

***

The house in Glenworth allowed Leonard to dream big dreams and aspire to greatness, but next to Lela, he actually spent the least amount of time there. Leonard was one of the first ones Gena had brought to the United States. He left Essie's house at the age of sixteen to live with Gena in New York City. Many decades later, although it was almost ten years after the death of his mother, he was able to fulfill his delayed promise to pen a book about her and about her house in Glenworth.

***

Essie's house in Glenworth was a serious motivating factor in Bunny's life. The greatest benefit of the house started taking root when the rest of his family emigrated to the United States, leaving only him and his wife and two kids in Jamaica.

It's true that Bunny had a thriving leather business in Jamaica, but there's another story behind why he chose to remain in Jamaica. In Gena's gutsy glory days, when she was determined to make good on her promise to her mother to pave the way for all her family members to relocate to the United States, she came up with a big, ambitious plan.

After the smooth success of Denise and Myrtle making it past US immigration at the airport a few years earlier, Gena felt overly confident. She was as confident as Usain Bolt when he started his premature celebration of his world-record-breaking win in the 100-meter race at the 2008 Olympic Games in Beijing. She therefore devised a big plan to get three people in at the same time: Bunny, Lela, and Faith. Faith was the twelve-year-old daughter of her friend Fay. Fay had heard about Gena's big plan and wanted Gena to do her a favor by delivering Faith to her aunt in Brooklyn.

Gena had no fear, and she was ready for action. She was determined to make good on her promise by whatever means necessary. Bunny's passport contained his correct picture, but it had the name and information of someone else who was a citizen of the United States. Gena's plan was now in full swing. She went to Jamaica as she usually did, and she instructed Bunny, Lela, and Faith on what they needed to do. She drilled the new information into them so that their new names would become second nature.

When Gena thought that they were ready, she scheduled their make-believe return flight to New York City. The flight went off without a hitch. It was about eight in the evening, and they were now nervously approaching the United States immigration officers. Gena securely held Faith's hand as if she were her daughter, while Bunny and Lela trailed right behind them.

Gena stepped up to the stern, angry-looking older black officer and handed him the documents for both her and Faith. She sensed that something wasn't right. Based on the atmosphere and the questions that the officer was asking, she realized that immigration expected three people who were not supposed to be on the flight. However, the officers wrongly expected the three people all to be together.

While the immigration officer calmly processed her paperwork, she watched with regret as a young Hispanic-looking male officer pulled Bunny and Lela aside for extra questioning. Gena knew then that someone must have informed the US embassy about them. It had to have been someone who knew about her plan, and very few people did.

It turned out that she was right. Karl, who had followed them to the airport, had left the family for a quick few minutes. But in those few minutes, he was able to notify the Jamaican embassy, which in turn notified the US embassy. Karl did so because he viewed this as a similar situation to the time his family had left him in the country with his father while the rest of them were living a modern city lifestyle. The family was conveniently heading off to live the American dream while he was being left behind to suffer in Jamaica. He didn't care if his sisters and brother got caught and sent to jail. His grudge ran deep and was unyielding.

Gena was ahead of the game. She knew that if anything went wrong, she would have to quickly separate herself from the pack and bail out. That was exactly what she did. As soon as her papers were processed, she did not linger. She calmly walked by Bunny and Lela, who were still being questioned. Gena held her head straight as if she didn't know them and had no part in other people's affairs. As the old Jamaican saying goes, it was like "when chicken a pass by dentist office," meaning, since chickens have no teeth, they have no concern with dentists, and therefore, they hold their heads up high with pride when passing by a dental office because they have no reason to care.

Gena held on tightly to little Faith's hand and headed straight out through the doors of the airport.

She took a quick glance back just before she disappeared through the main doorway, and disappointment slapped her squarely in the face. She saw that the immigration officer was leading Bunny and Lela away to a special room. She noticed the sad looks on their faces. They were as disappointed as the inarguable favorite to win the Brazilian team was when they got surprisingly knocked out of the 2010 FIFA World Cup. The Brazilian team was knocked out by the Netherlands team in the stage-two round of the sixteen knock-out phase. Gena walked away feeling as sad as Maradona, the famous one-time soccer player and now coach of the Argentinean team. He stood on the sidelines of the same 2010 FIFA quarter finals and watched his team get brutally beat down by Germany, four goals to zero.

Gena knew then that her mission had partly failed. She was, however, still thankful that God had protected her through it all, and she had made it through with her friend's daughter, Faith. She had gotten one out of three people, so her trip to Jamaica and her efforts were not in vain.

Gena had hoped that her brother Bunny and her sister Lela would make it through, but like the Brazilian team and Maradona, she concluded that it was just not their time. The immigration officers held both Lela and Bunny overnight in jail and returned them to Jamaica on the next flight out early the following morning.

Luckily for Gena, neither Lela nor Bunny gave any incriminating information during their interrogation that would affect her. Gena scheduled a second try at a later date. Bunny refused to make any more attempts, but Lela was willing to try again. This time, Gena was able to get her through the immigration system because she didn't make anyone else aware of her plan.

People often speak about the heroes of their country. Gena was the true, bold, unsung hero of Essie's family.

Many years later, that experience still left a bad taste in Bunny's mouth. Even when Mrs. Essie Brown became a US citizen and filed for all of her kids, Bunny refused to be included in the group. He had developed a stronger love for his homeland, Jamaica. He decided that he would make himself more comfortable in Jamaica, and if he had to travel, he would travel to everywhere but the United States.

Bunny was never the same. He was ready to live and die in his bittersweet, struggling island of Jamaica. However, his brother Dr. Leonard went ahead and added his name against his will to the documents Essie filed so that he could obtain his green card like all his other siblings.

Prior to that time, Bunny had been slowly getting his life together. Being Essie's youngest child, he felt that he had a lot of time to do that. However, when he met Joyce, who later became his wife, she became a strong motivating force in Bunny's life. He started going to the main library in downtown Montego Bay to do research on leather crafts. He also started developing a strong interest in local politics. One day, he made a call to his brother Leonard in Florida, asking for his insight on his new leather project. "Hey there, brother. How're you and the family doing this wonderful day that the good Lord has made for us?" Bunny asked.

"I'm doing well, my brother. My wife and my stepson are doing great also. I can't complain. He gave us life, and as you said, this wonderful day. Thanks for asking. How are things going with you in Jamaica?"

"Well, I met a nice girl named Joyce. She's really a go-getter, and we're looking for ways to start our future together. She does buying and selling in the local tourist market, and I'm doing some self-educating in the library. I'm looking at getting into the leather craft business. I noticed that there are lots of crafts in Jamaica, but very few use the raw material of the cows here. I want to start from the basic raw material and build a strong network chain as a foundation of my business."

"That sounds great, bro. I'm proud of you. You're taking a stand to strengthen your future. I like your idea. It sounds like you've got yourself a niche market. But you know, you have to jump on it real fast before it gets cold."

"No, mon, this idea cannot get cold. I've had this fire burning inside of me for a while now, and I'm just trying to see how I can get started. There are some little things that I'm going to need—the proper tools, for instance. I'm taking things step-by-step."

"Hey, tell you what, bro. I'm going to look around and see what I can find over here in Florida. As soon as I see anything, I'll give you a buzz."

"Hey, brother, you read my mind. You saw that I could use the help. Thank you. May the good Lord bless and keep you and your family. Say hello to them for me."

"I will. Bye for now. Love you, bro."

"Love you too, brother. Bye."

Within two weeks, Dr. Leonard located a leather shop called the Tandy Leather Company and purchased a spiffy little starter kit with all the necessary tools needed to do leather crafting. He sent it to Bunny, and that was the start of Bunny's leather business.

Bunny never looked back. His business got

stronger and more profitable each day. They say that if you give a man a fish, he will eat well for a day, but if you teach him how to fish, he will be well nourished because he will have food for a lifetime. The gift that Leonard sent Bunny, even with its small price tag, was worth more than a million dollars in the long run.

Now that he had a strong, growing business in Jamaica, and his wife's business endeavors were also growing, Bunny wanted to start a family of his own. They had two lovely boys to begin with, and later on, they added a little princess girl and also adopted another charming girl into their family unit.

They were flourishing in Jamaica, living well in Essie's house in Glenworth. They took full occupancy of the house after the rest of the family emigrated to the United States. They were very proud of their home, so they kept it clean and neat. They also made some major improvements to the house to make it look more presentable. They were truly comfortable, and they benefited directly from Essie's house in Glenworth.

That benefit started dwindling when Betty decided to return to Jamaica to rebuild her beauty salon business. This was a major disappointment for Bunny and his family, because they never thought that they would have to share Essie's house with anyone, let alone someone who had emigrated to the United States.

Moreover, Betty was not domestic and didn't care to make the same effort at keeping up the house as Bunny and his family did. There was a brewing rivalry between the two siblings, which eventually escalated into an outright verbal fight.

It was now time to call in the big chief, Mrs. Essie Brown, living in the United States at this time. After being notified of the rising animosity between the two siblings over issues concerning rights and means for a peaceful coexistence in the Glenworth house, Essie immediately packed her bag and headed to Jamaica to settle the fuss between them. Once Essie got there, the fire only escalated more, since Mrs. Essie Brown, being a strong advocate for female rights and safety, was partial to her daughter. Mrs. Essie Brown believed that Bunny, being a man, should be the one to leave her house if he couldn't live peacefully with his sister.

Anger can be a brutal force, and Bunny's anger blazed up in a fury. He was wretchedly angry at his mother, as angry as the typical Cuban American against Fidel Castro's regime. He was as angry as they were when they were forced to leave their home and emigrate to the Miami shores via unsafe, makeshift boats.

However, Bunny found enough chivalry deep within him to compose himself as he calmly brought his mother outside and pointed to a humongous two-story white house across the street. "Do you see that house, Mother?" he asked. "Take a good look at it. I, Bunny Dun, am going to build myself a house like that. Believe me, I don't need to live in your house. Mother, listen to me and listen well. You and Betty can go to hell in this house. I don't care to live here anymore." Bunny lost some of his composure. His eyes were as red as fire. He was burning with fury, and he couldn't hold it back any longer.

That very same day, he turned his back on his mother's house in Glenworth and started moving his things out. For now, he and his wife would go to live with his wife's mother in a small, worn-out, two-bedroom house.

The conflict with Essie and Betty lit a fire within Bunny that never died. It motivated him to find a spot and build a house exactly like the house across the street from Essie's house. This was one of the other major benefits that the house in Glenworth offered Bunny.

This was also a strong driving force for Bunny

and his wife to resurge back to the top. They were forced to take their game plan to another level. Joyce started traveling abroad, where she would buy clothes and other items at a low cost in places like Miami and return to Jamaica to resell them for a big profit.

Bunny also stepped up his game, as he started working longer hours in his business and making some stronger social and political network connections, which helped his business even more. In a relatively short time, he and his wife found a piece of land on which to build their dream home.

It was a beautiful spot on a hill that overlooked Montego Bay's Sangster International Airport and the beautiful picturesque ocean behind the airport. They started with a modest two-bedroom basic structure. Over the years, they added to it slowly, one room at a time, until it started taking shape. Finally, it became a true duplicate copy of Essie's neighbor's house, as Bunny had so confidently promised.

Then Essie won her lawsuit against the Catholic church in New York where she had fallen. Essie sent the ten thousand US dollars of award money in two portions to Bunny for him to use to complete her dream of adding a second level to her house in Glenworth.

For the life of her, she could not imagine the depth of built-up emotions that her little beloved wash belly had and the grudge he held against her. She always thought that she had done the right thing, so it was hard for her to see why her son wouldn't forgive her for taking sides with her daughter.

Bunny knew in his heart, just like Karl, that he could not forgive his mother, but he was more than happy to take the job and the money to get the job done. Being only human, he did the best he could do with the funds, but Essie's house was not completed as expected. Bunny reported that the money ran out because most of it was spent on labor. Essie was very disappointed, but she was more than happy to see the new improvements to Bunny's enormous, elaborate, attractive home on top of the hill on the other side of Glenworth.

Many years passed, and things began to seem normal. Betty was enjoying Essie's modest and incomplete house, and Bunny and his family were enjoying their gigantic, showy two-story dream home. Betty and Bunny became somewhat cordial and polite to each other.

After Essie passed away in New York City and her body was shipped to Jamaica for her second funeral service and her burial, Bunny and his wife were put in charge of the funeral preparation and related activities. They both did an excellent job as far as the preparation of the funeral was concerned. After all, it was Bunny's mother, and he couldn't afford to give her anything less than what the Glenworth society expected.

However, bitterness and anger ran deep within Bunny's veins. That bitterness could be seen at the gravesite at Essie's funeral.

Chapter 32

"If this was the Army, this occasion would be a pin ceremony rather than a regular funeral service." Dr. Leonard Brown read Mrs. Essie Brown's eulogy from the pulpit with a fierce, strong, almost angry tone. "This is so because a pin ceremony follows an act of bravery, or comes after someone has completed a lifetime of outstanding achievement, or has performed some brave act of heroism. If this were the Army, we would all be here awarding this fallen soldier with one of life's highest personal honors."

Karl and Bunny sat stoically at the front row of the unpretentious district church, joined by other members of the family, all dressed in black.

Dr. Leonard believed that this was categorically the moment to celebrate Essie's life and to let the world know that his mother was a virtuous woman of substance. He knew that he had failed miserably in his promise to write a book about her before she passed away, so a detailed eulogy was the best he could do for her. He had a lot to say and very little time to do so. The world needed to know about her life, but he would have to settle for this small district church audience.

"Honorable heroine Essie Brown, also known affectionately to her hometown folks as Miss Pretty, was born in Cascade, a small town in Hanover, on March 26, 1922." Dr. Leonard shuffled his papers in his hands as he scrambled to find the correct page to read. His nerves got the better of him for a moment, but he quickly collected himself and continued reading. "At nine months of age, she was brought to Cascade to live with her new parents, Aunt Rose and Amos. She was schooled in Cascade, but later moved to Montego Bay and went to work for a registered nurse named Sandra Ferguson and her husband, Dr. Roan Ferguson. Forced to leave that situation, she bravely went on her own as a grown teenager."

Some of the members of the congregation at the back of the church whispered to each other.

Dr. Leonard cleared his throat and projected his voice so he could be heard above them. "She bore four boys and four girls: Gena, Junior, Betty, Lela, Myrtle, Karl, Leonard (myself), and Bunny. She was blessed with more than twenty-six grandchildren, the youngest of which are Alexander M. Brown and Algivanni G. Brown. She had more than twenty-one great-grandchildren, all of whom she loved and cherished with all her heart. She always said that children are blessings sent from God.

"She was also blessed with a whole host of nieces, nephews, cousins, friends, and extended family members." Dr. Leonard paused for a quick second and adjusted his collar. He braced himself for his next statement. He was mad as hell and wanted everyone to know clearly who Essie was. He continued speaking with an undertone of rage. "Today, for what it's worth, I

263

bestow the honor of heroism on Mrs. Essie Brown. She fought a raging, long, and hard battle to give her family a better home and a better life and to make this earth a better place.

"A hero is an unselfish person who greatly risks his or her life to save another. Well, my mother did just that. As a shy, vulnerable little country girl, she came to town to make a living for herself. Instead, she ended up dedicating her whole life to her family, giving up everything else just so that her family could see a brighter future."

Sitting with the other family members, Myrtle wiped tears from her eyes.

"Success did not come easily, however. She struggled to play the role of both mother and father to her eight children." Dr. Leonard gazed at his handwritten notes. "As if that weren't enough, she benevolently took care of many other kids along the way. Often, she went into town to shop and saw a young lady in the streets with nowhere to go, and she did not hesitate to take that young lady home to join her already-too-large family. This kind act she performed numerous times in her life. Today, as I speak, one or two of these ladies might be among us in this church because of her kindness."

In the front row, Pauline-the-twin, once a young girl in need of help, sat with the family. Essie had found Pauline-the-twin and her sister sitting on a wall in downtown Montego Bay, had realized they needed help, and had taken them home. Pauline looked up at Dr. Leonard and nodded.

"By this time, Essie had learned to put her troubles behind her with a little whisper of prayer." Dr. Leonard softened his tone, though he was still eager to let the congregation know the caliber of human being that this world had lost. "She struggled in life, but she was, nonetheless, a true fighter when there was a battle

264

to be won for her family. She gave her absolute all. The biggest turning point in my mother's life came when she was fifty-four years old. This was the time when she found herself through religion. She also got married on April 11, 1976, to Mr. Timothy Brown.

"Thanks to another junior hero, Essie's oldest daughter, Gena Murray, Mrs. Essie Brown enjoyed the best of both worlds—the USA and Jamaica—in her golden years. She traveled extensively between New York, Florida, Washington, DC, and Jamaica.

"At one o'clock on the morning of April 17, 2001, she left us for a better place, a place where there is no more pain, nor sorrow. She has gone to a place where she won't have to fight as hard as she did in this life. She has left us the legacy of hope: if you fight very hard for what you want, you will by all means succeed." Dr. Leonard closed dramatically as he suddenly raised his voice. "Honorable heroine Mrs. Essie S. Brown was in no way short of being a true hero in her family's and friends' eyes. Heroes live on forever, long after their bodies are gone. As we advance in this new era of life, we will always remember Mrs. Essie S. Brown and keep her living on forever in our hearts. We know that the Lord holds her blessed."

At this point, Dr. Leonard let it all out in tears as he made his way to the front row of the church and sat down next to Karl.

Everything went as planned, and everyone was pleased. For the most part, it was a wonderful funeral, one that Essie herself would have been pleased to attend. No expense was spared, but it was money well spent, resulting in a calm, decent, well-polished service with top-of-the-line performers, including a choir and soloist. Some would even say it was sophisticated. The procession from the church to the gravesite was neat and orderly. Everything went off without a hitch.

Once the body was lowered into the ground and the workers at the cemetery started to cement and seal the grave, the minister proceeded with a short graveside ceremony, which he ended with a short prayer. It was now time to read the will and testament that Mrs. Essie Brown had quickly put in place after her first devastating stroke.

It was no secret that Myrtle would be the one who would get the house in Glenworth, but no one was quite sure about who would receive the hefty savings account that Mrs. Essie Brown had left behind. Junior believed that his mother would be very considerate to him in her will and most of the money would be left for him.

Mrs. Essie Brown had made it clear that she would like for the will to be read in public over her body in the casket so that everyone could hear the contents of her will. Although no one knew why she wanted it to be done this way, Karl assumed that his mother was using this method so that she could openly condemn him and embarrass him by leaving absolutely nothing in her will for him. Therefore, he was strongly against the idea that the will should be read out loud in public. He would rather it be read in private after the funeral was over.

Myrtle and Junior, on the other hand, were more than happy to have the will read in public as their mother had so clearly stated. Myrtle knew that a good portion, if not all, of Essie's possessions would be respectfully allotted to her and Junior.

The minister stood in front of the more than one hundred people at the gravesite as they were about to break out into a series of songs. He beckoned them with his hands in the air to stop and give him their undivided attention. "Hello, ladies and gentlemen. I have with me a will. Today, I was instructed by the directives of the deceased to read this will that she wrote when she took sick and had her first stroke in a hospital in New York City." He reached for an envelope in his left bosom jacket pocket, but he was stopped abruptly by a voice on his right side.

"Pastor, please, sir, don't read that will out here. Please wait until we get inside to a private room." It was the coarse voice of Karl pleading with the minister.

A wave of shocked silence swept through the crowd of people as they gazed in astonishment at the minister, who was seemingly at a loss for words.

"Okay, we will have to read it at another time." The dumbfounded minister put the envelope back into his jacket pocket.

"Why do we have to read it at another time? Junior asked. "Pastor, please read the will as instructed by my mother."

"Okay." The confused minister proceeded to retrieve the envelope from his pocket again.

"Pastor, mi say don't read it out yah," Karl insisted. "Pastor, I say don't read it out here."

The pastor stood in front of the crowd as everyone looked on, baffled by what was happening. They were astounded by the level of irreverence at what had been a wonderful, respectable funeral up to that moment.

"Okay, okay," said the minister. "Ladies and gentlemen, obviously we have a serious problem. We will not read this will out here." He returned the envelope to his jacket pocket.

Myrtle moved forward to the front of the crowd. "You can't do that, Pastor!" she shouted. "You can't do that. My mother wanted the will to be read out loud right here in front of these people, and you have to honor her wishes."

"Yes, that's true," the minister said in a firm voice. "I have a job to do, and I must do it. Please, no more bickering. I will read this will right here as instructed." Having arrived at his final decision, the minister reached for the envelope in his left jacket pocket and opened it. He swiftly took the certified letter of will out of the envelope and held it in front of him to read.

"Gi mi that bom bo clart letta." Karl quickly rushed forward and aggressively grabbed at it. He tried to snatch the letter out of the hands of the minister before he was able to read the first word from it.

Junior, who was now close to the minister on the opposite side from Karl, quickly reached over the minister's shoulder and latched onto the will before Karl could snatch it out of the minister's hands.

Karl then pushed aggressively at Junior's hand, hoping to make him let go of the will. Instead, Junior gave Karl a hard, swinging left punch that connected with his right upper chest area. Karl swiftly and aggressively punched back at him.

Leonard dashed through the stunned crowd to stop the embarrassing fight between his brothers. The minister was still holding onto the will. After all, he had been entrusted with it, so it was his responsibility to secure the contents and to properly register and store it in its rightful place.

Kenneth, Betty's boyfriend, who was way in the back of the crowd, also made his way forward. When Bunny saw Betty's boyfriend rushing forward through the crowd, he pounced on him, pushing him down to the ground. Betty's kids saw what happened and immediately rushed to counterattack.

Complete pandemonium and chaos resulted. People ran frantically in all directions for cover and safety. Punches and kicks were flying all over the place, and before anybody knew it, a chaotic barroom-style fight had broken out all over the funeral grounds.

Siblings and relatives with old feuds, grudges, and rivalries were releasing years of built-up fury over unsolved matters. It was a clash of emotions out of control. It was a battlefield of white and black three-piece suits, jackets and ties, stilettos, Gucci, Dolce & Gabbana handbags, dinner gowns, miniskirts, and three-piece formal dresses.

It was embarrassing, a funeral gone wild. This was certainly not the legacy that Mrs. Essie Brown had intended to leave behind.

Chapter 33

Dr. Leonard gave a lengthy, eloquent eulogy in honor of his mother at her funeral in Jamaica. He cleansed his guilt as he bid Mrs. Essie Brown farewell and prayed that her soul would rest forever in peace. It was the final closure of the life of a naive, beautiful girl from the countryside of Cascade who chased her dreams relentlessly.

But there's more to Essie's story.

There is a story about a minister who was preaching one Sunday at a large church. This particular day, the church was full. It was said that the minister was a very good minister. When he preached, he moved people to action. Today's topic was injustice. As the minister preached hard and strong about all of the injustices in this world, one particular member of the congregation was deeply touched. This member was heartbroken to see how much injustice there was on this earth.

As the minister continued his sermon about

injustice, this church member got angrier and angrier. For the first time since he had been attending this church, he was moved to do his part to stop all these injustices. He was so fired up that he felt he had to do something about this problem right now.

He sprang up out of his seat and raced out of the church in a mad rage. He was on his way to fight injustice. As he reached the outside of the church, he stopped abruptly in his tracks. It dawned on him that he didn't know where to start. Who was responsible for all these injustices? Whom should he attack? Where should he go? How should he fight injustice? Eventually, he turned around and calmly walked back into the church and took his seat. He sat down peacefully and enjoyed the rest of the minister's sermon just like all of the other church members.

Being an orphan child, Essie knew that life was devastatingly unjust to her. The only thing she was not sure about was if, as a single parent, it was unjustifiable to sacrifice one of her precious children for the sake of the others. Who, she wondered, had experienced the most injustice?

Was it Karl, who had unfortunately sacrificed a healthy childhood life in the city for a hard, tiresome country life with his father, just so the rest of the family could move on? While his family in the city was comfortably getting ice-cold drinks from the refrigerator and drinking water from a convenient indoor pipe, he was getting his drinks from a little homemade icebox outside of the humble, rundown country house. He was also walking miles to get his drinking water supply because there were no indoor pipes in his home. While the rest of his family in the city was being comfortably driven to school, he had to walk miles upon miles every day just to get an elementary education.

Was it Lela, who had been given up virtually at

birth to her cousin Miriam? Did Lela sacrifice a life with her biological mother just so the rest of Essie's family could move on?

Who suffered the most injustice because of the poverty in Essie's early family life? It is often said by the rich that poverty is the greatest sin on earth.

***

"Hey, my brother!" said Myrtle, who was calling long-distance from New York. "How're yuh doing today? How're the kids?"

"They're doing fine," said Dr. Leonard from his home in Florida. "Much better than I am. They have their bread buttered on both sides. My oldest son, Alexander, is growing tall. He's not talking as clearly as he should, but we have him in speech therapy. We're still looking for a good babysitter for Algivanni. How about you, Myrtle? How're you doing? Are you behaving yourself?"

"I'm doing fine," Myrtle replied. "Yuh know that I stopped smoking and drinking and doing all that wild stuff. I started going back to church in a very serious way."

"Oh, yes! I forgot you told me about that the last time we spoke. You also told me that you were getting married and that you wanted me to play the role of your 'give-away' father, and I told you I would be honored to do so."

"Yes, will yuh do me that favor, my wonderful brother?"

"Sure! You have to tell me the date of the wedding early enough so I can request some time off from my job. But you still didn't tell me who the lucky young man is. Who is he? Are you ready to tell me now?"

272

"No, not yet, my brother. I'll tell yuh more about the whole thing soon, but I think the date might be around February thirteenth."

"Myrtle, did you tell your fiancé about your newly diagnosed condition?"

"Yes, mon, I told him my whole story, and he's fine with it," she said confidently. "I told him everything, and he loves me even more. My brother, yuh wouldn't believe it. I found someone who accepts me just the way I am, with my big belly and all." Myrtle giggled.

"Oh, that's so good. It's very unusual when someone loves you unconditionally. You're so lucky. Where did you meet him?"

"I met him at the church that I attend. He's a very nice person. Yuh'll love him when yuh meet him."

"Oh, he's a Christian? That's so good to hear. He's already a good match for you with him being a Christian and all."

"Yes, mon. Leonard, I'm telling yuh, he's a very nice guy."

"He has to be. I remember the last time we spoke, you told me about your secret that you've been holding back from me and almost everyone. I was shocked when I heard what your ex-boyfriend Roy did to you."

"Sorry. I should've told yuh earlier, my brother."

"What balls! Can you imagine? He knew that he had the human immunodeficiency virus even before he got divorced from his wife in Florida, but he didn't tell you a word about it. If it wasn't for his ex-wife in Florida, who called you and told you about him herself, you probably still wouldn't know anything."

"Can yuh believe that, my brother? I'm really sorry I didn't tell you earlier. I just didn't know how to deal with it."

"Myrtle, if I sound like I'm angry, it's because I'm so mad and fed up with what's going on these days. Do you know the popular song by the famous rap singer Nas, called 'If I Only Had One Mic'?"

"Yes, I believe I've heard it before."

"Well, if I only had one mic that I could use to speak to the whole world, I would love to set the record straight about AIDS," Dr. Leonard said with a tone of outrage and frustration. "There are many cases like yours happening every day. People need to hear stories like yours. Can you imagine someone who knew he was infected and yet slept with you repeatedly, over and over again, without condoms?"

Fury hit Dr. Leonard, leaving him almost breathless. Just the thought of Roy passing on HIV to his sister made him angry all over again. He was as angry as the New Yorkers and the other American patriots all around the world as they acknowledged the atrocious act of terrorism upon the World Trade Center on September 11, 2001. He was equally as angry to know that there were people out there terrorizing other people's lives on a smaller scale by intentionally passing on HIV to them.

He felt the pain and sorrow that his sister must be going through. He wished that he could help it go away by enlightening her more on the topic of AIDS.

"Let him go about his business," Myrtle said. "Time will take care of him. I'm very upset with him, too, but I don't want to create any scandal. I don't want anybody to know about my personal life."

"Let me tell you the truth about this whole thing," Dr. Leonard said. "HIV is not an embarrassing thing or anything to be ashamed of. But unlike HIV, AIDS is totally preventable. AIDS can be prevented with some of the best combinations of medications in these

274

modern times. There's no reason not to get tested for HIV. Early detection means the possibility of effective drug treatment to prevent the diseases related to it, diseases that we now refer to as AIDS. Those are the facts. As long as you're taking your medications and being proactive with your health, you have no reason to be ashamed. Take it from me, your brother." Dr. Leonard's voice shook as if he was out of breath or about to break down and cry.

"Oh, I see. I see." Myrtle acknowledged her brother's explanation as she willingly soaked up the vital information that he was pouring out on the other side of the long-distance line.

"Do you understand now?"

"Yes, my brother, believe it or not, that was why I called yuh today, before yuh started yuh long, everlasting preaching." Myrtle chuckled. "I'm just kidding. Anyway, I wanted to let yuh know that since I stopped taking all my meds, I feel so much better."

"What? Nooo!" Dr. Leonard was alarmed. "Myrtle, did your doctors tell you to stop taking your meds? I know that sometimes they have a thing called drug holiday, but I don't believe you would benefit from that situation. I'm almost sure that you did that on your own."

"Yes, mon," Myrtle confessed. "I tried it last week, and I noticed that it made me feel a lot better."

"What about your digoxin and other medications? You didn't stop that, right?"

"I stopped everything. I never ever felt so good and strong in my body for a very long time," Myrtle bragged.

"No, no, no!" Dr. Leonard said hysterically. "Myrtle, you can't do that. It isn't only about how you feel. It's about what will keep you alive. You're only forty-five years old; you're too young to be taking those

275

chances with your life. I'm so glad that you called me, because you have to start back taking all of your heart medications. I can see it maybe being possible to hold off on your HIV meds since you're getting too many unwanted side effects. If you choose to do that, you'll have to see your special immunologist or HIV care doctors to let them reevaluate better dosages and probably change your HIV meds to a different set that you will tolerate much better." Dr. Leonard pleaded with his sister. "Myrtle, please promise me that you will start back on your Lasix and digoxin and the rest of your heart medications as soon as you hang up the phone. Is that a promise?"

"Yes, my brother, but I have to go back to the clinic tomorrow to get my meds refilled."

"Why not today, Myrtle?" Dr. Leonard insisted. "I think that you still have time to do it today."

"Okay, my brother, I'm going to try and see if I get dem today. Okay? I love yuh."

"I love you too, Myrtle. Bye for now." Dr. Leonard ended their conversation, his mind troubled.

***

Myrtle, at age fourteen, had been a pretty little light-skinned girl. She got her good looks from Essie. If Essie was as pretty as a little terrestrial mermaid of the tropical island of Jamaica, then Myrtle was the little Jamaican "roughneck" terrestrial mermaid of the raving tropical cannabis island.

She was skinny and tall, with a perfect model shape. Her skin was as cool as the tropical island breeze in the late evening. She had long, slender legs just like Essie did when she was fourteen years old.

The main differences between Essie and Myrtle when they were fourteen were that Essie had noticeably

276

bigger hips and much longer hair. Though Myrtle had a slightly better shape than Essie, and although she also had comely features, she was in no way as beautiful as her mother.

The real shortcomings that Myrtle had were her hair and, eventually, her attitude. Her short, dry hair earned her the nickname "Dry Head Adassa." That used to be a popular nickname in Jamaica for girls who had very short hair that was hard to comb and style. It was originally created by a famous Jamaican poet named Miss Louise Bennett, also known as Miss Lou.

Myrtle was a pretty, quiet, well-behaved little girl up until the age of fourteen, when she dropped out of church. Though still pretty, she was not quiet or well behaved anymore.

She had started going to the Glenworth SDA Church at the age of twelve after being invited one day by her neighbor, Mr. Benjamin Mulgrave Sr.

"Good morning, Myrtle," Brother Mulgrave said one Sabbath on his way to church. "Why don't you come to church with me one of these days?"

"I'll ask my mom if I can come with yuh next week, Brother Mulgrave," Myrtle said. She was sitting on a large stone just outside her front gate.

"Okay, I'll check back with you then."

The following week, Myrtle was excited about going to church. She got dressed very early that Sabbath morning and went to church with Brother Mulgrave and his wife and family. She loved it so much that she couldn't seem to stop going. She continued to attend every Sabbath and got baptized that same year.

However, she regrettably dropped out of church around the time she was diagnosed with rheumatic fever. The illness caused her to lose many school days, and she had many sick days off from school to allow her to attend her numerous doctors' appointments. Myrtle became rebellious and less interested in school. When she did go, she would return home in the evening with her uniform dirty and torn up from being in countless fights with other students. It was as if Myrtle's sole purpose for going to school was to start a fight.

Myrtle not only picked fights at school, but she also picked fights with anyone just about anywhere she went. The person's age, size, or gender didn't matter. If anyone stared or as much as looked at her, that would be enough cause for a fight. She wouldn't hesitate to attack viciously, like a wild animal.

"What are you looking at?" Myrtle said to an older gentleman who was maybe twice her age and three times her small size. "Don't look at me. I'm not a showcase. I'll punch you in your face."

"Little girl, just behave yourself and go and learn some manners," the stranger said. He was busy and on his way to work.

"What did you say, face-T boy? You think I'm afraid of you, huh? Do yuh think I'm afraid of yuh, batty boy?" Myrtle zipped across the street with lightning speed. She pointed her index finger at the gentleman's face and dared him to fight with her. "Yuh want to fight, haw? Yuh want to fight with me, dutty boy?"

Myrtle would start every fight, and she would pretty much lose every fight, but that neither bothered her nor stopped her. It was as if she had a death wish, but she wanted someone else to pull the trigger. Someone could have had a gun pointing at her, and she would no doubt still have been in his or her face trying to start a fight. She had no fear. She became more and more ruthless.

The funny thing about it was that her bad behavior did not in any way match her pretty, innocent looks and her petite, heavenly body. A man, or even a woman, who saw her for the first time, would be more inclined to think of making love to her than of fighting or making war with her.

One day Myrtle went to school and never came back home. Her family became very worried. Knowing Myrtle's new violent attitude, everyone expected the worst. A week went by, and there was still no sign of her.

One month later, Myrtle sent a message to her family letting them know that she was doing fine. She was living with her new boyfriend, Dudley—who was a rich drug dealer—in a large, fancy, fabulous house in the parish of Saint Ann's Bay. Dudley was a tall, handsome yet nerdy black guy in his twenties. He was soft-spoken, but his full, bulging eyes were red most of the time, and he wore a mean look on his face.

Everyone was happy to know that Myrtle was alive, but no one thought for a minute that she was doing well. Essie was afraid for her being in such bad company. She was also concerned that her health was not being properly attended to by a physician. Essie sent a message back to her asking her to come home. Eventually, she did come home, but not because she wanted to. She came home because she was feeling seriously ill. By this time, she had tried marijuana and loved it. She had also become an avid beer drinker.

Essie took her to the hospital, where she was admitted. Shortly thereafter, she was rushed to Kingston Hospital to have emergency open-heart surgery. Myrtle had a mitral valve prolapse and was given an artificial heart-valve replacement. Thanks to early detection and to swift action, the doctors saved her life. They cautioned her to stop her dangerously unhealthy smoking and drinking habits and to live a less volatile lifestyle.

Myrtle did eventually drop the fighting attitude, but after the surgery and when she was fully recovered, she resumed her bad habits of smoking and drinking even more than before. For the life of her, she would not break those habits; they only got worse.

Her doctors also explicitly warned her that it would be very dangerous for her to get pregnant; she could die. However, it seemed as if Myrtle only took that as a welcome answer to her death wish. Shortly after her surgery, she got pregnant by a nice, courteous, good-natured Christian fellow named Ralph. It was as if she had gone looking for someone just to get her pregnant. As soon as it happened, she broke up with Ralph without ever telling him she was going to have a child.

When Myrtle went to her doctor for prenatal care, he recommended that she abort the child because either she would not live to see the child, or the child would not survive the birth. Both mother and child would not make it together. However, Myrtle refused to listen to her doctor's advice. She insisted that she would keep her pregnancy all the way to full-term delivery.

Both the baby and Myrtle survived the pregnancy. Her son, Dean Myers, was delivered prematurely at seven months due to complications.

Myrtle lived the rest of her life in the same defiant manner. Anything that her doctors said she shouldn't do, she did. It was as if she still had a death wish, and she dared death to happen as she went up against the odds. If you wanted her to do something, all you had to do was tell her not to do that particular thing. You could bet your only remaining silver dollar that she would be doing it, if it was the last thing on earth that she did.

There is a popular saying that goes, "If at first you don't succeed, skydiving is not for you." Myrtle got bored with the normal activities of the day. She liked only the risky activities and risky challenges. She continued the risky behavior of heavy drinking and smoking of both marijuana and tobacco. She enjoyed a life rich with negligence and rebelliousness.

It is easy to see why it was so necessary for Gena to have delivered Myrtle to the U.S. at the time when she did.

Myrtle, her brother Leonard, her niece Denise, and Gena's own daughter Desiree were now happily living with Gena in New York City in her large three-bedroom apartment.

Myrtle quickly made friends and started enjoying the New York lifestyle. She liked to be the talk of the town. To say that she tasted the Big Apple was an understatement. It was more like Myrtle gobbled up the Big Apple as if she were a character in a Pac-Man game. She quickly developed a large circle of friends, both male and female. Myrtle was having a wild and wonderful time. She was truly happy as she tried to find herself in New York City.

However, she refused to quit smoking and drinking and was very set in her old ways and bad habits. She partied hard and always seemed to find the weirdest and strangest guys to be her friends. Although Gena had worked as fast as she could to deliver Myrtle, it seemed as if she was a little too late.

Against her doctor's orders, Myrtle decided to get a job. She wanted to earn some money of her own, so she took a job in the discount department of a small retail pharmacy store conveniently located in their neighborhood.

She was very happy with the job. However, one day her boss had to fire her because, as he said, she was losing her mind. Angry and even violent, for no reason, she began breaking things left and right, aisle by aisle, in the store.

Gena quickly rushed down to 125th Street in Manhattan and took her to the closest hospital, where she was given sedatives and antipsychotic drugs to calm her down.

Myrtle was stable for a long time. However, every now and then, she had an outburst. One day at home with the rest of the family, she got agitated and started walking back and forth, pacing the floor. Hysterical, Denise immediately summoned Gena, who fearfully rushed to see what was wrong with Myrtle.

Myrtle gave her big sister a stern, condemning look and started shouting at her. "Gena, you owe me. Did you know that you owe me? Momma owes me. Did you know that? The whole family owes me. Did you know that? You all owe me. You owe me. It's because there is a God why I'm still alive. Everybody owes me."

"Myrtle, I know, I know. Just calm down. We love you, Myrtle. We love you." Gena patted her on her shoulder. "Just calm down, Myrtle. Calm down."

Myrtle rested her head on Gena's shoulder and began to sob deeply.

Gena comforted her as she cried and told her to make sure to take a dose of her medication to relax her mind. From the day of that incident on, Gena made sure Myrtle took her medications before she left the house in the mornings. Once Myrtle took her medications, she was as good as normal.

Myrtle even continued to party as she usually did and had fun with her friends. One Friday night, Myrtle was at a big party in Brooklyn, New York, partying and having the time of her life. While she was blissfully doing the sexy Butterfly or the backbreaking Bogle to the get-up-and-dance "Ting-a-ling" by DJ Shabba Ranks, she suddenly fainted and fell to the floor because of pulmonary congestion.

Paramedics came and rushed her to the hospital, where doctors recommended an immediate second open-heart surgery to replace the old mechanical heart valve with a new one. The old one had stopped functioning the way it should. Myrtle had the surgery, and she recovered well. However, after the second open-heart surgery, she was in and out of the hospital regularly, mostly for heart-related problems.

Once, when she was admitted into a very large teaching hospital in Manhattan, a team of cardiologists carefully studied her heart and her overall condition. They sadly gave her a poor prognosis. They told her that, based on her cardiomegaly—or superenlarged heart—and overall poor cardiovascular condition, she had about three weeks to live, if that long.

Myrtle, who was not a stranger to these types of terminal prognoses, openly laughed at the medical team as she informed them that such a prognosis had been given to her many times before. "At one point," she explained to them, "a young doctor saw the size of my heart and gave me three days to live. That was thirteen years ago."

The first such terminal prognosis had been given to her about fifteen years earlier, when she was eighteen years old. Since then, she had been receiving one such prognosis every six to twelve months.

Myrtle cheerfully encouraged the cardiologists to be strong and be of good courage and to understand that she was a living, walking medical exception. Ten years later, Myrtle was still cheering up the pessimistic cardiologists with a high five whenever she saw them in the hospital hallways or on the streets.

Another unusual thing about Myrtle was how comfortable she became when she was admitted to the hospital. Whenever she was not feeling well, she would check in with her cardiovascular clinic or the closest hospital center. Usually, once the staff took her vitals or did any medical workup, they would admit her to the hospital ward. Myrtle's vitals were usually literally off the chart and almost always required some attention. The funniest thing about it all was that, while Myrtle's family was in a panic and distressed that she was in the hospital and could die at any moment, Myrtle remained unbelievably calm and relaxed.

She was as calm as the intrepid ocean liner that was now peacefully parked on the Hudson River in Manhattan, posing as a museum. She was sometimes more relaxed in the hospital than she was at home. When she checked into the hospital, it was like she was checking into a five-star hotel. The first thing she did was order her television hookup. Then she made sure that her phone line was on. Immediately after that, she called all of her family and friends to inform them of where she was and how she could be reached. She then investigated the food menu for dinner and found out who would be her personal doctor in charge of her care during her stay.

Finally, she got back on the phone to make all of her personal calls as comfortable and cozy as she would be if she were at home. Myrtle visited the hospital so often, it was a home away from home.

When Mrs. Essie Brown came to the United States and got an apartment next door to Gena, Myrtle left Gena's apartment to live with her mother.

Mrs. Essie Brown was very attentive to Myrtle in her illness, just as Gena had been. Myrtle eventually got her legal status in the United States and also got her son, Dean, to immigrate from Jamaica. Dean lived with her and his grandmother for a while, but for whatever reason, he later decided to return to Jamaica to live in Essie's house in Glenworth.

Myrtle met an old boyfriend she used to know back in Jamaica. Roy supposedly had divorced his wife in Florida and come to start a new life in New York City. They did everything together, and Myrtle was very happy with him. Roy even moved in with Myrtle in Mrs. Essie Brown's oversized two-bedroom apartment. They were madly in love, and they were supposed to get married soon.

They all lived together well in their Manhattan apartment until, unfortunately, Mrs. Essie Brown had her stroke. After a year and a half being paralyzed in a nursing home, Mrs. Essie Brown passed away. Because she was unable to go to Jamaica before she died, Gena and Dr. Leonard decided that they would give her two funeral services. They would have one in New York, and after that was through, they would send her to Jamaica for her final service and burial. They felt that Mrs. Essie Brown's soul would not rest in peace if they did not send her back to Jamaica to her home in Glenworth, whether dead or alive.

Dr. Leonard was passionate about making sure people knew all the good things that his mother had done with her life. He insisted on presenting a long eulogy that dispelled any negative thoughts that people might have had about his mother. He was determined to set the record straight even between siblings who were not very fond of some of the things his mother had to do to survive.

Moreover, Dr. Leonard felt deeply saddened and guilty that he had been unable to write a book about Mrs. Essie Brown's life before she died, as he had promised her he would do when he was ten years old. He was saddened and dejected, because he had had a whole lifetime since then to get it done, but he hadn't.

He felt disconsolate and guilty because he knew that his mother was patiently waiting on him. She was patient because she believed wholeheartedly in him. Of all his seven siblings, he was the only one who had made it to college and beyond. He knew that he was her only hope to shine her light around the world so others could see the warmhearted woman of substance and virtue that she was.

Thus, a simple funeral turned out to be much more than a funeral to him; it was his chance to redeem himself for failing to keep his promise to his mother by writing and reading a summary of her life. He was, therefore, more than delighted to travel from Florida to New York City to present his lengthy eulogy of his mother and then to Jamaica to do the same.

Myrtle was not the same after her mother died. She was sad and depressed, and her mood was melancholy most of the time. She was taking more than twenty different medications and became very compliant in doing so. She started going to church seriously and cut down on her undesirable drinking and smoking habits. Myrtle was fighting to live again, but this time, she wanted to live honorably in the sight of God. She broke up with her boyfriend, Roy, without explaining why. She said that she could "do bad" all by herself. Everyone was very proud of her sudden maturity and sobriety.

Two years after her mother died, Myrtle called Leonard in Florida to let him know that since she had stopped taking all her meds, she felt so much better. Dr. Leonard was shocked to hear what his sister had to say about stopping all of her medications without her doctor's knowledge. He strongly urged her to restart all of her meds, or at least all of her heart medications. He encouraged her to go and talk with her doctor about making changes to her therapy to decrease any major side effects that she might have been experiencing. By this time, he knew that Myrtle had been diagnosed as HIV positive, a present from Roy.

Myrtle had not been the same happy-go-lucky person she used to be before Mrs. Essie Brown passed away. The reality of the loss of her mother hit her hard.

She once told Dr. Leonard that when her mother died, she felt like she had truly lost her best friend. Mrs. Essie Brown was her crutch in life. Mrs. Essie Brown stood by her words when she promised to always be there for her. One solid thing about that family, they genuinely stood by their words. When they made a promise, they zealously kept it to the end.

Mrs. Essie Brown taught her kids that if a man does not have his word, he has nothing. She was the one who encouraged Myrtle to take her medications. She was also the one who constantly showed her why life was worth living to its fullest potential.

After Mrs. Essie Brown passed away, Myrtle felt alone. She never held any grudges against her mother, because she knew that her mother truly loved and cared for her. Her mother told her that just about every day.

Myrtle truly believed those words because she knew that Mrs. Essie Brown was as honest as the tropical sunshine was to the Montego Bay white-sand beaches and as the twinkling lights were to the New York City nights. She wished that Mrs. Essie Brown was around to comfort her in her times of despair.

Sometimes Myrtle felt so sad, she believed that her whole life had been a mistake from the beginning. She believed that her mother had tried to end her relationship with Myrtle's father a little too late. It was too late because Essie was already pregnant with her. It was a mistake then, and she believed that her whole life had been one big mistake ever since that day.

Myrtle died on February 13, 2003, two months after speaking to her brother. After she passed away, Dr. Leonard realized that although Myrtle had promptly restarted most of her medications the day after their phone conversation, she had not restarted her digoxin medication, which was one of the main medications for her heart.

287

She had been dutifully taking that cherished medication since her teenaged years. Myrtle and her digoxin heart medication were closer than twins. After all these years of devoted medication compliance, she was now in one symbiotic accord with her digoxin medication. She knew her meds so well that she could accurately estimate the effective outcome based upon the timeline of the omission of her digoxin medication.

Dr. Leonard realized that his sister was simply fed up with life. She was fed up with the inequitable hand of disparity that life had dealt her. That was why she told him over the phone on their long-distance call that she was getting married on February 13, 2003, and that she would love for him to be her "give-away" father at her wedding.

It wasn't until the eleventh hour, so to speak, that Dr. Leonard realized that his heartbroken sister was being very honest with him during that call. She was as honest as a heartbeat was to a stethoscope and blood pressure was to a sphygmomanometer when she told him, in all sincerity, the bona fide truth that she was getting married to someone who wholeheartedly loved and accepted her for who she was. She was honest when she said that she had confessed her undisguised story to Him and He loved her even more.

It was after her death that Dr. Leonard was sucker-punched with the reality that his sister had been faced with one disaster more than she could bear. It was a brutal TKO blow that he never really recovered from.

Along with having to deal with a major lifelong heart disease and its accompanying medications, Myrtle could not deal with the barefaced crime of intentional HIV infection by her ex-boyfriend, Roy. She finally decided that she was going back to where she had first found refuge. She went back to church, and she decided that this time she would marry the man who would always love her unconditionally. Accordingly, Myrtle was married on February 13, 2003, one day short of Valentine's Day.

THE END

Made in the USA
Charleston, SC
04 March 2013